ALMOST EDEN

Also published in Large Print
from G.K. Hall by Dorothy Garlock:

Homeplace
Ribbon in the Sky
Tenderness
Forever, Victoria
Sins of Summer

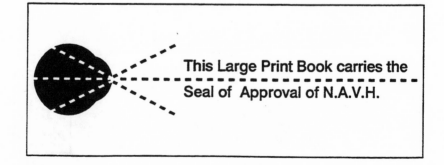

This Large Print Book carries the
Seal of Approval of N.A.V.H.

ALMOST EDEN

Dorothy Garlock

G.K. Hall & Co.
Thorndike, Maine

Published in 1996 by arrangement with
Warner Books, Inc.

G.K. Hall Large Print Romance Collection.

The text of this Large Print edition is unabridged.
Other aspects of the book may vary from the original edition.

Set in 16 pt. News Plantin by Rick Gundberg.

Printed in the United States on permanent paper.

Library of Congress Cataloging in Publication Data

Garlock, Dorothy.
    Almost Eden / Dorothy Garlock.
       p.   cm.
    ISBN 0-7838-1638-3 (lg. print : hc)
    1. Frontier and pioneer life — Missouri — Fiction.
  2. Man–woman relationships — Missouri — Fiction.
  3. Large type books. I. Title.
    [PS3557.A71645A54 1996]
    813'.54—dc20   95-47885

for Janet and Max Lillienstein

CHAPTER ONE

Jason Picket was mesmerized. His mind scarcely registered what he was seeing, but he was alert enough to grasp the possibilities this chance encounter could mean to his miserable life.

He gripped the reins, staring, staring.

She stood beside the bole of a spreading elm tree, her small perfect body blending with the background of thick grapevines that clung to the massive trunk. A brown linsey skirt swirled around the calves of her bare legs. Her face, perfect as a cameo, was framed by gorgeous blue-black hair. Even from this distance he could see her clear green eyes and red mouth. A mystique that bordered on the supernatural surrounded her.

"My luck has finally turned," he murmured to himself.

If just looking at her stirred *his* jaded blood to the boiling point, what would she do to the bored young blades in New Orleans? Jason chuckled to think of how it would be with her on his arm. Every rich dandy within a hundred miles would be clamoring for his company. With his skill at cards he would clean their pockets.

Oh, God! Excitement made his heart knock against his ribcage and his sex swell in his tight britches until he thought he couldn't stand it. *She would be worth a king's ransom in New Orleans.*

After a night of tossing and turning, Jason Picket had made up his mind to leave his half-brother's homestead on the Missouri River west of St. Charles. He would leave his wife, Callie, and their two sons with Jefferson. Sucker that he was, Brother would see that they didn't starve.

Jason had felt like a fool when he had found out that Hartley Van Buren was an agent for Aaron Burr and had been using him to prevent his half-brother from taking the evidence of Burr's treachery to Thomas Jefferson. Plotting with General James Wilkinson, commander of the army and the governor of the Louisiana Territory, Burr had planned to take over the territory. But Hartley's scheme had gone awry and he was dead. Now there was nothing to keep Jason here in this godforsaken wilderness.

At first he had felt he had been dragged back into this backwoods for nothing. But he realized now that it had all been worthwhile. He had found a jewel! With a little polish this girl would make him a fortune in New Orleans. He had no intention of leaving this disgusting place without her. He'd had a glimpse of her once before and learned that her name was Maggie and that she was the daughter of a homesteader struggling to eke out a living on a patch of uncleared ground.

She was alone. His for the taking.

Jason yanked the reins so suddenly that the horse reared. Forced to gentle the animal, he had to take his eyes off the girl, and when he looked again, she was gone. He cursed under his breath and angrily jerked on the right rein to punish the animal. The horse went around and around in a circle. Maggie couldn't have gone far, he reasoned. She was probably watching him from behind a bush or tree. He smiled slyly at the thought and, deciding to try another tactic, dismounted. He walked around his frightened horse, patting him and talking softly to him, all the while scanning the edge of the woods.

Jason could picture her in a beautiful green gown with a voluminous skirt that emphasized her tiny waist. He would draw her hair up to the top of her head and tie it with a ribbon. With her ethereal beauty she would be worth anything he had to do to get her. His heart pounded like a hammer on an anvil. Exerting every ounce of self-control, he turned his head slowly and saw that, like a small, shy animal, she was moving toward him. Suddenly, she stopped and stood as still as a doe scenting danger. One hand rested on the rough bark of a tree.

"Hello, Maggie," he said softly. "I think you frightened my horse."

He glanced at her and then away, but the picture of her stayed in his mind.

The familiar sounds of the woods surrounded them. Wind stirred the leaves overhead. From far away a whippoorwill called, and, closer, jays scolded a blackbird who was poaching in their berry patch.

"Ya hurt yore horse. Why'd ya hurt him?"

He held his breath as she approached. Her movements were so fluid that she seemed to skim the ground. She had eyes only for the horse. She passed easily beneath the animal's head, reached up, put her hands on either side of its face, and pulled its head down so that she could whisper in its ear. The sounds she made were soft coos and low murmurs. The animal stood quietly, its ears twitching as if listening.

Close up, the girl's beauty had a more devastating effect on him than it had from a distance. He sighed, and at that instant she looked up at him, fixing her magnificent eyes on him. They held a faintly sulky expression. They were long eyes, genuinely emerald green in color, like flashing gems between her beautiful thick, dark lashes. They attracted and held his attention irresistibly, as did the pale warm glow of her skin and her soft red mouth that looked so innocent.

"Why'er ya lookin' at me that way?" she asked.

Jason had thought his scrutiny had lasted no more than a few seconds, but it must have been longer because she looked suspicious and resentful, like some tiny shy bird that would take wing and fly if he made a sudden move. He was careful not to do so.

"I like to look at you. You're very beautiful."

"I know." She shrugged.

"How old are you?" He offered his most charming smile.

10

"I'm not a youngun," she said quickly. The sulky expression dropped from her eyes and was replaced with one of haughtiness. "I've had my woman's time for this many years." She held up four fingers.

"Oh, I never for a moment thought you were a child," he answered gravely. "I knew you were a woman full-grown."

She moved around to the side of the horse, then behind it.

"Don't go behind the horse!" Alarm caused him to speak rather sharply.

She laughed.

Suddenly Jason realized that he had seen that smile before, on a painting in one of the great mansions in New Orleans. An artist had painted a portrait of a girl he said he had seen in a dream. The painting was considered a great work of art, and many people would have paid a high price for it; but the artist refused to sell. He had carried his picture all over the world searching for the girl. Many years passed; and it was said that when he failed to find her, he had killed himself.

This was the girl.

This beautiful, elusive creature of the woods was the girl in the painting. Good Lord! If he could only get her to New Orleans —

"Don't go behind the horse!" he warned again.

"He won't hurt me. See?" Maggie swung gently on the horse's tail, patted his rump and the hind legs that could lash out with such murderous force. The animal remained perfectly still.

11

Dear God! She was not like anything he'd ever seen before. If she beckoned, a man would cross half the world to get to her. She whirled around suddenly. The full skirt of her dress flared out to reveal perfect ankles and calves and tiny feet encased in low, beaded moccasins. Jason had never seen a woman who could compare with her, had never known anything like the tide of feeling that swept over him when she looked at him and smiled. Whatever he had to give, whatever he had to do, he had to have her.

"Do you have a horse?"

"No."

"Do you want one?"

"No. I like t' run."

"Do you dance, Maggie?" he asked casually when she whirled again.

"Sometimes."

"Will you dance for me?"

"No."

"I'll give you something pretty."

"I don't dance for pay," she answered disdainfully.

"I meant no offense." He cursed himself for a fool when he saw that he had offended her. "I just meant that you are so very beautiful that you should have beautiful things."

"I'm beautiful, but I don't want anythin'." She spoke completely without vanity.

"Where did you live before you came to Missouri?" Jason was desperate to keep her talking.

"Kaintuck."

"Have you been to a town bigger than St. Louis?"

"I don't like towns. Folks are hateful." Her mouth turned unhappy and sullen.

Jason laughed. "Not to you. I don't see how anyone could be hateful to you."

"Womenfolk hate me. In Kaintuck they called me a witch and were goin' to burn me. Pa brought us here."

Jason laughed again. "Are you a witch?"

"I don't know." She lifted her shoulders in a shrug. Not a trace of a smile touched her mouth. "When I looked at the men, they'd leave their women and come to me." She tilted her head defiantly. "I did it sometimes 'cause they'd been mean to me and Ma and Pa."

Jason felt a tightness in his chest and a throbbing ache in the pit of his belly. He had never practiced abstinence, and it had been a while since he'd had a woman. Although he had pleasured himself with women of every color and creed, none of them had ever set his blood afire like this little backwoods nymph.

"How would you like to see New Orleans and wear fine silk dresses and have men bow at your feet and bring you jewels?"

"What for?"

"Why . . . because they admire your beauty." Jason showed her a ring he had taken from Hartley's pack just before he left the homestead. "This is a fine gem. Very expensive. See how it sparkles?" He held it so that shards of light

13

gleamed from the stone. "Would you like to have it?"

"I don't like it."

"It's worth a lot of money."

"I don't need money."

"But it's beautiful. The color matches your eyes. It would make you even more beautiful if we put it on a ribbon and tied it about your neck."

"I don't want t' be more beautiful."

Jason's patience snapped. His hand lashed out and grasped her arm.

"Then what the hell do you want?" he growled angrily.

She struggled and hit at him with her free hand, but her strength was nothing compared to his. He held her easily and drew her to him.

"I didn't want to do this, but I will if it's the only way." He was breathing hard, not from the exertion of holding her, but from the lust within him that tore at his loins like cruel, sharp spurs.

Like a small spitting cat, she hissed and clawed and used every ounce of her strength to pull away from his grasp. She tried to bite him; and when she failed at that, she butted him with her head. Her struggles only made him the more determined to have her. Pursing her lips, she let out a long shrill whistle before his mouth clamped down upon hers. Holding her wrists behind her with one hand, he pried her jaws apart with the thumb and forefinger of his other hand. His tongue

14

lapped the sweetness of her mouth. White hot flames licked at his groin.

When he paused for breath, she whistled again. Jason scarcely noticed that, nor did he observe the fact that their tussle had frightened the horse into shying away. With a grunt he threw her to the ground and fell on top of her. Her struggles were beginning to irritate him and he slapped her. Almost instantly he was sorry, but it was too late to recall the blow. She would never be his now, except by force. By God, if that was the only way he could have her, that's the way it would be!

He yanked her skirt up and saw that she wore nothing beneath it. Dark curls nestled between her thighs, and he buried his hand there while she writhed under him. She whistled again. He withdrew his hand and slapped her again, hard. It rocked her head but she didn't cry out.

"Stop that!" he snarled, and jerked at the fastenings on his britches. His fingers fumbled in their frenzied haste to release the part of him that was swollen and rigid and ached so desperately.

Small mewing and gasping sounds came from her as she fought to free herself from his pressing weight.

"God, but you're beautiful! Even fighting mad, you're beautiful. Will I be going where no other man has ever been?" His happy jubilant laugh rang out.

He shifted his body to lie full-length on hers, pressing his sex against her wriggling body. She whistled once more, but the sound was lost as he clamped his mouth to hers and ground his lips against her clenched teeth. He lifted his head just enough so that he could see her face.

"You wild little . . . slut! I'm going to ram this up into your belly!" He flexed his hips and pushed the hard length of his arousal against her. "I can't wait to feel *that* inside you!" He pried her legs apart with his knees and lowered himself onto her, breathless with anticipation. He grasped his elongated sex in his hand, desperately seeking admittance into her small, writhing body.

Jason felt something hit his back.

Seconds passed before he felt pain. Then strength suddenly left his arms and he toppled over onto his side, unaware when the girl slipped out from beneath him. Something warm and wet gushed from his mouth. His fingers turned into claws, reaching out . . . seeking. A foot against his chest pushed him over. He felt an icy chill start in his legs and then cover his body. He was cold . . . cold.

"Help . . . me —" Jason looked up into a fierce, dark face; the eyes were wild, the lips drew back in a vicious snarl.

The devil! The devil had come for him!

This was Jason Picket's last thought before a knife slashed a bloody path across his throat.

Baptiste Lightbody looked down on the mutilated body of the man he had just killed. Jason Picket's trousers were open and his male parts lay exposed to the sun. Such fury consumed Light that he could hardly restrain himself from slicing them from the body. Instead, he spit on them.

"Dog!" He spat again, this time on the still, lifeless face. He wiped his knife and returned it to his belt, then rolled the body over with his foot and held it there while he pulled the thin steel from between the shoulder blades. Then he rolled Jason Picket back over and left his face and privates uncovered as if to add more insult.

Light turned from the dead man and opened his arms. Maggie flew into them. Not a whimper had escaped her lips, nor was there a tear in her eye. Her arms encircled his neck and he lifted her off her feet, burying his face in the soft curve of her neck. She could feel the trembling in his body and sensed his desperation by the way he strained her to him.

"I'm a'right," she crooned in his ear. "I knew ya'd come. I waited for ya."

"*Mon Dieu*, my little pet!" He set her on her feet and brushed the tangled hair back from her face. His fingers gently touched her bruised, swollen flesh. He cursed in French. "Did he violate you, my pretty one?" His dark eyes examined her anxiously. Her eyes questioned him. "Did he go inside you?" he asked gently.

Maggie shook her head vigorously, and he clasped her to him again and held her for a long, quiet moment.

"*Oui, chérie.* You are very much a woman, *ma petite.*" His voice quivered with tender emotion. She stood quietly while his hands moved over

17

her, brushing the dirt and leaves from her skirt and hair. He put his hands on her shoulders and held her away from him so he could examine her face. Anger gleamed in his dark eyes.

"I would kill him again and again."

She lifted a hand and her fingers traced the frown that drew his brows together and softly stroked the hair over his ears.

"I'm a'right now, Light." Her crooning voice had a soothing effect on his anger.

"How did you know that I was coming this way?"

She smiled, but only one side of her swollen mouth moved. She lifted her shoulders in a shrug.

"I called t' ya, Light. I knew ya'd come."

"You were waiting for me to come to you," he repeated softly and tenderly kissed the injured side of her soft, red mouth. "It is enough to know for now. *Mon Dieu,* my sweet pet! I must guard you well, my jewel. You have become most precious to me!" He cupped her face between his palms and kissed her again and again, finding the broken flesh and licking it with his tongue.

"Does it make ya happy t' be with me, Light?"

"Very happy, my pretty one."

She laughed a soft, trilling, happy sound that echoed like music in his ears. Her arms tightened around him, hugging him. At that moment a great swell of joy washed the torment from his soul. When he held her away from him so that he could look down into her face, it was with gentle firmness.

"Do not be so foolish again, my sprite," he scolded gently. "When you are alone, you must not get so near a man that he can pounce on you."

"He hurt the horse, Light."

Her palm was against his face. He turned his lips into it. She smiled, holding his eyes with hers until his dark features relaxed. She loved this quiet man who moved so silently through the forest, constantly vigilant. Though his copper skin and straight black hair that grew well-back from his forehead revealed his Indian heritage, his endearments were often French words, his accent ever-present.

"Come, my sweet pet," he said softly. "We must go from this place. I have first the painful duty of telling my friend that I have killed his half-brother. Then we must go tell your papa that I'm taking you with me to my mountain."

"Yore mountain? Where's it at, Light?"

"To the west, *chérie*. I've seen it in my dreams — a shining mountain where the trees grow tall, and clear rippling streams sparkle in the sunlight. At night the stars are so close you can almost reach out and touch them. It's a virgin land of peace and quiet, unsullied by man. I want to go to my mountain, build a stout cabin and live out my life there."

"Ya'll take me with ya, Light? I want t' go where I can sing an' dance and folks won't think me strange. I want t' go where no man can find me but you, Light." Maggie stood on her toes

19

and kissed his cheek.

Light looked down at her for a long while. He had been irresistibly drawn to the fey girl since first he had seen her traveling with her family on the Missouri River. Light had grown accustomed to a solitary life. He had fought against loving another woman, but the little woods sprite had crept into his heart. When he gazed into her eyes, it seemed to him that she was looking into his soul and he into hers. It was unthinkable to him that a man, any man, should capture her and break her spirit. He must protect her forever.

"You are my woman, *ma petite*," he said, and the words were a pledge. "Come. We first go to Jefferson, then to your papa."

CHAPTER TWO

"Isn't that Light coming in on Jason's horse?" Jefferson asked and moved out away from the house.

Jefferson's friend, Will Murdock, narrowed his eyes and watched the riders approach. Light rode Jason's horse and Maggie sat astride the spotted mare that Light favored. Will observed Jefferson's set face and felt a premonition of trouble.

Light rode up within a few feet of them. He tossed the reins to Will, slid down, and reached up to lift Maggie from his mare. He turned and looked Jefferson in the eye.

"I have killed your half-brother."

Both men stared at him with astonishment. Light stood with his feet spread, his body rigid. His piercing black eyes held Jefferson's. Maggie stood close to him, both hands clasped around his upper arm, looking up into his face.

Jefferson looked steadily at the expressionless, dark face of the man who had been more like a brother to him than his own kin. It took a while for the import of the words to hit Jefferson.

Jason was dead!

Light had killed him!

"I know you, Light," Jefferson said slowly. "You wouldn't have killed him without a powerful reason."

"I killed him while he lay on top of my woman. I did not know who he was when I threw the knife. Had I known, I would still have thrown it." A rush of fury reddened Light's face. "But I knew who he was when I cut his throat," he said quietly, despite the anger that washed back over him.

"He was forcing himself on . . . Maggie?" Jefferson's gaze went to the girl. She turned her face to him. It was swollen and bruised, her lip cut and bleeding still. He knew what Light said was true without seeing any further evidence. Light did not lie!

"I was on my way here when I heard her whistle. He was forcing his way into her." Light's voice shook with rage.

Maggie took his hand and rubbed his arm soothingly. He looked down at her, his face softening. He placed his hand behind her head and drew her to him.

"I'm sorry," Jefferson said slowly. "I didn't know that side of Jason."

"He lies yonder, on the trail to St. Charles. I would not soil my hands to bring him to you."

"I understand." After a silent moment, Jefferson heaved a big sigh. "I'll go tell his wife. Then we'll go get him."

"I'll hitch up the wagon." Will walked away,

leading Jason's horse.

"I will tell the *madame*," Light said.

"No, my friend. I'll do it. Jason has not been a good husband and father. Callie is a free woman now." Jefferson laid his hand on Light's shoulder. "Will and I feel that now that Hartley is dead the investigation of Burr is over. Tom Jefferson left a purse with me to pass on to you when we completed our mission. What are your plans, Light?"

"I'm going west and I'm taking Maggie."

"It will be a dangerous journey."

"*Oui.*" Light sprang onto the back of his horse and pulled Maggie up behind him.

"Will we see you before you go?"

"*Oui,*" Light said again, and rode away.

The sun sent streaks of light fanning up from the eastern horizon when Light arrived at the Gentry homestead riding his horse and leading a small mare. His flintlock was under his arm, a tomahawk hung from his belt and the handle of a long hunting knife protruded from the top of his left legging above his moccasin. His hair was tied at his nape, and he wore a flat-crowned, round-brimmed leather hat.

Wearing a newly sewn doeskin shirt, leather britches and moccasins, Maggie waited in the yard beside her parents clutching a bundle tied with a thin thong.

After greeting the Gentrys, Light motioned Maggie's father, Orlan, to one side.

23

"It still be yore notion t' go clear t' the mountains?" Orlan asked, although he knew the answer. He had spent several hours talking with the scout about his plans.

"*Oui*. I am a man of the forest, *m'sieur*."

" 'Pears t' be plenty a woods 'tween here and there. Plenty a Indians too."

"That is true. Are you thinking that Maggie would be safer or happier here, *m'sieur*, where she is scorned by women and lusted after by men who would dishonor her?"

"No," Orlan admitted sadly and wondered why God had given him this special child.

"I will love her and protect her with my life, *m'sieur*. I do swear it to you."

"Will you wed her?"

"We will speak our vows."

From where she stood beside her mother, Maggie watched anxiously. When his conversation with Light was over, her father came to her and put his hand on her shoulder. He cleared his throat before he spoke.

"If it still be in yore mind t' go with Light, ya have my blessin'. He'll be a good husband to ya. He do swear it. Me and yore ma be knowin' it ain't yore fault ya ain't had no easy time with folks. Go from here to a new land" — the words stuck in his throat — "an' . . . God be with ya."

"Thank ya, Pa." Maggie kissed his cheek.

"Mind yore man now, daughter."

"I will, Pa. I'm Light's woman. I go where

24

Light goes. Don't fret for me, Ma," she kissed her mother's cheek. "He'll keep me safe. I'll be happy."

Light flung a blanket over the mare's back and lifted Maggie to sit astride. He tied her bundle to a burden strap he had slipped beneath the horse's belly. Taking the reins of Maggie's horse, he mounted his own and they rode away from the homestead.

Maggie turned for a last look at her parents. Her eyes were aglow, her lips curved in a happy smile. She waved and called to them.

"Good-bye, Ma. Good-bye, Pa. 'Bye! 'Bye!"

The day was balmy with light breezes rustling the leaves of the tall forest. White pine, hemlock and oak towered two hundred feet high. Subdued sunlight struck the woodland floor of dense matted leaves. A marten slunk through the brush ahead of them, momentarily pausing to bare its sharp teeth. A cathedral silence surrounded them on all sides, broken only by the crackle of twigs under the hooves of their horses.

Maggie was wildly, ecstatically happy. Her heart sang. She puckered her lips to whistle a merry tune. It was as if this were the first day of her life. She had only existed until now. She and her man were going into the vast wilderness beyond the great river. The unknown held no terrors for her . . . because she was with Light.

She was going home to Light's Mountain.

He turned and smiled.

25

The sun beamed down when they came to a break in the forest. The breeze brushed her face and stirred the brim of the straw hat her mother had insisted that she wear. She breathed deeply of the green, sweet-scented grass, the towering trees and the muddy smell of the river.

They stopped on a bluff and looked toward the west where they could see the path the great Missouri River had sliced from the wilderness. It was noon, the top of the day. Maggie slid from her horse, and she and Light walked to the edge of the bluff. He turned her toward him and looked earnestly down into her upturned expectant face.

"I brought you to this godly place to exchange our vows, *chérie*. I told your papa we would marry. Here I will pledge my love. It will be more sacred to me than if we stood before a man of God."

"We marry here, Light?"

"Yes, *chérie*. Is it your wish that we go to St. Charles and find a priest?"

"No. Let us marry here."

Light took off her hat and his and tossed them to the ground. He placed her hand over his heart and looked earnestly into her eyes.

"I, Baptiste Lightbody, take you, Maggie Gentry, to be my wife. I swear to honor and cherish and protect you for as long as I live." He looked up toward the heavens. "God be my witness."

While Maggie listened to the words her face was solemn and her eyes reflected the seriousness of the moment. She had known since first she saw him that this moment would come. He was her heart, her soul, her mate.

"Does it mean I'm truly yore woman? Like Ma and Pa?"

"Yes, my precious pet. I have vowed to love and protect you. You and I will be as one. We will be together for as long as we live."

"Forever an' ever," she said solemnly. "I promise all that ya did, Light. I promise t' honor and obey ya and be a good wife." She looked up at the heavens as he had done. "God be my witness."

They looked into each other's eyes, the small girl and the dark scout, and spoke their vows as solemnly as if they were truly in a great cathedral.

He held her close. "From this day forward, *chérie,* for as long as we live we will never be apart."

"Never be apart," she echoed.

Her arms moved up and around his neck. He held her firmly to him and kissed her reverently. She looked up at him with such adoration that he was suddenly fearful in his happiness that something would happen to snatch her from him. He would do everything in his power to keep this precious treasure, this wonderful small creature who was now his wife, safe from all harm.

"Will we sleep together, Light?"

"*Oui,* my love. Every night."

"I'll like that." She snuggled closer in his arms.

"We'll eat our wedding dinner here." His smile altered the usually grave lines of his face.

"Annie Lash sent pie."

Maggie clapped her hands. "And Ma packed hard-cooked eggs and corn pone and maple sugar sweets."

The first two nights he and his bride were together, Light only caressed her and kissed her, holding his trembling desire in check lest he frighten her.

Maggie loved being close to him. Each time his arms reached for her, she gladly went into them, delighting in the shelter of his wiry, warm body. Never, never had she felt so safe and so complete as here in their private world.

On the third night, as they lay on the grassy riverbank, Maggie rolled over and stared down into Light's face in the gathering dark. As she traced his thick dark hair and his straight nose with her light fingers, his firm mouth relaxed and softened.

"Don't you want to mate with me?"

"Oh, *chérie.* I didn't know if you knew —"

Maggie laughed. " 'Course, I know. I've seen couplin'."

"*Mon Dieu!* Where?"

"When we camped near St. Charles. A man an' a woman were in the woods. She pulled up her skirt an' he pulled down his britches. I watched them. I didn't think I'd like it then. But now I want t' be with ya like that." She took his hand and placed it on her lower belly. "Do ya want t' do that with me, Light?"

"Sweet pet." Light laughed. He turned her and leaned over to kiss her again and again.

Eyes closed, Maggie felt herself in some kind of warm paradise without borders of time or space. Light stopped kissing her for a moment and, smiling tenderly, put a finger on her eyelids to open them so that he might look deeply into her eyes. She shook her head impatiently as passion seized her. She tightened her arm around his neck and pulled his lips back down to hers.

Slowly he pulled off her britches and pulled up her shirt to bare her breasts. A tremor raced through him. He crushed her to him and kissed her deeply. His hand trembled as he cupped her breast and began caressing it slowly. Maggie's hands traveled searchingly over his body. She felt the hardness between his legs and gasped. She held onto it, excited by its length and rigidity.

Light groaned with pleasure and held her hand there even as, with his other hand, he touched and felt the moistness between her thighs. Knowing he could not wait much longer, he fumbled to unfasten the tie at his waist and release his aching, throbbing, elongated sex.

Light covered her mouth with his when he plunged into her, and remained still. He waited until the shock of entry receded and he felt the tight sheath surrounding him relax. Maggie clung to him as a fire ignited in the pit of her stomach. She began to move and then found herself gasping with exquisite pleasure.

For both the sweet agony became more and

more intense, then peaked. Maggie whimpered. Light lurched suddenly and violently.

They lay quietly with Light still inside her for several minutes. When he withdrew, he lay at her side with his arms around her.

"I'm yores and yo're mine, Light."

"*Oui,* my precious pet. I am yours."

They traveled for a week without seeing anyone. Then late one evening they met a party of Osage. Light identified himself and they were greeted warmly. Light explained to Maggie that the Osage had heard of him and that they knew his mother's sister, Nowatha, the healer. That night they all sat around a fire and ate strips of venison, fish and boiled kernels of corn.

The hunters were plainly puzzled when Light prepared the food and his squaw sat beside the fire. After the meal they smoked and spoke in a language Maggie didn't understand. She curled up on a blanket and went to sleep.

When she awoke, she and Light were alone once again. He had traded a bit of gunpowder and tobacco to the Osage for a bow and a quiver of arrows. They had given Light a black rawhide whip they had found when they came upon a mule skinner who had been killed by the Delaware.

After a breakfast of tea and biscuits, Light showed Maggie how to snake the narrow strip of rawhide out behind her and how to bring it forward. He left her to practice while he broke camp and prepared the horses for their departure.

"You must practice each day," he told her gravely. "There may come a time when we will be set upon. You must know how to defend yourself."

Each evening during the following weeks Maggie practiced with the whip and the knife. Crack after crack sounded through the still forest air as she gradually learned how to control the long, writhing snake of rawhide, until she could use the tip with enough precision to snap off twigs and weeds and blossoms.

"It is an extra weapon, *chérie*," Light explained.

Light taught her to use the bow and arrow, but she did not have the strength to send the arrow with force for any distance and his flintlock was too heavy for her to lift, let alone control. The gun was a colonial make called the "Kentucky rifle" and was four inches over five feet in length. Light was one of only a few men west of the big river who could manage to hit his target at two hundred yards. Even so, he would much rather use a knife, and some evenings he and Maggie entertained themselves with contests between the two of them.

The following weeks were a heavenly time for Maggie as they rode through the wilderness, skirting the flooded lowlands and Indian villages. Deep forests surrounded them, and at times Maggie wondered how Light knew which way to go.

One afternoon Light left Maggie in a secluded place along a small stream so that he could scout ahead. She lay quietly, listening. No voice came to her. She turned her head to listen very carefully. Still no sound but the sounds of nature.

A golden eagle soared down out of the sky from the south. The huge bird settled on the dead, barren arm of a tree long ago splintered by lightning that had forked out of the sky to end its one-hundred-year-old life. The eagle arranged itself on the limb with the composure of one who truly believed that he was lord of all he surveyed.

"Yo're thinkin' I'm dead. Ya come t' pluck out my eyes." Maggie laughed softly. "Well, I ain't." She lifted her hand and wiggled her fingers.

The great claws loosened a piece of dead bark from the limb. It splashed as it fell into the river. The bird shuffled its feathers into place and turned a coolly benign eye on Maggie. It winked at her solemnly. She laughed again — silently.

"A grass lizard passed here a while ago. Did ya see it? It'd make ya a good supper."

The golden eagle tilted its head and glared down at her.

"Don't ya pluck up that rabbit over there under the brush. Hear me now? That's supper for me an' Light."

"Awrrch!" The eagle squawked, ruffled its feathers again, then sat stone still, its yellow-rimmed eyes staring down at her.

Maggie slowly and carefully reached over her shoulder and drew an arrow from the quiver on her back. She placed it in the bowstring and waited. Her intention was not to kill the eagle, only to discourage it should its mind be set on the rabbit.

She waited.

The eagle waited.

Suddenly the great bird dropped from the limb. It caught just enough air under its great wings to become airborne. Spreading its black talons, it dipped out of sight, then soared upward with a large snake hanging from its powerful beak.

"Good-bye," Maggie whispered and watched until the majestic bird was out of sight.

The sun had been directly overhead when Light had stopped and held out his arm to halt Maggie. As they had listened, two deer had shot out of the woods ahead of them, frightened by some unknown presence. Light had dismounted and moved the horses some distance behind a screen of brush. He had dropped the pack from his horse in a spot concealed by thick willows and motioned for Maggie to stay with it while he moved along the forest path warily, watching carefully on either side. His flintlock had been tucked under his arm, loaded and cocked. In his belt was his tomahawk.

Maggie had waited beneath the willows, her knife in the scabbard against her thigh. She carried a bow and a quiver of arrows on her back now. She looked like a young boy, except for the long rope of hair hanging to her waist.

They were on course. Light had checked his brass-bound compass earlier in the morning and had pulled out a creased map and consulted it as well. They had followed the river to this point and then left it to travel cross-country.

The Osage had told Light that ahead lay a large encampment of Delaware who had been pushed across the Mississippi River by Mad Anthony Wayne. The Delaware were resentful of the Osage, who had an agreement with the government to supply pelts to Manuel Lisa, an important trader in St. Louis.

Had he been alone Light would have skirted the encampment in full daylight; but life was more precious to him now, and he took every precaution. He and Maggie were on their way to the unknown, the unexplored, the unmapped — the vast territory beyond the barrier of the Mississippi. The Lewis and Clark expedition had returned from their journey with tales of mountain ranges, rich with game and untouched by man.

Now, as she lay beside the small stream that fed into the Missouri, it seemed to Maggie that Light had been gone for a long time. But according to the shadow of the dead tree creeping across the water, it had been but an hour.

Light was not more than six feet away when Maggie finally heard him. She turned, the bow in her hand, the arrow strung and pulled back.

"Light! Ya were close before I heard ya." She lowered the bow.

"I did well then, *ma petite,* for you have a fine set of ears."

Light dropped down beside her and reached for the water pouch. His dark hair, pulled straight back from his forehead and held behind his neck with a thong, was wet with sweat that rolled down the sides of his face. His dark eyes caressed her face, then surveyed the edge of the forest.

"What did you see?"

"Delaware."

"Friends?"

"Not these men, pretty pet. They are outcasts. Not even their own tribe will permit such as they among them."

"What'll we do, Light?"

"We stay here and rest until the moon comes up. By then they'll be so drunk they'd not hear a herd of buffalo pass through their camp."

He stretched out beside her and extended his arm for her to come close. Maggie snuggled beside him, her head on his shoulder. She would be content to travel with him through the forest and up the river forever.

"What did you see, Maggie, as you waited for me?"

"A great golden eagle. He sat on the limb of that dead tree."

"You must have been very still."

"I wiggled my fingers so he'd know I wasn't dead." She laughed. Her palm against Light's chest told her that he laughed too. "There was a rabbit under a brush pile not far away. I would have caught it and cooked it for ya — but ya told me t' stay where I was. I do what ya say, Light."

"You're my sweet *amour*." He bent his head

and kissed the lips she offered.

One kiss was never enough. They turned eagerly to each other. Maggie's hand wiggled inside his doeskin shirt to caress his smooth chest, then down beneath the drawstring of his britches.

"What do you do, my love?" He sucked in his breath to hollow his stomach and give her access.

"Do ya like it when I do this, Light?" she murmured, her nails scratching into the hair at his groin. "Does it make you happy?"

"*Mon Dieu!* My sweet —" The words came on a husky whisper. "*Oui,* it makes me very happy."

"Does this feel good?" Her small fingers danced up and down his hardening flesh.

"Very good, my treasure."

"It makes me feel good too, Light." She covered his face with quick damp kisses, nibbled his lips, licked them with her tongue.

"I should swat your round little bottom, my little pet," he threatened in a raspy voice, and rolled her onto her back. "It's the middle of the day."

"We did it before — in daylight."

"We did? When?"

"Ya know it. Yo're teasin', Light." Her laugh was warm and moist against his mouth.

Beneath the shelter of the willows they bared their bodies like two children in the Garden of Eden. When they were ready, he slid smoothly over her, seeking entrance while she waited in

36

rapt and arching anguish. He moved between her legs and pressed into her tightness. He stayed there, gulping air into his lungs, savoring this wondrous moment. They kissed and moved together, joined their hungry flesh.

Maggie felt him hard and deep inside her body and became caught up in an overpowering desire to give to him. He was part of her, he was her world, her universe, and she vibrated with all the love she had to give to him. She reached up and ran her fingers through the dense mass of dark hair over his temples. Her lips spread in a beautiful smile.

"I'll always be where ya are, Light."

CHAPTER THREE

"Boat comin' upriver, Jeff."

Will Murdock removed his hat and wiped the sweat from his brow. Splitting rails was back-breaking work. He and Jefferson had been at it for two days, and the pile was growing; but not fast enough to suit Will.

Jefferson's eyes squinted against the sun. The long, narrow flatboat, poled by four men, moved easily against the gentle current close to the bank. The man at the sweep oar was bareheaded; the brown hair that swept his shoulders was lighter than his close-cut beard.

"Know 'em?" Will asked.

"I've seen three of them down around St. Charles. Can't say as they're anythin' to sing about."

Will picked up his muzzle loader and followed Jefferson to the sandbar where the boat was being moored.

"Howdy," Jefferson called.

"How do?" the man at the sweep oar replied. He motioned to a stocky dark-haired man, and they jumped off the craft and crossed the sandbar to where Jeff and Will waited.

"I'm looking for Jefferson Merrick," the bearded man said. Up close Jefferson could see the beard was shot with gray; he reckoned that the man had lived a few years more than his own twenty-seven.

"You've found him."

"Eli Nielson." The man offered his hand to Jefferson. "Paul Deschanel," he said, indicating the stocky man beside him.

Jefferson shook hands with both men and introduced Will Murdock.

"I was told," Nielson said, "that a man by the name of Baptiste Lightbody was a friend of yours and you could tell me where to find him."

"Light *is* a friend of mine." Jefferson looked the man in the eye and said no more.

"Do you know where I can find him?"

"Depends."

"I'm taking a cargo upriver to Bellevue. I hear he's the best scout around."

"That's true. Light is the best woodsman, tracker and scout west of the Mississippi."

"Part Osage, isn't he?"

"You got something against Osage?"

"No. Where can I find him?"

"He left a week ago."

"He's gone upriver?"

"It's what he said."

"Did he go alone?"

"When he left my homestead he was alone."

"How long will he be gone?"

"Didn't say."

Eli Nielson looked steadily into Jefferson's dark eyes. "I guess that's that. I'm obliged to you."

"Welcome."

Eli and Paul walked back to the craft. Eli was cursing under his breath.

"Missed him by a week."

"Give it up, *mon ami.*"

"Not on your life."

"What will you do now?"

"Go upriver."

"*Mon Dieu*, Eli. Lookin' for that feller in the wilderness will be like lookin' for a flea on a buffalo."

"You don't have to go, Paul."

Paul swore for a long while in French, then said, "What will we do upriver?"

"Depends."

As soon as Will saw that the boat was headed back downriver, he voiced the question that was in Jefferson's mind.

"What do ya reckon he *really* wanted with Light?"

"Damned if I know. I can't see Light hirin' on with that crew."

Will laughed. "Puttin' Maggie on a boat with a bunch like that would be like touchin' a spark to a keg a gunpowder."

"He'll not catch up with Light."

"Do you reckon he'll try?"

"I'd not doubt it."

Light was uneasy about the presence of Delaware in the area. He wanted to get past them and over into Osage country. In a few more days, if he read his map right, he'd reach the spot where the river made an abrupt turn northwest. He intended to cross over there and head straight west to the mountains.

Each day after they had skirted the Delaware encampment, he would leave Maggie concealed in a thicket and backtrack. Then he would ride swiftly through the thick woods to a high point from which he could see the open space below and scan the terrain with his spyglass, a gift from Jefferson Merrick. One day his vigilance paid off. He saw two warriors loping along the route he and Maggie had taken, following the tracks made by their horses.

The braves were on foot. Light reckoned they had broken away from a hunting party when they spotted the horses' tracks and were planning to try to steal the animals. A Delaware brave who owned a horse would have considerable prestige among the people of his tribe.

Light collapsed his spyglass, dropped it inside his doeskin shirt, and hurried back to where Maggie waited. Without telling her of his concern, he insisted that they press on and keep to the higher ground.

In the late afternoon, the sky darkened as thunder clouds rolled in from the southwest. When he and Maggie came to a break in the trees, Light used his spyglass again to survey the land ahead and behind. Although there was no sign of the Indians, that did not mean they were not there. The Delaware would follow for days, if not weeks, in the hope of seizing the horses.

On one side of the knoll where Light and Maggie stood, the ground sloped down to the river, and on the other lay a vast open space.

Light carefully scanned the bank where the river made a sharp turn and he noted, above the bushes along the wall of rock, a dark hole that could be a small cave. He motioned to Maggie and they rode toward it. Blackthorn bushes grew thickly along the riverbank; and, as Light expected, on a rocky shelf above the river, partially covered with the bushes, he found the entrance to a cave.

Waving Maggie to a stop, he dismounted and handed her the reins. With his rifle in his hands, he approached the opening. He tossed a large stone inside, waited a few seconds, then tossed in several more. He walked back to hand Maggie the rifle, then gathered a handful of dry grass and twisted it into a torch. On a flint he drew from the bag tied at his waist, he struck a spark with his knife.

In the torchlight he could see that the cave was quite large. Its floor was sand and the ceiling was high. The remains of a fire was evidence that it had been used by man, but not recently.

Light checked carefully for snakes, then went out to bring Maggie and the horses inside.

Leaving Maggie to unpack the horses, he gathered firewood before the rain began, then cut brush to conceal the cave opening.

Light and Maggie worked well as a team. Quickly and quietly they set up camp for the night while thunder rolled and lightning flashed. The small fire Light had built so that they could see was almost smokeless. What little smoke there was disappeared overhead. While Maggie made the last of their cornmeal into mush, Light took the horses one at a time to the river to drink.

The rain came suddenly. It spilled out of the sky like water pouring from a bucket. The raindrops were large and wind-driven. Light welcomed the rain. It would wash away any tracks they might have left; and the Delaware, if they were still following, would hole up somewhere until the rain lessened or stopped. He and Maggie sat cross-legged on a blanket and, in the dim light of their small fire, ate their meager meal.

Maggie had added a few dried berries to the mush. While water was heating for tea, she cracked a handful of nuts with Light's tomahawk. With loving generosity, she fed him two of the nutmeats for every one she ate.

"What are you thinking, my pet, when you gaze at me so seriously?"

"That yo're beautiful," she replied and popped a nutmeat in his mouth.

"Ho! *Ma petite!*" His face creased with the

smiles she loved. "I fear your brains have turned to water. *You* are beautiful. The sunrise is beautiful. A rainbow is beautiful. I am but a man."

"My man!" She put her foot on his chest and playfully pushed him over onto his back. "My man," she repeated as she followed him down to lie on his chest and kiss his lips. "Say it."

"My man." He laughed at her.

"No! *My* man!"

"Ah, *chérie*. You're my treasure." He held her to him and kissed her soundly.

"Tell me what we'll do when we get t'our mountain, Light." She laid her head on his shoulder and nuzzled her face into his neck.

"We'll find a place where no man has been before. The trees will be tall and the grass deep. We'll build our cabin beside a small stream, *chérie*. Before the first snow we will hear the geese go over on their journey south. We will listen for their return in the spring. Spring, summer, fall and winter. We will live there, grow old there, together."

"But that will be a long time from now."

"A long time, my love."

"Do ya want us t' have babies, Light?"

"We'll have a whole nest full if we keep doing as we have been." He chuckled against her upturned face.

"I'll love ya the most," she said seriously.

"A mother's love for a babe is different from her love for her man, sweetling. You'll love our babes, wait and see."

"If my woman time stops it will mean a babe is growing in my belly. My mamma said so."

"That is usually what it means. Go to sleep, my treasure. We are safe here for now."

The heavy storm clouds moved away, but the rain continued for most of the night. By dawn, it had settled into a light mist. Light left Maggie sleeping in their blankets and ventured outside the cave. He heard the cooing of doves and the sound of a whippoorwill in the distance but no sound nearby. He was instantly alert.

He stood as still as the rock at his back, only his eyes moving from left to right and back again. Then he caught movement. Turning his head ever so slowly, he identified what had drawn his attention: a scrap of red cloth tied to the top-knot on the head of a Delaware. The brave's buckskin shirt and leggings had blended in with the limestone rock and dead brush.

As Light watched, the Delaware discovered the fresh cuts on the branches Light had made the night before when he had gathered brush to pile in front of the cave entrance.

Light's gaze traveled in a widening circle until he was reasonably sure the brave was alone. Then he slipped back behind the thicket of thornberry, flattening himself against the wall, and waited.

With tomahawk raised, the Delaware moved along the cliff toward the mouth of the cave. Light could hear the scrape of the Indian's buckskins against the rock wall. He came to a spot where Light could see him through the concealing

45

brush. The man was short, no longer young, and dirty even for a Delaware.

A chill of apprehension washed over Light. *Should Maggie awaken and come to the opening, the brave would be sure to attack her with his tomahawk.*

Now the Indian moved to the other side of the opening within an arm's length of where Light stood. At that moment one of the horses stamped and blew air through its lips.

At the instant the Delaware crouched and made ready to spring inside, Light's two hands snaked out and circled his throat. With one ferocious powerful squeeze, he throttled the brave's outcry. Then he wrapped his legs around the Indian's thrashing body. The two fell to the ground. Light held on as the brave struggled in his death throes.

For what seemed like an eternity to Light, the body writhed. Finally, it went limp, and he let go. The Delaware lay crumpled at his feet, the head lolling at an odd angle.

"*Chérie?*"

"Here, Light."

"Stay inside. There may be another one."

Light stepped into the cave to pick up his rifle and then set out into the misty morning. He headed in the direction the Delaware had come. He moved swiftly and soundlessly, constantly scrutinizing the ground and the stunted shrubbery on the rocky ledges. A half mile downriver he found the overhang where the Delaware had waited out the rain. Only one set of tracks led away from the overhang.

The braves had split up before reaching this place. One of them was still out there. Light set off in a fast trot toward the cave.

Maggie did not brood over the killing of the Indian any more than she had when Light killed Jason Picket as he tried to rape her. They both had been bad men intent on evil. The body of the dead Indian lying in the doorway of the cave, however, did have an effect on her and the horses. The odor from his unwashed body and dirty clothing, coupled with the stench of his bowels, let loose when life left him, was nauseating to Maggie.

The smell frightened the horses. They whinnied, rolled their eyes and pawed the sandy floor. Maggie crooned to them and partially calmed them, but still they moved restlessly.

The struggle between Light and the Indian had trampled the brush that covered the cave opening, allowing morning light to come in. Maggie longed to leave the cave, to get out into the fresh air, but Light had told her to stay.

She was whispering in the ear of one of the horses when she looked toward the entrance and saw that it was blocked by the figure of an Indian with tomahawk raised. The horses, sensing the strange presence, tossed their heads and crowded against each other.

While the Indian's eyes were becoming accustomed to the dim light, Maggie quickly moved behind the horses and slipped the knot in the rope that held them to the log Light had used to secure them. When they were free, she pricked one of them on the rump with the tip of her knife. The horses bolted for the cave entrance. Maggie's first thought had been to leap on one of the horses and go with them, but she decided not to chance being scraped off or snatched off by the Indian. As the horses crashed through the brush, Maggie, with her knife in one hand and the whip in the other, watched and waited.

The cave was well lighted now. Carefully Maggie uncoiled the whip, took a deep breath and let out a piercing whistle. She was not sure how far the sound would carry from inside the cave, but Light would hear and he would come.

When the Indian sprang through the entrance, she was ready. She lashed out with the whip, and the tip struck the arm that held the tomahawk. Stunned momentarily by shock and pain, the Indian paused, giving Maggie time to strike again. She aimed for his face, but the tip missed the mark and hit his shoulder. The warrior put his arm over his face to protect it and ran at her. Maggie stepped back and struck again. The next blow caught him on the arm, drawing blood. Snarling with rage, he backed away from her.

Maggie knew she was fighting for her life, yet she was calm. If only she had more skill with the whip! Her next strike was one Light had warned her against, allowing the lash to snake out too far before she snapped her wrist to bring it back. The leather wrapped around the Indian's leg. Quickly she dropped the handle and shifted her knife to her other hand.

The Indian's grin was hideous.

The small woman meant to fight him with a knife!

Knife ready, her eyes on the brave, Maggie sidestepped to face him squarely. Gripping the blade of her knife between her thumb and fore-finger, Maggie waited until the Indian had inched to within a few yards of her. When the triumphant grin on his face changed to one of evil intent and his arm lifted higher to deliver the killing blow, Maggie threw the knife.

The slender blade flew from her hand with the speed of an arrow and buried itself to the hilt in the Delaware's chest. Maggie covered her mouth with her hand and watched the surprised look on the man's face as his legs melted out from under him.

When the tomahawk fell from his hand, she darted past him and ran out of the cave. Drawing in a deep breath of clean tangy air, she whistled again. An answering whistle came immediately from nearby. In a matter of seconds Light was beside her.

"In . . . there —" Maggie pointed. She had no breath to say more.

Long minutes passed before Light came out. He slid her cleaned knife back in her scabbard and looped the coiled whip over her shoulder before he put his arms around her and held her to him.

"Is he . . . ?" Maggie whispered.

"Dead. Your aim was true. Ah, *chérie*, I do not know if my heart can endure another scare like that. It will turn to stone and drop into my belly."

"I'm all right, Light." She put her palms against his cheeks and turned his face down to hers. "They were mean men who would kill us for our horses, not like animals who kill only to eat."

"I should not have left you."

"I am your mate, Light."

"You're my treasure." He held her so close he could feel the beating of her heart. After he kissed her, he raised his head and looked into her eyes. "You did well, my pet. You make me proud."

"Light . . . I let the horses go."

"Don't worry, love. They won't go far."

"I'll go catch 'em."

"We go together."

Light took two knives, a quiver of arrows and several fish hooks from the Indians before he dragged the bodies to the back of the cave. Although he covered the entrance again with the brush, he knew that it would be no barrier to wolves when they smelled the dead flesh. It would, however, conceal the opening should a war canoe come upriver.

Light and Maggie rode until noon. The sun came out and the land looked sparkling clean. Light led the way along the riverbank until they reached a sheltered sandy beach where reeds grew at the river's edge. He held up his hand and Maggie stopped. He sat for a minute with his ear turned toward the river. She, too, heard the sound that alerted him. Water was splashing among the reeds. Light dismounted and walked ahead along the bank. He paused and motioned for Maggie to join him.

About six feet out in the river a young doe, with large frightened brown eyes, struggled to free herself from the reeds.

"Her leg is broken, *chérie*."

"Ah . . . how did she do that?"

"She was frightened by something up there and" — he looked toward the rocky shelf — "jumped to the beach, broke her leg, and dragged herself to the water. She was here before it rained, there are no tracks."

"What'll we do, Light?"

Light looked upriver and down. He scanned the area in every direction before he spoke.

"We camp here. We need food."

"Ya'll kill her?"

"Yes. Quickly. If not, she will die slowly. Leave our packs over there on the high ground. Take the horses to water downstream, then hobble them in that grassy patch."

Maggie moved the animals away from the river, not wanting to see the necessary death of the doe. The horses followed her as if they were pets. She took off the blankets and the burden straps that held their packs and moved them next to the bluff. Murmuring softly to urge them to fol-

51

low, she led them upriver.

When she returned, Light had removed his clothes and had waded naked into the river with his knife clamped between his teeth.

While Light butchered the deer, Maggie built a fire using dry cedar knots and splinters. It burned with a clear hot flame and gave off little smoke. She strung hunks of the meat on a green willow stick and hung it over the fire. Other chunks she prepared for burial in the hot coals to cook overnight. Light dragged the rest of the carcass out to let the current carry it downriver.

Still naked, he waded out into the river beyond the reeds and, using a hand line, cast a hook to which he had tied a bit of the deer liver as a lure. The hook had scarcely hit the water when it was struck by a giant pike. In a short time Light had caught a bass and a small white catfish. He knelt at the water's edge and cleaned his catch on a flat rock.

After washing himself in the muddy river, Light dressed. Maggie, thinking of the clear pool she bathed in at home and the clear streams they had used since beginning their journey, refused to immerse herself in the muddy water. She removed her britches and shirt and washed herself while squatting on the shore.

Later, after eating their fill of the meat and fish, they lay on a blanket in the soft sand. When night fog began to rise from the river in wispy patches, Light covered them with their extra blanket to hold off the damp chill. All was quiet and peaceful; the fog surrounded them like a cloak.

Light held Maggie close to his side, her head on his shoulder, her arm across his chest. Visions of her fighting the Indian had weighed upon him all day. His stomach lurched when he thought of how close she had come to death and, in reaction, his arm tightened around her.

Two attackers were dead, and this was only the beginning of their journey. Had he been foolish and stupid to bring her into the wilderness? But to have left her behind would have broken her heart and his. For a long moment he considered taking her back to St. Charles and homesteading a piece of land there. How long would he be able to endure planting, plowing, raising hogs on a plot of land? How long before Maggie would again be called a witch for her "odd" ways? New folks would be moving in. Would they want to burn her as the folks in Kentucky had been ready to do?

"My treasure, are you asleep?"

"I was thinkin' of the deer, Light. It made me sad ya had to kill her."

"She gave her life so that we could eat. If not us, the wolves would have had her so that they could eat. It's nature's way, love."

"I know. I'll try not t' think of it anymore."

"Listen to me, *chérie*. You were almost killed today."

"But I wasn't. I knew what I could do."

"We will face danger as we did today many

more times. We should think about going back to St. Charles." Light spoke the words softly and held his breath while he waited for her answer.

It was a long time coming. Maggie lay perfectly still, then lifted herself so that she could peer down into his face even though she could see only the shape of it.

"Ya don't want t' take me t' yore mountain? Am I a bother t' ya, Light?"

"Ah, *chérie!* You are my life, my joy. But I fear that I might fail to keep you safe."

"I can help, Light. I'll practice with the bow and the whip and the knife."

"If we go back, you can be with your ma and pa, with Biedy Cornick, who makes you pie. You can visit with Callie and Annie Lash. When winter comes, you'll be safe and warm and your belly full of roasted goose and suet pudding."

Maggie was silent for a long while — and still. Only her fingers moved, stroking his cheeks.

"But ya'd not be there."

"Ah . . . my treasure. I long for my mountain."

"I want what you want, Light. I'm yore mate. We promised each other. And . . . when winter comes t' our mountain, we'll roast a goose an' make suet pudding."

"It will be a long journey."

"I'm not afraid."

"We are not yet half-way to the mountains," Light said with a deep sigh.

"I don't care." Maggie fitted her small body tightly to his. "I belong with you."

While his wife slept beside him, Light stared into the foggy night. The Missouri rolled on past them out of the distant land he longed to see.

He had heard the astounding stories of snow-peaked mountains, green meadows and sparkling streams from men who had returned with the Lewis and Clark expedition. They had never before seen beaver like the ones in the streams coming down from the mountains — beaver that had never been hunted sat out in the open and gaped at you, they said. And the mountains were rugged and beautiful beyond belief.

"I love you," he whispered to the woman cuddled against him. "We will go on to our mountain together. If we should die on the way, we will be together."

CHAPTER FOUR

Dawn came swiftly.

High above the river, a pair of hawks swooped and circled in amorous pursuit of each other. A pleasant slap, slap, slapping sound came from fish frolicking in the river beyond the reeds. Always when he first awakened, he listened.

Light lifted his head to look out over the muddy water, then up and down the river. The horses stood sleeping next to the cliff. Satisfied that everything seemed to be as it should, he gazed down into the face of the woman pressed tightly against him, depending on him for warmth and protection. Just looking at her filled him with intense pleasure.

Every day that Light was with Maggie he learned something new and puzzling about her. Not only was she spunky and quick-thinking, she was braver than any woman he'd ever known. She had calmly stood her ground against the Delaware, a man twice her size. Could it be true that she was a witch? She had certainly bewitched him.

He chuckled softly, reveling in a happiness he

had never expected to have. He had loved his first wife, Little Bird, with all the love a young boy had to give. When she was killed, his grief was deep. But the love he felt now, a man's love for this wild child, filled every corner of his heart. Light pressed his lips to her forehead and tasted the sweetness of her flesh. She stirred and the blanket slipped down, exposing her soft naked breasts peeking through the dark silky hair that lay in a tangle over her shoulders and curled between the soft white mounds.

A rush of warm blood through his veins spread an unwanted arousal throughout his body. Reason won out over his hunger to gather her close in his arms and seek the "sweet hurty feeling," as she called their lovemaking. Green was fading from the tops of the oak trees and soon leaves would fall. He and Maggie must make every day of good weather count if they were to reach the bend in the river and fashion a shelter for winter.

"Wake up, my treasure." His whisper came against her ear as his palm stroked her breast. "It's a fine day."

"I'm awake. Ya were lookin' at me."

"How do you know? Your eyes were closed."

"I can see ya with my eyes shut," she whispered, and he believed her.

Her arms moved around his neck. She reached for his lips and pressed hers firmly against them. He kissed her back, slowly, deeply, enjoying the way she gave herself to him so freely. He stroked her arm and shoulder and kissed her froth of hair over and over again.

After a while, Light lifted his head and looked down into her face framed in the mass of tumbled ringlets. Her smile was pure enchantment. Was this fairy-like creature from another world? Another time? Light felt himself to be in some kind of warm paradise. He looked down at her searchingly for a long moment, then dipped his head to kiss her face once more. Slowly he shook his head.

"I'm tempted to stay here in the blankets with you till the sun goes down. But it would be foolish, *chérie*. We have many miles to travel before the snow comes."

Maggie stretched herself to her full length, her arms still about his neck.

"Don't ya want t' stay and make love with me? I want t' be with you . . . like that, Light." Her fingers feathered over the evidence of his desire.

Her frankness always amazed, aroused and amused him. He had never heard a man say his woman had asked him to mate with her. Light considered himself the luckiest of men. Reluctantly he pulled back from her searching hand.

"We'll have long cold winters on our mountain, my pet. We'll lie in our blankets all day and all night and make love whenever you want. But now, my lady of the woods, we must break camp and travel."

He pulled the blanket off her naked body and stood. Maggie jumped up and grabbed for the blanket. Light twisted away from her, laughing, holding the blanket out of her reach.

"No. No, sweet one. Get dressed. Someone beside your husband is looking at you."

"Who? Who?" Maggie spun around, her crossed arms over her naked breasts.

"Squirrel. Up there." Light pointed to a tree branch, threw back his head and laughed.

"Pooh on ya, Mr. Squirrel."

Maggie spread her arms and, naked as the day she was born, bowed to her husband and began to dance. She dipped and swayed and skipped on the sandbar to the tune she was singing.

"Squirrel in the big tree, what'll I do?
Squirrel in the big tree, what'll I do?
Squirrel in the big tree, what'll I do?
What'll I do, my darlin'?"

Mesmerized, Light watched his child-wife. She danced with such innocence. He was dazzled by the sight of her white, bare flesh, the symmetry of her rose-tipped breasts, rounded bottom and slim legs. Her red mouth smiled. Her tangle of dark hair floated around her white shoulders. Beholding her perfection, Light decided that no one of this world could express her emotions with such swift honesty as his Maggie. Then she whirled into his arms.

Only with her physical warmth pressed against him, her arms about his neck, her mouth lifted to his, could he convince himself she was a flesh-and-blood woman. He lifted her off the ground and swung her around before he sat her down. Then he hungrily kissed the mouth she offered and lightly slapped her on her bare bottom.

"— Get yourself dressed, my sweet naked nymph!" He patted the top of her head and stroked the soft curve of her breasts. "Now obey me."

"I do what ya say, Light, for . . . now." Her musical laugh came against the flesh of his neck.

He was reluctant to let her go even though he had ordered her to get dressed. He turned his eyes away as she quickly stepped into her britches and pulled her shirt on over her head.

In a happy mood, they ate the deer meat and drank hot tea from their one cup. When they had finished, Light carefully packed the remainder of the meat and fish. It was enough to last for several days. They would not go hungry. In the forest were a dozen kinds of wild fruits, ranging from persimmons to chokecherries and enormous grapevines with clusters of their ripening fruit. Light knew where to find wild peas, onions and root vegetables to make a thick stew. The wild served up a banquet for those who knew where to find it.

When their packs were ready and Light had started to fasten the burden straps on their horses, flocks of waterfowl rose from the river to circle in wild, noisy confusion.

"Something's coming." Light looked downriver

and then hastily kicked sand onto the remains of their campfire.

Shouldering the packs and motioning for Maggie to lead their horses, he hurried with her up the embankment and into the shelter of the woods.

"Who's comin', Light?"

"Stay here," was his only answer. He dropped the packs. Taking his spyglass, he went back to the edge of the woods and squatted among the foliage.

Maggie tied the horses and silently slipped through the woods to kneel down beside Light. If her man was in danger she was going to be beside him. The quiver of arrows rested on her back, the bow on one shoulder and the coiled whip on the other. Her knife was in the scabbard at her waist. Her green eyes questioned him when he looked down at her.

"I stay with ya, Light," she declared.

Light frowned. "When I put you somewhere, Maggie, I expect to go back and find you there." He lifted the glass back to his eye.

"I'll mind ya next time." She smiled at him beguilingly.

"Imp!"

"Who's comin'?"

"Flatboat. Three men, that I can see. Two at the poles, one at the sweep oar."

The flatboat that approached was one that had been put together by a master craftsman. Light knew that at first glance. It was long and narrow and, judging by the way it rode the water, lightweight. A railing ran along the two long sides and a low open-ended shed squatted in the middle with a mast pole rising from its closed end. It was a worthy craft that could be sailed, poled, or rowed.

The man at the sweep oar stood on spread legs. He was broad-shouldered and slim-hipped. His shoulder-length hair glinted red, and the close-cropped beard was a darker brown. Two pole-men moved the craft along the water outside the reeds.

"Down," Light said suddenly. One of the men had raised a nautical glass to his eye and was scanning the riverbank.

"Are they Delaware, Light?"

"No."

"Why are we afraid of them?"

"It's best to make sure who they are, pet, before we show ourselves."

As the last word left Light's mouth, a blood-curdling screech came from behind them.

Caught in an unguarded moment, Light turned to see two Delaware braves leap from a thicket of wild rose with tomahawks raised for the kill. Sure of their success, the braves had given their victory cry before the battle began.

Light had no time to raise his gun and fire; but, in swift reflex, he stepped back and swung the butt end, smashing one warrior in the face. Bones crunched and blood gushed from the man's broken nose and cheek. With an agonized howl, he fell back holding his hand to his face.

Maggie had bounced to her feet like a cat and ducked as the second brave swung his tomahawk at her head. Too close to the Indian to throw her knife, she plunged it into his bare side and fell back away from him. In pain and shock the Indian hesitated for only a second, just long enough for Light to swing the end of his long gun around and fire. Blood blossomed on the brave's chest as the shot tore into his flesh and flung him back.

The other brave, still howling in pain, took to his heels and disappeared in the bush. Light dropped his rifle and leaped after him, easily overtaking him. Without mercy he ran his knife through the Delaware's back to his heart. He stooped over the fallen warrior to retrieve his blade, then raced back to where he had left Maggie.

The small clearing was empty except for the dead Indian. Light's breath was stopped by a dread so acute he was unable to breathe.

His precious treasure was gone!

"Maggie!" The agonized cry came roaring up from the depth of his soul. "Mag . . . gie!" He grabbed up his gun and, half-blinded by fear and dread, tore through the brush to where they had left the horses.

He reached the clearing and found Maggie, standing with hands on her hips, peering after two braves riding away on their ponies.

"They took our horses, Light. Don't that beat all?"

"To hell with the damn horses!" His next dozen words were a mixture of French and Osage. He said them crossly while shaking her. Then he pulled her to him and hugged her fiercely. "*Mon Dieu, chérie!* You scared me. After this, stay where I put you!"

Maggie nestled in his embrace for a brief moment, then moved back to look up at him. She caressed his cheeks soothingly as if she were quieting an excited animal.

"If I had, I'd be gone with the horses."

"*Mon Dieu,* that is so, my treasure." He held her against him for a moment.

"What will we do without our horses?" Maggie asked sadly.

"I don't know. I was hoping to meet some of my mother's people and trade them." Light echoed Maggie's disappointment. "We will need stouter horses for our trip across the plains."

"We'll make out, Light. Don't worry." Maggie reassured him with a sweet confident smile.

"It is good that we had not put the packs on the horses," he answered, looking for a way to support her optimism.

"What now, Light?"

"We'll see who's on that flatboat coming upriver. There are only three of them to worry about, and Lord only knows how many Delaware between here and the bend."

Since sundown the day before, Eli Nielson had been aware that there was a man upriver and that he was traveling light. Only a man alone would have butchered a deer in such a way, taking only what he could use before the meat spoiled and leaving the rest of the carcass to float downriver. After spotting the dead deer, Nielson, Deschanel and a German named Kruger had moved the flatboat upriver until it became too dark to spot a dangerous sawyer or an unruly current.

At dawn Nielson had taken his turn at the steering oar while Otto Kruger, possibly the best carpenter in the territory and also the most ill-tempered, and Paul Deschanel, Nielson's friend and companion for most of his life, took the poles.

"You think it's him?" Paul asked as he pulled his pole from the muddy river bottom.

"Could be. Merrick said he was a week out of St. Charles."

"If it is, *mon ami*, you'll get a look at him before nightfall, that's if the Delaware don't take a notion to set on us . . . or him."

"I was sure that he wouldn't have turned inland. Merrick didn't say, but it's logical that he would follow the river if he was goin' to the Bluffs."

"*Mon Dieu.* Merrick didn't say he was going to the Bluffs."

"Cautious man."

Paul snorted a reply.

"Trappers comin' down riffer two days back see no vhite man." The German spoke with a heavy accent.

"They might've thought he was an Indian."

"*Eh, bien!*" Paul took one hand off the pole to remove his fur cap. "Is he not?"

"He iss a saffage?" Kruger's bald head swiveled on his thick neck.

Eli was looking through his spyglass and didn't answer.

"If he has any sense, he's cut a wide path round them Delaware." Paul grunted and heaved on the pole. "If he went through them, he could'a come out without hair. *Mon ami*, them Delawares is mean sonsabitches."

"If he planned to get to the Bluffs before winter, he took to the river." Eli lifted the spyglass to his eye again.

"Who knows, *mon ami*, why a Frenchman does anything." Paul grinned over his shoulder at Eli. "A Frenchman with Osage blood is" — he waved his hands — "crazy like fox. Knowing about Baptiste Lightbody's been eating on you for going on five year now."

The tall sharp-eyed man agreed but showed no outward sign of it.

Had it been only five years since Sloan Carroll, of Carrolltown up on the Ohio, had sent word that he had a spot of business to discuss with him? What Carroll had told him had changed his life. From that day on he had even viewed himself in a different way.

A few months after his visit to the Carrolls, he had received another blow to his pride. Sloan's daughter, Orah Delle, had told him that she was going back to her father's ancestral home in Virginia to study music. To give the lady credit, he was sure that she had no idea that he had lain in his bed night after night dreaming of her and had come to the Carroll home as often as possible in hopes of seeing her.

Five years ago he had been so young and inexperienced, unable to recognize that the beautiful and gracious Orah Delle had offered him only the same courtesy that she would have shown any of her father's acquaintances.

Eli Nielson had heard about the profits to be made by freighting up the Mississippi. It was one of the reasons, a minor one he admitted to himself, that he had left the Ohio Valley, come down the Ohio to the Mississippi and up to St. Louis, where he had bought guns, gunpowder, tools, blankets and tobacco with the intention of taking them upriver perhaps as far as the French settlement of Prairie du Chien.

From a word here and a word there he had learned that Baptiste Lightbody was a well-known scout that Zeb Pike had tried to hire. It seemed that he had no close ties to anyone other than the men Sloan named, Jefferson Merrick and Will Murdock. That information had led Neilson to Jefferson Merrick, and now here to this wilderness.

In this country Eli felt marvelously alive. He would never regret this journey no matter how it turned out. He fully intended to spend the rest of his life in this land beyond the great river.

Flocks of disgruntled waterfowl squawked and

rose as the flatboat approached each group feeding in the reeds along the bank. On a sandy bank a raccoon washed a squirming crayfish and did not observe the flatboat until the sudden smell of it startled him into releasing his grip on his meal. The crayfish scampered into the water; the raccoon scampered into the underbrush.

While the two men poled in silence, the other scanned the riverbank. After they had bought the flatboat from him, Kruger had joined Paul and Eli in St. Louis. The German owed a sizeable gambling debt at the saloon and was being pressed for payment. With the money from Eli, he had paid up and proceeded to beat the saloon keeper senseless; then needing to leave town in a hurry, he had joined them on the trip up the Missouri to the homestead of Jefferson Merrick. Aware that the barkeeper and his cronies would be lying in wait for him back in St. Louis, Kruger had continued on with the pair up the Missouri.

The morning quiet was abruptly broken by the screeching of a Delaware attack. Almost before the men on the boat could recover from the surprise, they heard the sound of a shot. Eli scanned the upper bank and saw nothing. He dropped the spyglass and swung the steering oar to head the craft to the sandbar.

"Turn in! Turn in!"

"*Verdammt!*" Kruger snarled.

Paul cursed in French and pulled mightily on the pole to do as he was told.

As soon as the flatboat touched the sandy bottom next to the sandbar, the three men grabbed rifles and crouched behind the shed. The flatboat floated gently among the reeds.

"Mag . . . gie!" The shout echoed up and down the river. "Mag . . . gie!"

"Maggie?" Paul said. "Maybe that's his squaw, or his horse. Leastways it wasn't him what was shot." When Paul grinned at his friend his teeth gleamed white against his black beard. "You'd not be fit to live with, *mon ami*, to come all this way and find the bastard dead."

Eli didn't reply. His eyes were fixed on the small ridge above the sandbar. The minutes ticked away. It suddenly occurred to him that if it was Lightbody up there, he might not have survived the attack or if he had, he might be injured. Eli stood and cupped his hands about his mouth and shouted.

"Lightbody!" Again the shout echoed up and down the river. After a moment of strained silence, Eli yelled again. "Lightbody."

Paul, squatting on his heels, shook his head.

"*Mon Dieu!* You damned Swede! Someday you're going to get your foolish head shot off."

CHAPTER FIVE

Light peered through the bushes toward the river. He had watched the flatboat hit the sandbar and the men take shelter behind the shed. He couldn't have been more surprised when the man stood and shouted his name.

"He called yore name, Light. Do ya know him?"

"I don't think so." He looked down at her. "Button your shirt up to your neck, pet. And stay close."

"Are they bad men?"

"I don't know. But we've got to risk it. It's them or the Delaware."

Light stood so that he was in plain sight of the men on the boat and lifted his rifle over his head. Sun glinted on the hair of the tall man who waved back. Leaving their packs on the edge of the ridge, Light and Maggie walked hand in hand down to the sandy beach.

The men jumped off the boat and one of them secured it to a stunted tree that grew along the river's edge. They stood waiting, rifles in hand, and watched the pair approach. Light had his long gun ready. Maggie's whip was coiled and looped over her shoulder.

A sudden hotness crawled over Light's skin. These men, he was sure, had not seen a woman like Maggie, ever in all their lives. Were they honorable men like his two friends back in St. Charles, or the other kind like Jeff's brother, Jason? Would he be able to protect her if the three of them jumped him? He sized up the men as they drew near them.

The one who had called out was obviously in charge. Light knew that instinctively. A wide-shouldered man with a lean, strong-boned face, the boatman seemed to be thirty-odd years old.

The dark one appeared slightly older. Gray streaked his hair. He was thick in the chest and his legs were like tree trunks. Light suspected that he was not a leader, but a man with strong convictions who would fight for what he considered his due. If he could be judged by the jaunty angle at which he wore his fur cap, he had a cheerful disposition.

The other man was as tall as the light-haired one but much heavier. The hand holding his fire-piece was the size of a ham. He was hatless and hairless, his head slick as a peeled onion. Intuition and experience had taught Light to read men as he would a forest trail. The bald head was small for a big man, his features lean and vulpine, his eyes like those of a weasel. This was a man to watch.

Maggie could feel the intense gaze of the men as they approached, and she hated it. Men always stared at her. She glanced at each one briefly, then kept her eyes turned away but furtively alert for sudden movement.

She freed Light's hand should sudden action be required, and hooked her fingers in the belt at his back where he carried his long hunting knife. Her other hand hovered over the thin-bladed knife in her scabbard.

Maggie was worried. Sensitive to every change in her husband's demeanor, she knew he was tense, untrustful of these men.

Light stopped a good distance from the men. He studied the still face and squinted eyes of the one who had called out to him. The man was looking at *him* and not at Maggie as the other two were doing.

"How do you come to know my name?" Light asked, breaking the silence.

"Baptiste Lightbody?"

Light nodded.

"Jefferson Merrick said you were the best."

"Best at what?"

"Best woodsman, best hunter, best riverman."

Light shrugged. "Merrick is my friend."

"We heard you shoot."

"Delaware."

The man nodded. "We better get the hell out of here. They're all along this part of the river."

"Why did you call my name?"

"Figured it was a lone . . . white man who sent the partially butchered deer carcass downriver."

"I'm Osage."

72

"French and Osage," the man said, then added, "Baptiste is French."

"What do you want with me?" Light asked impatiently.

"You're headed for the Bluffs. So are we. Merrick said you're the best scout in the territory. And we could use an extra hand on the poles."

Light had no intention of going to the Bluffs, but he let the statement stand.

"What happened to your crew?"

"Two men deserted the first week. Two more took our canoe a week back and left in the night. 'Course they won't make it. None of them had the brains of a flea. Loss of a good canoe is what it amounts to. We put in thinking you were in a tight spot and needed help."

Light's dark eyes met blue ones and held. There was something familiar about this man, but he couldn't quite put his finger on it. Caught in the scope of Light's vision, the bald-headed man's eyes were still on Maggie.

"We've had two run-ins with the Delaware. They wanted the horses and they got them this time."

"I heard that they take prisoners if they can."

"Death by torture is a ritual among the Delaware."

"That's not exactly my idea of a good time." The stocky man's worried eyes searched the forest.

"I'm a trader. Name's Eli Nielson." The leader of the group introduced himself. "I'm taking a

73

small cargo upriver. I plan to buy furs and bring them back to St. Louis."

He would not get that boat anywhere near the Bluffs with two crewmen. Light kept his thoughts to himself. He looked straight at the bald-headed man, whose lustful eyes were so blatantly ogling Maggie.

"I'll kill a man who lays a hand on my wife . . . and I won't wait for him to face me."

Eli Nielson's eyes flickered down to Maggie's face, then back to Light.

"Good enough. I'm from Kentucky country along the Ohio. We feel the same about our women. This is Paul Deschanel." He indicated the short stocky man.

"Pleased to meet you." Paul Deschanel pulled off his cap and bowed slightly.

"And Otto Kruger." The bald one acknowledged the introduction with a darting glance at Light, then his gaze returned to Maggie.

"We'll get our packs. Knowing that we're on foot, the Delaware will be back."

Eli nodded. "I'll lend a hand."

Light was hesitant about turning his back. If they were going to kill him and take Maggie, now was the time. He turned, tense and ready to take action if need be. Taking Maggie's arm, he propelled her ahead of him. He looked down and slightly to the right where he could see the shadow of the man behind them. When they reached the packs, Nielson was several paces back.

"Merrick didn't mention you had a woman with you."

"Maggie is my wife. She goes where I go."

Nielson looked searchingly at Maggie. The only change in his expression was a narrowing of his eyes, and for only a second his brows puckered.

Light knew this man was probably thinking the same thoughts he had had when he had seen Maggie for the first time almost a year ago: that she was more than just a pretty woman. The combination of her beauty and the innocent woman-child spirit that was reflected in her clear green eyes made her very desirable.

She stared openly up at Nielson with the curious naiveté of a babe tempered with the age-old wisdom of a woman. Light watched the man's expression soften under Maggie's close scrutiny. Suddenly she smiled.

When Maggie smiled the world stood still.

"It'll be all right, Light. Ya'll see." Her hand slipped into the crook of Light's arm and shook it gently. "Ya'll see," she said again.

Nielson was only a couple of inches taller than Light and heavier, but in his duck pants and heavy boots he seemed much larger. Light was clean-shaven; Nielson had a close-cropped beard. It was impossible to tell which of the men was the older.

Light was puzzled by Maggie's acceptance of this man. What was it about him that caused her to trust him? She was usually leery of any man.

"We need to leave this place. Those damn Delaware make me uneasy." Nielson spoke softly and to Light, as he didn't want to frighten Maggie. He stooped and shouldered one of the packs.

"Go ahead. We'll be down."

Nielson nodded, picked up a roll of blankets and walked back toward the boat.

Light waited until Nielson reached the boat before he spoke.

"*Chérie,* you must be careful of all the men and especially the one with no hair."

"I will, Light. That one is bad. This one" — she nodded toward the boat — "is not like him."

"How do you know that?"

Maggie shrugged. "I dunno."

"Come. Relieve yourself in the bushes. There will be no privacy on the boat."

Nielson stepped on the boat and stowed the pack and blanket roll in the shed. When he turned Paul was there.

"Are we getting out of this place?"

"As soon as they get on board."

"That's a damn relief. Where'd they go?"

"They'll be along."

"You got your look at Lightbody. What now?"

"He's not what I thought he'd be."

"*Mon Dieu,* Eli. You knew he was Osage."

"Guess I didn't think he'd be quite so civilized."

"He's got enough French in him to sweet-talk that woman into going off with him."

"She's . . . different —"

76

"She's comely. Otto's foaming at the mouth."

"He'd screw a snake if you held its head," Eli said with disgust.

"You think to take her from him?"

"Dammit, Paul, why'd you say that for?"

"You want to hurt him, don't you?"

"Hell yes, I want to hurt him!"

"Otto wants his woman."

"He'd have to kill Lightbody to get her. I'll not stand for that . . . yet."

"Wonder why Merrick didn't tell us that he had a woman with him."

" 'Cause he never reckoned we'd catch up to him. Findin' a man in this wilderness is like finding a fart in a whirlwind."

Kruger's heavy boots landed on the flatboat, rocking it gently. He stood on the end of the boat holding onto the mooring line and looked over his shoulder at Paul and Eli. His eyes were unusually bright. He was grinning like a cat ready to pounce on a crippled bird.

"I neffer see a voman like dot one."

"She's married to the scout. Leave her be."

"Dot voman bein' vit a breed ain't right. *Mein Gott,* it ain't right a'tall. His vife? Vot preacher marry a Indian to a vhite voman?"

"You got a mind to do somethin' about it, Otto?" Eli asked quietly.

"She ain't fer no . . . breed."

"You got something against breeds?"

"Vot? I say she iss not for breed. I ain't neffer had me no use fer a stinkin' saffage. He stole

77

her, is vot he done. Bet she'd be plenty tickled to be shed of 'im. Ain't no voman vantin' no Indian offer a vhite man."

"Gawddamn you! I'm telling you to stay away from her. I want no trouble."

Kruger laughed.

"Lightbody's not like those rattleheads back at the saloon. He'll kill you and not bat an eye. He's had two run-ins with the Delaware and he's still on his feet."

"Dot don't mean shit."

"I'm warning you, Otto. Keep your eyes and your hands off the woman."

"She gott yore pecker up too, Eli?" Kruger laughed again, nastily.

"You'd be wise to remember what I said."

"Vat ya vant to find 'im fer? Ya ain't needin' no scout. Any fool can follow the riffer." When Nielson merely stared at him, he said, "Shit, I ain't carin' vhy ya was lookin' for 'im. I'd a poled dis ting to the Bluffs all by myself to get a look at dat voman. I ain't neffer seen one like 'er. Her bottom's round as melon in dem britches."

"She's not for you."

"Yore vantin' her fer yoreself, Eli? *Verdammt!* I can see it."

Eli scowled, turned and walked to the far end of the deck.

"Don't push Eli." Paul told the German. "That Swede'll give you more trouble than you can handle."

"I ain't neffer asked, but vat's that breed done

dat Eli vas set on findin' him?"

"If he wanted ya to know he'd tell ya."

Paul did not like Otto Kruger. He had not liked him since the day they bought the boat from him. But as long as he did his work and kept his mouth shut, he could tolerate him. Seeing the woman had loosened Otto's tongue.

Paul feared it was only a matter of days before Eli or Lightbody had a run-in with Otto over that little whip-slip of a girl.

With four men on the poles and Maggie, after a bit of instruction, holding the steering oar, the narrow craft moved upriver. They stayed close to the shore in the gently moving water. Light, on the shore side of the craft, constantly watched for a sign of the Delaware.

They poled for several hours without stopping to eat. The men were drenched with sweat when they rounded a bend and saw a straight sweep of river ahead. Eli took the steering oar while Paul unfurled the sail. The wind took hold and they moved out away from the shore to catch the breeze. The craft glided smoothly onward as long as Eli stayed away from the swift current in the middle of the river and the thick growth of reeds along the bank.

While Light sank down on the deck, his back to the shed, and continued to watch the shoreline, Maggie opened their food pack and laid out the meat they had cooked in the pit the night before. She brought Light a cup of water and a piece of meat and left the others to serve themselves.

Light was thirsty and downed the cup of water quickly. When Maggie went to the barrel to fetch him another, Kruger stood there. He lifted the lid from the barrel. Maggie dipped the water and hurried away, but not before he managed to rub his hand along her bare arm.

In the middle of the afternoon, Light, scanning the riverbank ahead with his spyglass, suddenly rose to his feet. He pressed his hand on Maggie's shoulder in a signal for her to stay, and went to where Eli sat at the steering oar.

"Take a look at that patch of water grass ahead. No waterfowl are there and none has flown out of there for a while. The reeds are bent."

Eli lifted his glass to his eye. A deer came to the river but spun around and left without drinking.

Light braced himself with spread legs and searched the red clay riverbank and the grasses that grew in the shallows. He took the spyglass from his eye and pressed it shut.

"There's a war canoe in there."

"Paul," Eli called softly. "Break out the muskets."

Paul ducked into the shed and came out with four long guns. He lined up the firearms atop the low roof of the shed.

Light checked the load in his own weapon, slipped an unstrung bow from the straps of his pack, and hooked the string of two twisted buffalo sinews to the notched end. He looped it and the quiver of arrows over his shoulder.

"What's happenin', Light?" Maggie asked.

Before he could answer, a war canoe came streaking out from the far end of the reeds. A chorus of war-whoops became louder as the six Delaware braves paddled furiously to intercept the flatboat.

"Get in the shed, Maggie!" Light commanded sharply. Without question, she jumped to obey. "Don't shoot unless you have to," he said to Paul. "Every Delaware within five miles will know where we are."

"C'mon, ya saffage deffils!" Kruger shouted. "C'mon ya sonsabitches."

Eli sat calmly at the steering oar as the wind pushed them toward the oncoming canoe. Light strung his bow and waited for a brave to stand. As the canoe neared, a brave, reckless in the excitement of the battle, stood and shook his war club. Light's arrow pierced his chest, pushing him back into the river. Without missing a stroke, the paddlers powered the canoe onward. Backs were bent and heads were down.

A sudden puff of wind came from the south, filled the sail and pushed the flatboat along faster and faster into the path of the war canoe. Too late the eager bloodthirsty Indians saw their danger and tried to evade the craft bearing down on them. They had just managed to turn the canoe broadside when the flatboat smashed into it, turning it over and flinging the yelling warriors into the river.

The Delaware swimming toward the raft tried to scramble aboard. Paul and Kruger waited on one side, Light on the other. As heads came out of the water, the poles came crashing down on half-shaven skulls.

The Delaware were heroic as long as they were winning the battle; but when they faced odds not to their liking, they were more likely to flee. They did so now. The few who had survived the head-bashing struggled in the river mud and cast fearful glances over their shoulders as the white man's boat moved away from them.

CHAPTER SIX

"I don't like bein' on this boat." Maggie's words came out on a breath of a whisper, her lips close to Light's ear.

"It's best for now, pet."

The night was dark. A layer of clouds dimmed the quarter moon that was making its way across the sky. The mooring line attached to a tree allowed the flatboat to rock easily on the gently flowing river water a few yards from the steep bank. A big trout broke water alongside with a silvery splash. Somewhere in the woods to the north a wolf howled contentedly as if enjoying the night.

"I don't like it here," Maggie insisted, her lips moving against his cheek. "When can we get off?"

They had spread their blankets on the deck and sat with their backs to their packs. Light pulled the blanket up over her shoulders more to protect her from the mosquitoes than from the night air.

"As soon as we can." He pressed her head to his shoulder. "Get some sleep."

"Are you goin' to sleep?"

"In a while."

"I don't like that bald-headed man, either."

"Has he bothered you?"

Maggie thought for a minute and decided not to tell him about the incident at the water barrel.

"Mr. Nielson doesn't like him."

"How do you know that?"

"I just know, that's all."

"Not much gets by you, pet."

"Mr. Nielson likes you."

"I suppose you *just* know that too," Light teased.

"He looks at ya . . . but not in a mean way."

"If you don't stop talking, I'll have to kiss you."

She laughed silently and nipped the skin on his neck. "It's what I been hopin' for."

He kissed her softly on the lips and tucked her head beneath his chin.

"Sleep while you can."

When he was reasonably sure she was asleep, he moved and eased her head down onto his thigh. Nielson had said he would fix her a place inside the shed, but she had insisted on staying with him. He was glad now that she had. Here in the velvet blackness of the night, with the sound of the water lapping against the raft, the feel of her warm, trusting little body made him realize how much he would miss her if she weren't there.

Kruger had the first watch. Light did not trust him. The man's face was easy to read. He was hungry for a woman and allowed his lust to rule his brain. His resentment stemmed from the fact that he didn't understand why a white woman should prefer an *Indian* over a white man — any white man.

That the German was an angry man with a cruel streak was evident when the Delaware had tried to board the craft. Light had known immediately that they were young boy-warriors, out on their own. An experienced warrior wouldn't have been so foolish as to attack the boat in such a brazen way.

Kruger had taken delight in repeatedly jabbing a young one with his pike as the boy tried to swim away from the boat, and he had laughed uproariously when the Indian sank beneath the water.

Sitting in the dark with Maggie across his lap, Light listened for movement from atop the shed where Kruger sat. He would not shut his eyes while the German was on guard.

If he and Maggie stayed with the boat for another week, they should be far enough upriver to be in Osage territory, that is if the two Osage he had met after they left St. Charles had read the map correctly. If the Osage were friendly, and he assumed they would be, he and Maggie would stay with them for the winter.

The night passed uneventfully with Light taking the last watch. If the Delaware planned an attack it would occur just as dawn lit the eastern sky. Maggie had awakened and sat beside him atop the shed where she had moved when Light took his turn to stand guard. She could see in the dark like a cat. There were times when Maggie could see things that Light couldn't see but that his brain told him were there.

Sitting shoulder to shoulder, their hands clasped, they listened to the chirping of birds along the shore an hour before dawn and the splash of fish in the deep channel in the middle of the river. Together they watched the stars dim as the sky lightened in the east.

Daylight came quickly without anything to disturb the tranquility.

Otto Kruger arose, stretched and went to the edge of the boat and let water. When he finished, he made no attempt to shield himself before turning toward the shed where Maggie sat. Light had turned her away and was staring over her head with hard cold eyes at the German.

"You're a crude son of a bitch, Kruger," Eli said angrily.

Kruger laughed. "Ven a man's got ta pee, he got ta pee."

Paul grunted his disgust and began to build a fire on the flat stone beside the shed. Soon water was heating for tea.

Light lifted Maggie down from the roof and went to Eli.

"We will go to the woods."

Eli glanced past Light to Kruger, who watched with a smirk lifting his thick lips. He brought his gaze back to Light.

"You don't have to go to the woods for your wife to have privacy. Come." Eli ducked his head and entered the long low shed. "I forgot about

86

this until this morning."

Walking stooped over, he led them to the far end of the shed. He reached behind several canvas-wrapped bundles and pulled out a tin chamber pot.

Obviously uncomfortable, Eli set the pot down and headed for the door. "You can hang a canvas across the corner," he said over his shoulder.

When they were alone, Maggie put her hand on Light's arm. He looked down at her. She pulled down his head and whispered in his ear.

"I want to go to the woods."

"Use the chamber, *chérie*. Maybe tonight we can go ashore." Light arranged the bales of goods to give her privacy. "When you finish, stay inside and I'll bring you a pan of washwater."

Paul was squatted beside the cook fire when Maggie came out of the shed to throw the washwater over the side. Fish were frying in one black iron skillet and hoe-cakes in another.

"That smells good." She hung the pan on a nail above the water barrel.

"Ain't nothin' better'n river pike, *chérie*." Paul grinned at her and turned the fish with a long, thin knife.

"Light calls me *chérie*. You call me Maggie."

Paul lifted his dark brows. "I stand corrected, *madame*."

"What's your name?"

"My name is Paul, *mon petit chou*." The Frenchman grinned.

"What's that mean?"

"Pretty little cabbage."

Maggie smiled. "I like cabbage." She looked pointedly at Eli. He and Light were studying a map. "What's his name?"

"Eli Nielson."

"I knew the Nielson part. He's not a bad man like the other'n."

"I've known him most of his life, *madame*. You are right, he's not a bad man."

"I don't like that bald one. Light will kill him," Maggie said with a positive note in her voice.

"How do you know that?" Paul stood.

"I just know."

Maggie walked over to take Light's hand. Without looking at her, he put his arm around her and drew her close to him. His finger was on a spot on the map.

"At this point the river turns northwest. This is the Osage country."

"Have you been there?"

"No. There are half a hundred Osage camps between the big river and the mountains. Maggie and I will stay there. If you give the chief tobacco and a bit of gunpowder he'll furnish you with rowers for a week or two."

"Then what would I do?"

Light shrugged. "Clark said that most of the tribes, except for the Delaware, were friendly."

"Why not go on with us?"

"I'd rather go it alone."

"I'll pay you in trade goods."

"We have all we can carry."

"Dammit man. Be reasonable. Your wife will be safer if you stay with us."

"I am the one who decides what is best for my wife. We'll stay with you until we reach the Osage country." Light's tone put an end to the conversation. He folded the map and put it inside his shirt.

"Come and get it," Paul called from the cook fire.

The weather was hot and sticky and had been for the past two days. Sweat poured off the men pushing the raft upriver. Eli dipped a bucket in the river and poured the water over his head. It cooled his body for the moment. He glanced at the woman sitting at the sweep oar. In all his travels, up the Ohio to Pittsburgh, across the Cumberland Gap and on to Chesapeake Bay, he had never seen a woman to compare with her.

Most of the beautiful women he had seen had been rather plump and useless, having been put on a pedestal to be admired. Maggie was not only beautiful, she was quick and capable. Her great green eyes seemed to see everything. She could have had any man she wanted. Why had she chosen Lightbody?

Eli looked over at the dark-haired man toiling at the pole. He was not at all the dim-witted, half-breed savage he had expected. Half-breed, yes, but far from dim-witted. He hoped to know more about him before they parted company at the Osage camp. *If* they parted. It was damn hard to change five years of thinking.

By mid-afternoon of the fourth day, a sultry calm had settled over the river. Not a leaf stirred. Even the birds fell silent. Light began to listen and to sniff the air. As they rounded a bend, a fringe of iron-gray clouds appeared above the forested landscape. In an hour's time the dark mass had boiled upward until it towered into the sky. White wispy clouds scurried ahead of the storm.

The men moved the flatboat swiftly alongside a clay bank that loomed above their heads. Eli scanned the shoreline ahead with his glass, looking for a place to pull in and tie up. He knew the river was a formidable enemy during a wind storm and even moreso if it were accompanied by lightning, especially if the boat had a cargo of gunpowder.

Light watched the distant sky for a downward spiral of clouds that might indicate a tornado was in the making. Puffs of hot dry air traveled down the river ahead of the storm. Even the current seemed to slow, as if waiting. From far away they could hear the roar of thunder that accompanied the flashes of lightning that illuminated the dark clouds. The atmosphere seemed ominously still, like a hungry cat perched on a limb with its eyes on a nest of baby birds.

"Sandbar," Paul shouted.

The men increased their efforts and headed for the bar a few hundred yards ahead. A wave of water came rushing down and they strained to maintain what progress they had made.

"Somethin's let loose up ahead," Eli yelled, then, "Take 'er in."

They reached the sandbar seconds ahead of a great gust of wind that came from behind them.

"Vind's changed," Kruger announced as if he were the only one to notice.

A wind-driven wave coursed upward against the current, bearing the flatboat on its crest and casting it upon the bar that jutted out from the bank.

All hands sprang to do what was necessary to save the boat and themselves. Poles were sunk deep into the river bottom and lashed to the boat to secure it. Eli and Paul grabbed mooring lines and jumped from the craft. Light rushed to tilt and tie the sweep oar.

Moving swiftly, Light slung his rifle and his bow over his shoulder, tucked his powder sack inside his shirt, grabbed a heavy canvas and, pulling Maggie along with him, jumped off the boat and headed inland.

The storm broke over them with fury. Rain poured from the sky. Huge drops, propelled by the wind, whipped their faces. Streaks of lightning were followed by loud claps of thunder. Light ran through the thick grove of trees that grew alongside the river. Maggie easily kept pace with him. In the middle of a clearing away from the trees, the river, and the boat with its kegs of gunpowder, Light stopped, sat on the ground and pulled Maggie down between his legs. Setting his long gun beside him, he covered the two of them with the canvas.

They were both breathing hard.

Maggie loved the storm. Her hair was sopping wet, rivulets of water ran down her cheeks. Wrapped in her husband's arms, she tilted her head to nuzzle her nose into the warm flesh of his throat.

One particularly loud bark of thunder made her jump. Over the sound of the rain pounding on the canvas they heard the cracking and rending of trees hit by the fiery knife.

"I love you," Light said to the woman he held in his arms. He said it slowly and sincerely because he was not sure if he would have a chance to say it again. The next strike could end their lives, either by a direct hit, or by sending a tree crashing down on top of them.

"Yo're my heart," Maggie murmured, her mouth against his, her nose alongside his, her eyelashes tangling with his. She wrapped her arms tightly about his waist. "Don't be scared," she crooned. "We ain't goin' t' die here. It isn't our time. We'll have years an' years t'gether."

"Ah . . . my little witch. How can you be so sure?"

"I just know. That's all." She offered the familiar explanation and lifted her puzzled face.

"Maybe I *am* a witch, Light."

She was so serious that he chuckled. "Why do you say that?"

" 'Cause sometimes I just know thin's. Like

the first time I saw ya, Light, I knew I was yore woman. And I knew that Jefferson's old wolf dog wouldn't hurt me; an', that day when his brother tried to go inside me, I knew ya'd come. I only had t' hold him off an' wait for ya."

"*Ma petite,* you may be a witch, but a most beautiful one."

"I don't want ya t' love me 'cause I'm beautiful," she murmured.

"Ah . . . sweet one. I love you because you're my precious girl. I'll love you when your hair is gray and your teeth are gone. You're my life, my soul, my wife, my Maggie." He whispered the words reverently.

"Ya say pretty words, Light." She was quiet for a moment, then she leaned away from him and asked, "When my teeth are gone?"

Light laughed and hugged her so tight she could hardly breathe.

"You will be beautiful to me even then."

The first violence of the storm was followed by a steady drumming rain which seemed to last for a long while. When it lessened and stopped suddenly, Light threw off the canvas and they stood, stretching stiff limbs. Patches of gray light filtered through the scurrying clouds.

Around them in the clearing lay broken limbs and uprooted saplings. After the heat of the day, the air was cold on their wet bodies. As they walked back through the grove toward the river, the sun, low in the west, broke through, but it offered no warmth.

Eli joined them as they reached the bank above the sandbar, which was completely covered with swiftly moving river water. The flatboat had been struck by a sawyer. The top of a submerged tree was embedded in the muddy bottom of the river and a long strong limb jutted up hard and sharp through the bottom of the flatboat, thrusting it upward. Impaled like a butterfly on a pin, the raft thrashed about on the swift current. A foot of brown river water sloshed to and fro on the aft deck. The steering oar was gone. Two of the stout poles the men had sunk into the river bottom to help secure the boat were broken.

"Bloody hell!" Eli swore.

"Don't worry, Eli. It can be fixed. Light will know what to do," Maggie said soothingly and placed her hand on his arm.

Light's face was expressionless when he looked down at his wife. Maggie seldom touched anyone, and here she was stroking the arm of this man.

Eli appeared to be charmed. His expression held a mixture of awe and admiration. He lifted his eyes to Light's face. *The man knew of his desire for his wife.* Their eyes locked for a long moment, then Eli moved away and waded through the water to the boat.

CHAPTER SEVEN

The multitude of vultures and other river fowl that perched along the riverbank turned their backs to the sun and stretched their wings to dry. The deluge upriver had filled the creeks that flowed into the Missouri. The brown and muddy river raced on, carrying uprooted trees and broken branches. Dead logs pried from the sand and gravel bars along the river joined the parade.

The front of Eli's boat was tilted upward. River water washing over the stern had not yet reached the shed. Light and Maggie's packs were above water. Light pulled a dry blanket from his pack, wrapped it about Maggie and cautioned her to stay near the shed lest the boat lurch suddenly and she need to grab onto it.

Eli met the threat of disaster to his boat with calm. He knew it would not immediately sink. Its buoyancy depended on the thick timbers of which it was constructed. But strong and as tight as it was, it would not hold together long under the punishment of grinding against the sawyer that had impaled it and the buffeting of debris coming downriver.

Paul and Kruger came out of the woods and joined them on the slanting deck.

"*Mon Dieu!*" Paul exclaimed.

"I make goot strong boat," Kruger bragged.

Eli said nothing. He'd traveled the rivers on flatboats since he was a lad and knew that along with the unbearable exasperation one could cause a man, they possessed a single definite virtue. They could endure almost anything. A couple of strips of planking could mend a hole adequately if the understructure were strong. He'd not have attempted this venture if he hadn't been sure of that.

"What'll we do?" Paul asked.

"Cut her loose." Light and Eli spoke the same words at the same time. They looked at each other in surprise.

"First we unload." Eli went to the shed and came out with an armload of muskets, rolled them in a canvas, and placed them on the roof.

"Paul, you and Kruger start hauling cargo. Let's get it ashore. When she breaks loose from the sawyer, she'll either float or sink. The river current has made a deep cut here. She's on the edge of the bank. When she tilts back, if she does" — he looked pointedly at Kruger — "water will wash into the shed."

"*Verdammt!* It von't sink!" Kruger seemed to take it as an insult to his ability as a craftsman.

With the men carrying kegs of gunpowder and whiskey, sacks of salt, and bundles of tobacco, and Maggie bearing the lighter goods, they made numerous trips to the riverbank through the foot-high water that covered the sandbar. Paul stayed aboard the boat and lifted the heavy kegs over the side to rest on the shoulders of the men.

Maggie managed not to be onshore at the same time as Kruger. She was aware that not only was Light watching the man, but so was Eli. Once when she passed Otto on her way to the boat, his thick lips stretched in a grin and he eyed the way her wet britches clung to her bottom and thighs.

"The riffer iss full of vater snakes, missy," he murmured, his eyes lingering on her breasts. "Vatch ya don't get a bite on yore pretty little titties. Ja?"

Shortly after that Maggie had seen one of the snakes cutting through the muddy water, its head up, its long body making serpentine curves, winding its way downriver. She watched it until it passed the boat.

When all the cargo was unloaded except the tools that were hung on the sides and ceiling of the shed, they returned to the boat, wet and hungry. But there was no time to think of their discomfort.

Eli removed his shirt and boots and lowered himself into the fast-moving water on the river side of the boat. He groped in the dark until he found the tree limb. He came up gasping for breath.

"The son of a bitch is a foot or more thick. Give me the saw."

Eli took a deep breath and sank under the boat again. It seemed a long while before he came up to hang onto the side of the boat, gasp agonizingly for breath and then vomit some of the water.

"Kruger . . . come take a turn on the saw."

"*Verdammt!* Ya tink I fool."

Paul swore viciously and began to unlace his heavy boots.

"Are you refusing to take orders?" Eli spoke calmly, but his mouth snapped shut and his nostrils flared.

"Dis iss no fuckin' ship, *captain.* Vat ya gonna do? Make me valk ta plank? I ain't goin' down ta get bit by vater snake."

"Damn you! If we don't get off this sawyer before dark it'll rip this boat apart."

"Ain't *mein* boat. Ya gott it fer half a vat it vorth. Ain't no skin off *mein* arse if she breaks. I'll build me raft an' catch current down riffer."

Light reached for his rifle, checked the load and put it in Maggie's hands. He pulled off his shirt and moccasins, loosened the string holding the pouch about his waist, rolled them into a tight bundle and placed it on top of the shed.

"You know what to do, *chérie.*" He went over the side. "I can stay down for a count of thirty," he said to Eli before both men sank under the water.

With her back to the shed and the heavy gun in her hands, Maggie waited, her eyes roving from the place where Light had gone under to the men on the deck.

"Vat ve got iss Indian mitt book learnin'." Kruger laughed nastily. "Are ya figgerin' ta shoot me if yore man don't come up?" His lust-filled eyes traveled over Maggie.

"Leave her be," Paul snarled.

"Dem snakes likes to viggle in and outta timbers on the bottom of the boat. The Indian iss liable to get hisself snake bit."

"Shut up, Kruger."

"Ever see a man bit by a vater snake, pretty *fraulein?*" Kruger moved a step closer to Maggie. "Dey swell all up like a toad —"

"Hush your mouth!"

"Don't mind him, Paul," Maggie said quietly. "He's just a talkin' t' hear his head rattle. He's not scarin' me a'tall. Snakes is scared of what they don't know, and I don't reckon they've ever seen a man under a boat before."

Eli came up and took several deep gulps of air and went back down, and a few seconds later Light came up to hold onto the side of the boat and breathe through his open mouth. His eyes went to Maggie and she nodded that she was all right.

"Anything we can do up here?" Paul asked when Eli came up for another gulp of air.

"Cover the hole if she breaks loose."

For the next half-hour Eli and Light took turns struggling to drive the saw through the tough, water-soaked tree limb beneath the boat.

Then the completely unforeseen happened. The

limb, when partially cut through, bent under the weight it was sustaining and wrenched out of the hole in the flatboat's bottom, releasing the craft. The boat rose with its buoyancy, and the water on the deck leveled out and began to run outward through the hole made by the limb.

The German hooted. "*Verdammt!* Tol' ya I vas bess boat builder!"

Light came to the surface.

"Name of a cow!" Paul grinned, his white teeth showing through his black beard. "She's going to float." He took the saw from Light.

"River's coming up," Light said and pulled himself up over the solid low rail. Cold had tightened the skin over his high cheekbones, and his voice was hoarse from swallowing river water.

"Where's Eli?" Paul, on his knees, bent over the low railing, peering at the surface of the water. "Where's Eli?" Paul asked again anxiously.

Light turned, looked down, and then stepped over the rail and slid back down into the river.

Maggie waited beside Paul. Time seemed to go on forever. Light's head broke the surface. He took a gulp of air and went back down. Paul flung a foot over the rail.

"Wait." Maggie put her hand on his arm. "Light will get him." Something in her tone caused Paul to hesitate.

Kruger came and hovered over Maggie to look over the side. She moved the end of the long gun until it was poking into his belly.

"Move."

The bald-headed man laughed. "Ya effer seen a man vat vas drowned, *fraulein?* He look chust like vhite fish."

"Shut your blasted mouth!" Paul shouted and shoved Kruger with his foot.

Kruger drew back his fist. "Vatch vat ya do, ol' man!"

At that moment Light's head came up out of the water. He grabbed at the rail with one hand. His arm was around Eli's neck.

"Take . . . him," he gasped.

"Mon Dieu! Mon Dieu!" Paul was clearly distressed. He leaned down and grasped the limp body under the arms, but it was too heavy for him to lift over the rail.

While Light was climbing over the rail, Kruger, with his massive strength and a snort of disgust, hauled Eli up and unceremoniously dumped him on the deck. Eli lay there gray and lifeless.

"Det as doornail," Kruger pronounced without feeling.

"He ain't dead!" Maggie's eyes were as deep as storm clouds. She raised her small head defiantly and spat with all the fury of a vixen at bay. "Ya ugly old vulture!"

Far from being angry, the German stared at her with admiration.

Paul stared at his inert friend in disbelief.

Light quickly turned Eli over on his stomach and straddled his back. With the heels of his hands beneath Eli's shoulder blades, he pressed down hard, released and pressed again. Maggie handed the gun to Paul, knelt down and turned Eli's head to the side.

"Dat do no goot. He det already." Kruger stood, feet spread, hands on his hips.

Light ignored him and continued the rhythmic pumping. Suddenly Eli's mouth opened and water spewed out. He groaned. Paul let out a whoop. Light pressed several more times. More water came. Light stopped when Eli gagged. He helped Eli up to rest on his forearms, then stepped away while he vomited.

Eli rolled over on his back and looked up. What he saw was the face of an angel bending over him. *Have I died?* It was the first thought that crossed his mind. Then he remembered the terror of being there alone in the dark, his lungs bursting, his foot caught when the sawyer bent. Before consciousness left him, he had been sure he was going to die.

"Are you all right, Eli?" the angel said.

His vision cleared and his eyes focused on Maggie's face.

"Yeah," he croaked.

"Light saved ya."

Eli pulled himself up to a sitting position and looked toward his feet. The skin was scraped from his ankle. It was raw and bloody. He looked up at the slim dark man. Water was still running down Light's face.

"Thanks."

Light nodded, reached for his shirt and pulled it over his wet torso.

"*Mon Dieu,* Eli, that was close." Paul was still visibly shaken.

"Yeah. Close." Eli rolled over on his knees to stand. He grabbed onto Paul when he attempted to put his weight on his injured foot and leaned heavily on him until they reached the shed.

"Flood water has brought the river up," Paul said. "We can tie up to the bank."

"If it goes down as fast as it came up we could be stranded on the sandbar. Loosen the mooring and let her drift back down river a ways, then pole into the bank."

"Only got two left," Paul said and grabbed one of them.

Light used the other pole to keep the craft close to the shoreline. The men strained at the poles and finally maneuvered the craft close to the bank, and Paul tossed a mooring line up over a stump to hold the boat until he could scramble up the bank and secure it. Without a steering oar they would be helpless in the current.

By the time the raft had floated alongside a three-foot bank, twilight had descended. Gusts of cold air came off the river and chilled everyone. Maggie stood beside Eli, who was holding onto the roof of the shed. She had helped him pull his dry shirt on over his head. Shivering herself in the cool breeze, she draped her blanket up over his shoulders to protect him from the wind. Still he shuddered violently, and despite his clenched jaws, his teeth chattered.

"Come, *chérie*," Light called. He had stepped up on the railing and pulled himself up onto the bank. He leaned down to take Maggie's hand and lift her up. "Wait here," he said when she was beside him. He jumped down onto the deck of the craft.

A few minutes later Light and Paul had managed to get Eli up on the rail and then boost him onto the bank. During this effort, Kruger made no attempt to help. Hopping on one foot, his arm across Paul's shoulders, Eli managed to cover the short distance back from the river to a shelter under a thick stand of cedars.

Light's knowing eyes searched the area. "This is a good place. I'll build a fire after I get dry clothes for Maggie."

While he was gone, Maggie scrounged for dry wood and found some dead cedar branches. When Paul and Light returned, they were staggering under the weight of supplies they would need to set up camp. Light dropped the load and picked up his pack. He took Maggie by the hand and led her away from the others and into the woods.

The wet doeskin britches clung to Maggie's skin. Light had to help her get them off. He rubbed her wet body with a dry cloth shirt, and while she hurriedly dressed, he removed his own wet britches, dried his body, then put the shirt in Maggie's hands.

"Dry your hair, *chérie*. You will be sick."

"I'm never sick," Maggie said confidently.

She squeezed the water out of her braid and

rubbed her head with the cloth until tight curls framed her face. She wore a heavy shirt and a linsey-woolsey skirt that came to her ankles. Shod in their extra pairs of moccasins and carrying their wet clothes, they returned to where Eli sat on a dead log feeding a small fire with dry sticks. His feet were bare, but he was wearing dry britches.

"Paul's bringing up a keg of whiskey." Eli's throat was so raw he could scarcely talk.

"The German is trouble," Light said.

Eli didn't deny it. "He's turned sour of late."

Maggie knelt down to look at Eli's injured ankle. It was swollen to half again its normal size.

"Does it hurt much?" Her voice was rich with sympathy.

Staring into the clear green eyes so close to his, Eli almost forgot to answer.

"Some," he finally said.

"Tomorrow I'll find the *gonoshay* herb and make a poultice. It'll feel better," Maggie said as if she were speaking to a small child.

Eli glanced up at the man who had saved his life and saw a face devoid of expression and still as a stone except for the eyes. They were narrowed to slits and moved from his wife's face to Eli's. Eli's gaze traveled to Light's hands. The fingers were tense and curled into cups, although his arms and his stance were relaxed and loose.

The thought crossed Eli's mind that Lightbody was not so civilized as he had first believed him to be. He had the territorial instincts of an animal who would not allow any encroachment into his space, and he would do whatever he had to do to keep his woman.

Paul, followed by Kruger, came toward the fire. Paul carried an iron pot, and each man bore a keg of whiskey on his shoulder. As they eased them to the ground, Kruger glanced briefly at Light, then went back down the trail toward where they had piled the cargo.

Paul shrugged. "I told him we'd bring up the rest of the cargo in the morning."

After heating water in the iron pot, Paul made a whiskey toddy for Eli. He offered one to Light, but the scout shook his head. Kruger returned with another keg on his shoulders, accepted a mug from Paul and moved back from the fire to squat down on his haunches.

They were all weary and hungry. They ate cold fish left over from breakfast and hot mush laced with melted meat drippings. Maggie and Light drank tea while the others drank switchel, a beverage made with hot water and molasses. Afterward Kruger picked up his blanket and disappeared in the direction of the boat.

Paul bathed Eli's injured foot with warm water, then splashed it with whiskey before they bedded down beside the dying campfire.

Light led Maggie deep into the stand of cedars and threw their blankets down on a thick bed of pine needles. She snuggled close to him, her head on his shoulder, warm and secure in the home he had made for the night.

"I'll hunt *gonoshay* tomorrow for Eli's foot. I think Kruger hoped he'd drown. He don't like him none a'tall. He'll run off an' do mean thin's."

Light had ceased to ask her how she knew that things would happen. His Maggie had mystical knowledge of people and animals, time and places. She was truly the child of mother earth.

"But ya like Eli, don't ya?" She leaned over Light, her nose touching his, her breath mingling with his. "I want you to like him."

Light was still a moment longer, then said, "Nielson? It makes no difference if I like him or not."

"It'd be nice if ya did." She settled her face once again in the curve of his neck.

Never before had Light experienced jealousy. A physical pain gnawed at his chest and questions flooded his mind. Was Maggie attracted to the man because he was wholly white? In years to come, would she regret having taken a half-breed for her husband?

"Go to sleep, *chérie*." There was just a hint of impatience in Light's voice.

Maggie yawned against the skin of his neck. "Don't you want to love me in our special way? Hmmm?" Her hand found the bottom of his shirt and slid beneath to stroke the flat plane of his belly.

"I always want . . . that, pet. But not when you're so tired you can't keep your eyes open."

"I'm not tired," she murmured and yawned.

He chuckled and placed his fingers under her chin to lift her face. He kissed her soft mouth, forcing down the desire to share with her the sweet pleasure.

"This has been a hard day for both of us. Let's get some rest."

Almost before he had finished speaking, Maggie was asleep. Slumber did not come so quickly to Light. He held his wife in his arms, this precious being who had given herself to him so completely, and wondered at her sudden liking and concern for Eli Nielson.

CHAPTER EIGHT

The day broke bright and clear as it so often does following a storm. Eli awakened at dawn with a throbbing foot and a slight fever. His foot was swollen and black with bruising, but it was not broken. His throat was raspy, his stomach queasy, and he was in a sullen mood.

Maggie and Light searched for and found the *gonoshay*. They made a toddy out of whiskey and molasses and Maggie coaxed Eli to drink it.

"It'll help yore throat, Eli."

He sipped at the hot drink while she pounded the *gonoshay* into powder. Mixed with a little water it became a thick paste, which she made into a poultice and placed on the open flesh around Eli's ankle. He could immediately feel the soothing effect of the mashed herb.

Eli was able to examine Maggie closely as she worked over his ankle. Her skin was light cream and smooth as silk, her lips and cheeks naturally red. Even white teeth gleamed when she spoke, and when she looked up, her lashes reached almost to her brows. But it was her magnificent emerald eyes that fascinated him. They were a mirror of all that she was.

He took a deep shuddering breath.

"Oh . . . did I hurt ya, Eli?"

"No, ma'am," he mumbled numbly and looked away.

Light had the eerie feeling of being watched as he sat on a stump and peeled bark from a slender hickory sapling he intended to use to pole the craft. Several times he stopped his work to look and listen.

Now, while eating the noon meal, he set his tin plate on the ground beside him and picked up his weapon. He stood and scanned the edge of the woods on the north side of the clearing. Maggie, alert, as always, to every change in Light's mood, was instantly ready for action. She reached for her bow and the quiver of arrows and moved back beside him.

"What is it?" Paul got to his feet and picked up his rifle.

"Someone's coming."

"Indians?" Eli asked.

"No."

Light moved and Maggie followed. They stood apart from where Eli sat, his back against a stump, his leg stretched out in front of him. Paul was beside Eli, his flintlock in his hand. As they waited, the sound of a male voice became louder. And then out from behind a deep thicket of thornrose a big man and two boys appeared. After

110

showing themselves, they stopped. The man lifted his hand in greeting.

"How do?"

"Howdy," Paul replied.

"Made sure ya heard us a-comin'. Didn't want to come onto ya sudden-like."

"Come on in."

The man had a broad, bearded face and a thatch of gray-streaked curly hair that was pulled back and clubbed in a careless fashion. He was dressed in baggy duck britches and a cloth shirt. A pistol was tucked in his belt. The hand holding the flintlock looked thick enough to stun an ox with one blow. He stepped forward ahead of his two young companions. The man's sharp blue eyes, beneath heavy shaggy eyebrows, surveyed the campsite.

"Name's James MacMillan."

"Paul Deschanel." Paul extended his hand. "Eli Nielson," he said, gesturing to Eli, then to Light and Maggie — "Mr. Lightbody and his wife."

MacMillan bowed toward Maggie. Barrel-chested, with long arms, he had short legs for a big man so most of his height was from the waist up. His head was bare, but the two lads with him wore brimmed hats pulled down to their ears. Their duck pants were much too large for bodies slim as reeds. Each carried a firearm. Powder horns hung from their shoulders and shot bags from the belts around their waists.

"My younguns, Aee and Bee. Got three more: Cee, Dee and Eee. Eff's in his ma's belly, but

I'm figurin' to call him Frank when he gets here."
He announced all this without the slightest hint
of a smile.

Maggie moved close to Light and wriggled her
hand into his to get his attention. She stood on
her toes so she could reach his ear.

"They ain't boys," she whispered.

Light had already noticed the narrow shoulders,
the long slim fingers holding the barrels of the
Kentucky rifles, the butts of which rested on the
ground. The ends of the barrels were almost even
with the tops of the youngsters' heads. The dark
straight brows and high cheekbones were an indication of Indian blood, perhaps not half, but
certainly a quarter.

While Light was thinking this, Maggie let go
of his hand and walked toward the two girls.
She carried her coiled whip on one shoulder, the
bow on the other. The doeskin belt wrapped
tightly about her waist to keep her shirt in place
emphasized her soft breasts. Even armed with
weapons she looked soft and feminine. Her skirt
swirled around the ankles of her knee-high moccasins as she approached.

"I'm Maggie." She stopped within a couple of
yards and looked the two over. One of the girls
looked directly at her, the other girl's head was
bowed so low that all Maggie could see was the
top of her hat.

"I'm Aee."

"That's a funny name." Maggie walked behind
the girls, looking at them curiously.

112

Aee turned, keeping her eyes on Maggie.

"Why ain't ya wantin' me t' see yore backside?" Maggie asked.

"Why'er ya wantin' to?"

Maggie shrugged. She completed the circle and bent down to peer into the other girl's face.

"Is she older'n you?"

"No."

"Don't she talk?"

"Some."

"Them's ugly hats yo're wearin'."

A bit of temper showed in the other girl's face, but she didn't reply.

"Yo're Indian," Maggie said.

"I ain't 'shamed of it," Aee blurted angrily.

A smile lit Maggie's face.

"My man's Indian." She turned and gazed lovingly at the slim scout who was giving his entire attention to Mr. MacMillan. "His ma was Osage. His pa was French. Light and I married each other on a cliff down by St. Charles."

Aee's eyes went past her to the sharp-featured, buckskin-clad man who stood apart from her pa and the others. She had known he was a breed the second she saw him; but now that she knew what tribe he was from, she looked at him with greater interest.

Maggie saw the interest and stared at the girl, suspicious of the way her eyes dwelt on Light.

"He's *my* man," she said sharply.

Aee brought her eyes back to Maggie's frowning face and nodded.

"I ain't wantin' him," Aee retorted, her voice equally sharp.

"Even if ya did, ya couldn't have him."

She'd not have a chance anyway, Aee thought, with this woman around. She had strange ways, but she was so pretty it almost hurt the eyes to look at her. Was this the way women acted when they lived near other folk? Aee hadn't seen more than a couple of dozen other white women in all her seventeen years. All she knew about the outside world was what her ma or pa had told her.

"Want to see me use my whip? I can pluck a twig off that stump over there." Maggie gestured at a stump about a dozen feet away.

"If ya want to." Aee lifted her shoulders in a noncommittal shrug.

"I'll do it if ya take off that ugly hat and let me see yore hair."

Again anger showed in the soft brown eyes and tightened the girl's lips. She jerked the hat off her head and flung it to the ground. Two thick dark-brown braids tumbled down over her shoulders and a fringe of hair covered her forehead.

"Miz, yo're gettin' my back up!"

"Name's Maggie." Maggie smiled, not at all concerned at the girl's anger. "Yo're pretty."

Aee's mouth fell open and she gaped at this more than pretty woman who had said that *she* was pretty.

"Yo're . . . makin' fun —"

"Why'd I do that for? Yo're 'bout the prettiest

woman I ever did see, next t' me," Maggie said, so completely without guile that the girl continued to gape at her.

"Ya seen lots a women?"

"More'n I care to. Most women folk are spitey. I don't think ya are."

"Why?"

"I dunno." Maggie shrugged. "Light — that's my man's name. His name is Baptiste Lightbody, but ever'one calls him Light. He said t' stay away from folks that are mean. He showed me how t' use the whip in case I got cornered. Now I'm better at it than he is."

In the stillness of the clearing, Maggie's laugh was as clear and sweet as the song of a bird. Her sparkling eyes went to her husband.

"It's the only thing I'm best at. Light's best at ever'thing. Ya ort t' see him throw a knife. My pa swears that he can knock a pimple off a jay bird's arse."

"Naw! I ain't a believin' that!"

Seeing that Maggie was talking amicably with the girls, Light turned his attention to the conversation between the men. Paul had invited Mac-Millan to sit down.

"The woman was gatherin' *gonoshay* early this mornin'. Figured ya had a hurt man."

An uneasiness struck Light on hearing they had been spied upon. He had scouted the area before he let Maggie search for the roots.

"Got his foot caught in a sawyer," Paul explained.

"Sawyer can hurt ya. Hurt ya bad. Good ya moved off that sandbar. River 'long here goes down fast. Ya'd a been left high and dry. Happened to me oncet. Had a hell of a time gettin' off."

"You don't miss much, do you?" Paul looked past him to where Maggie was talking to MacMillan's youngsters.

"If I did, I'd not a lasted. Been here nigh on five year."

"Five years?" Eli looked impressed. "You were here when Clark came back downriver?"

"Shore was. Surprised he was to see me all settled like I was." MacMillan chuckled. "Had me a goin' tradin' business even then."

"That so?" Eli said. "What do you trade? We might do some business."

"Beaver, muskrat, shaved deerskins, whiskey, salt. Found me a rich deposit in a cave. Might be a deep salt mine someday. Folks are always needin' salt. Almost like gold to some folks. Trappers use it to cure leather and to salt hides. Indians learnin' to use it too. Salt keeps their meat and fish from spoilin'. Settlers need it for pork and for brine barrels. Barrel a coffee beans worth its weight in gold. You takin' trade goods up to Bellevue?"

"Yeah," Eli said. "Tools, cloth, whiskey and salt."

MacMillan laughed. "I was hopin' ya had tobaccy. Ain't had none for a spell."

"We got that too."

"Yeah? Might be we can barter before ya go."

Paul took off his hat and scratched his head. "*M'sieur*, aren't you a bit close to the Delaware for comfort?"

"A bit. But they don't bother us to speak of. This place spooks 'em. I give 'em salt and a little whiskey now and then. Got me a little barley patch and a still over at the place." MacMillan looked curiously at Light, who had not said a word. "Ya got ya a right sightly woman. My gals was sure worked up 'bout seein' her. They ain't never seen but a handful of white women."

"Where you from, Mr. MacMillan?" Eli asked.

"My folks come to Kaskaskia from somewhere in Ohio when I was a tad. My pa never liked bein' too near folks. Guess I took after him. Choosed me a woman, crossed the river and roamed for a spell with my woman's people. Later we met up with old Dan'l Boone and squatted on a piece a ground near him for a spell. Folks come movin' in there and scrounged us out. Ol' Dan'l still livin'?"

Eli and Paul looked to Light to answer.

"I've not heard that he died," Light said even as his eyes went past MacMillan.

Kruger, who had climbed the bank with an axe on his shoulder, was standing as if in a trance, his eyes on Maggie and the two girls.

MacMillan was aware when the scout went still, and every nerve in the man's body went on the alert. Turning to see what had taken Light's attention, MacMillan saw a large bald-headed man

117

staring intently at his girls and the scout's wife. The boatman's head jutted forward on his broad shoulders and it was clear that he was totally absorbed in his perusal of the women.

MacMillan's brawny body went on the defensive as Kruger continued to stare. An uncomfortable silence stretched for a full minute before the settler spoke.

"Mister, I ain't likin' the way ya stare at my women folks."

Kruger turned his bullet-shaped head to look at MacMillan. His eyes glittered dangerously. His lips pulled back in a snarl that bared his teeth.

"*Verdammt!* Tink I care vat ya like? Dey's breeds, ain't dey?"

MacMillan sputtered a vicious oath, "Keep a civil tongue in your goddamn rotten head!"

"*Mein Gott!*" Kruger snorted. " 'Tis plain as sin. 'Alf-breed sluts, is vat dey iss."

A stunned silence followed the German's words.

"Kruger! Damn you!" Eli struggled to get to his feet.

MacMillan took the two steps necessary to reach the musket he had leaned against a stump. His daughter, Aee, darted to him and took hold of his arm.

"He ain't worth it, Pa. Let's go."

Kruger's glittery eyes swept over the girl. He snorted an obscenity in German, gave MacMillan an impudent stare and turned his back.

"That son of a bitch yore man?" MacMillan

118

jerked around after Kruger disappeared into the woods.

"He's one of my crew. I apologize for his rudeness."

"If he comes sniffin' 'round my girls, I'll blow his blasted head off." MacMillan paused, then added menacingly, "It's been done before."

"You'd have a perfect right. We'll be gone from here as soon as we get the boat in shape." Eli was standing on one foot, resting his hand on Paul's shoulder.

"Dad-blamed horny river trash," MacMillan grumbled, his eyes on the spot where Kruger had disappeared in the forest.

"Pa. Pa —" Aee shook her father's arm to get his attention. "Don't forget Ma said you could invite them t' come and eat tomorry . . . if they were decent." Aee spoke aside to her father, but her words were heard by all.

MacMillan's face softened when he looked down at his daughter.

"Aye, she did say it. The woman thinks the younguns ort'a see more folks," he explained to Eli. "Ain't been nobody I could take to the place for quite a spell now."

"We could bring a canoe down for . . . him." Aee's eyes darted to Eli and then back to her father.

"I thank you for the invitation, that is if one is on the way, but I'll stay with my cargo." Eli's eyes passed fleetingly over Aee before he eased himself back down on the ground.

119

"Thinkin' somebody'll make off with it? Ain't nothin' moves on this river without me knowin'. How'd ya think I knew ya was here?"

Aee braced herself to offer her mother's invitation to Light and Maggie.

"Ma'd be pleased if *ya'd* come to our noon meal."

"Can we, Light? I like Aee. I like Bee, too, but she won't talk to me." Maggie clutched his arm with both hands, her eyes pleading. Light covered her hand with his before he answered.

"*M'sieur,* my wife and I will be pleased to accept your invitation."

"Yo're welcome t' come too," Aee said to Paul.

Paul doffed his cap and bowed. "I thank you, *Mademoiselle,* but perhaps it would be best if I stay with my friend."

Aee shrugged. "Suit yoreself." Her eyes darted to Eli and then away.

"My place is a mile upriver," MacMillan said to Light. "Ya'll have no trouble findin' it."

"Will you sell me a canoe?" Light asked bluntly.

The homesteader met Light's gaze steadily before he answered.

"Could be. We'll talk tomorrow."

Without another word the settler motioned to his girls, and they followed him to the edge of the clearing. Aee looked back one time, then disappeared into the woods.

By late afternoon the hole in the bottom of the boat had been repaired. While Kruger worked on a piece of wood he had selected for the steering oar, Paul and Light carried the cargo back to the flatboat and stored it in the shed.

Light had brought down a fat turkey with his bow and arrow. The bird was roasting slowly over a low fire. Maggie sat cross-legged feeding the blaze with small sticks. Each time Light came to pick up a load, his dark eyes took in the sight of his Maggie in earnest conversation with Eli Nielson.

Regardless of what was going on around him, the Ohio boatman's eyes never left Maggie's face. It was clear to Light that Nielson was fascinated with his wife, not that he blamed him. Maggie exercised her magical power to attract men without any intention to do so. In all her innocence, she appeared to be unaware of the foundation she was laying for trouble.

"Do you think Aee is pretty?" Maggie asked Eli when Light went over the bank to the flatboat.

"She's . . . fair." He shrugged his shoulders.

"Fair? She's almost pretty as me. I wish I wasn't pretty a'tall," she said with a sigh. "It makes trouble for Light. He'll have t' kill Kruger."

"Has Otto bothered you?"

"He wants to. He'll be gettin' 'round to it sooner or later. He'll get Aee or Bee if he can."

"MacMillan can take care of his women. It seems he's had to deal with rivermen before."

"He didn't like Kruger. I don't like him either. He's like a ruttin' hog!" she declared, then added,

121

"You and Paul ain't like him."

"Thank you."

"Jefferson's half-brother tried to rape me. Light killed him. He'll kill Kruger too."

"What makes you say that?"

"If it's not 'cause of me it'll be somethin' else. Kruger's bad."

"Maybe Otto will kill Light."

"He won't," Maggie said confidently.

"But if he did, you'd be alone."

"I'd kill him . . . slow — with my knife and my whip!" she said with teeth clenched tight.

Out of the corner of his eye Eli saw the scout linger before picking up a load to take to the boat. Was Lightbody resentful that his young wife was spending time with him? In all fairness, Eli thought, the man had every right to be jealous. He waited until he was sure that Lightbody was out of hearing before he spoke.

"How did you meet Light?"

"On the river. Our raft got caught in the current. He saved us."

"Did you know his folks?"

"No. They was killed a long time ago, I think. He had a wife before me. She was killed too. Light loves me more'n he did her."

"What makes you think so?"

Maggie frowned. "He calls me his treasure."

"Did he tell you he loves you more?"

"No. I just know."

"It's a long way to the Bluffs —"

"Bluffs? Where's that? Light said we'll winter

122

near the Osage, and when the snow melts, we'll go on to his mountain and stay there forever."

Eli's brows beetled in a puzzled frown. "Where's that?"

"Light's mountain? He knows where it is!" Maggie said crossly. "He'll build us a cabin right on top away from ever'body that's mean."

"Was his pa French or his ma?" Eli prodded gently.

"His pa."

"Where'd *he* come from?"

"I don't know. He trapped and traded with the Osage . . . Light said."

"His ma?"

"— was a princess. Her pa was the chief," Maggie said proudly. "Osage princess. Light had a sister. She died with their ma."

Eli nodded gravely. The only new information Maggie had given him was that they were headed toward some mountain and that Light had not talked to her about the Bluffs. Was it possible he was not going there? Eli wanted to keep Maggie talking; and not being much of a talker himself, he had to strive to think of something to say without asking direct questions.

"Your folks will miss you."

"Uh-huh." She tilted her head and for a moment there was sadness in her clear emerald eyes. "But I was trouble to 'em. Poor pa. Folks was mean t' him and ma . . . all 'cause of me. I was the only youngun they had, but Uncle Lube Gentry, that's Pa's brother, has lots of younguns.

123

Ma won't be lonesome. Pa gave me t' Light t' take care of."

"*Gave* you?"

"Light wouldn't take me with him less'n Pa said I could go."

"You married in St. Charles?"

"No. Light promised Pa we'd marry. We married each other on the bluff over the river the first day. Light promised t' love me 'n' keep me as safe as he can for as long as he lives. God was his witness. I said the words too."

"You didn't stand before a man of God, or a . . . magistrate or a witness?"

"God was witness. I told ya that."

"Nobody was there?"

"Me and Light was there. We didn't need nobody else."

"Then you're not *legally* married."

"Legally? What's that mean?"

"It means that the law may not recognize that you and Light are married to each other."

"We are too! I ain't carin' 'bout the law!" Maggie stood, placed her hands on her hips and glared down at him. "Why'er you sayin' that for, Eli? We promised before God."

"Folks usually get married by a preacher or by some public official, and it's recorded." Eli's brows came together in a puzzled frown.

"Why?"

"It's the law."

"Light took me t' wife and we mated! I don't like ya sayin' that, Eli."

"I just meant that —" Eli knew he had made a mistake. Her feelings ran deeper for Lightbody than he had thought. He groped for words to keep the conversation going, then said, "Sit down and tell me where you learned about *gonoshay*."

CHAPTER NINE

In the tops of towering elm trees, branches reached out and intermingled with one another, lacing over the forest trail. With an unblinking eye the creature perched on a limb watched Light and Maggie leave the camp and walk through the woods toward MacMillan's homestead. Sure-footed, it leaped lightly from spreading branch to spreading branch in order to follow their progress.

During the morning it had observed the man with the injured foot move around the camp with the help of a staff and the hairless man work with an adze to shape a steering oar for the boat. The bald man's eyes went often to the woman who kept her distance from him. The creature marveled at her persistence as she practiced with the whip and the knife while her man sat nearby carefully repacking their belongings. She appeared to be tireless in her endeavor to perfect her skill.

Her man was undoubtedly part Indian, but not she. Her skin was still startlingly white despite the summer sun. Not a single flaw that he could see marred her beauty. Hair, black as midnight, lay in tight ringlets around her face and hung to the middle of her back. She constantly pushed it back from her face until her man went to her and tied it at the nape of her neck with a thong. He watched over her as if he were starving and she was his last meal.

Now, desiring to get a closer look at the woman, the creature, high in the giant elm, made a misstep and knocked a scab of dried bark to the ground. Scurrying back into the concealing foliage, the watcher peered down through the lattice of leaves at the couple below.

Light stopped and threw his hand out to grasp Maggie's arm and draw her with him into the thick undergrowth. His sharp, dark eyes searched the overhead branches for movement and saw a fluttering of leaves.

"What?" Maggie whispered.

Light shook his head.

The quiet was absolute.

Not even a bird moved in the trees above them. After waiting several minutes until the birds began to chirp again, Light decided that they must have drawn the attention of a curious raccoon. He drew Maggie away from the animal path they had been following, and together they slipped quietly through the wood that bordered the river.

The creature, its face so grotesque it appeared not to be human, turned so that the unblinking eye could follow the couple until they were out of sight.

MacMillan's home was set in a clearing completely shielded from the river. Light was not sure what he had expected to see but it certainly wasn't a homestead as permanently established as this one. Several buildings of various sizes and a stockade fence surrounding a hog lot sat well away from the house. Osage plum bushes had been planted around the kitchen garden. The wiry shrubs had grown into an impenetrable hedge surrounding the plot, creating a veritable barrier between it and the wildlife that might devour it. The land around the homestead had been cleared of brush so that an enemy could not approach without being seen.

The cabin was of "poteau" construction: logs set upright in trenches and chinked with mud. Hewn shingles instead of thatch covered the roof. The noonday sun shone on two glass windows — a rare luxury this far from civilization. Wild rose vines climbed the cobblestone chimneys that rose above the roof on each end. A black wash-pot sat in the yard, and a stout clothes drying line stretched from the corner of the house to a tree. In the distance a small patch of barley grain stubbles lay golden in the sun.

In this territory where a man with a couple of mules and a wagon was considered well-off, MacMillan was evidently very wealthy.

"Can we have a place like this on our mountain, Light? Oh, looky, they got a well in the yard."

Light's sharp eyes caught movement near a

large open-ended building and saw a bare-chested Negro man wearing buckskin britches disappear inside.

As Maggie and Light approached, MacMillan came out of the cabin to greet them. He was followed by his pregnant wife, a tall, large-boned woman with shining dark hair parted in the middle, coiled, and pinned at the nape of her neck. Her back was straight despite the load she was carrying in her belly. She wore a loose blue-flowered dress with a white collar. MacMillan walked out into the yard, a smile on his face.

"Welcome to our home."

"It's a pleasure to be here," Light replied.

Maggie, eager as a child, smiled up at Mac-Millan.

"Where's Aee?"

"She's lookin' forward to yer comin', Miz Lightbody."

Maggie loosened her hand from Light's and stepped up to the woman standing beside the door.

"Hello."

The tall woman looked down and smiled. "Hello."

"Miz Mac," the settler said from behind Maggie, "this is Mr. Lightbody and his wife."

"Welcome to our home." She repeated the words her husband had spoken.

"*Madame.*" Light nodded politely.

"Where's Aee 'n' Bee?" Maggie asked.

The doorway was suddenly filled with children.

One by one they stepped shyly out into the yard, the smallest one first. They all wore freshly ironed homespun dresses with small white collars. Their hair, neatly combed and braided, ranged in color from dark to golden brown. When they were lined up, MacMillan proudly presented them.

"Our daughters, Aee, Bee, Cee, Dee and Eee."

Light bowed slightly. *"Mesdemoiselles."*

Maggie clasped her hands together. "Oh! They're all so pretty." Soft giggles blew from her mouth. She smiled up at Mrs. MacMillan. "Not a one of 'em is ugly, ma'am."

The red-faced girls, not knowing how to take Maggie's compliment, stood with downcast eyes.

Light glanced at MacMillan and his wife to see their reactions to Maggie's remark. He was relieved to see MacMillan beaming proudly and Mrs. MacMillan's smile.

"Thank you, Mrs. Lightbody. Won't you come in?" She turned to her husband. "The meal is almost ready, Mr. Mac. Why don't you and Mr. Lightbody sit in the shade until I call you. You can show him around the place this afternoon."

"All right, my dear." MacMillan waved Light toward a bench beneath a giant elm. "I'm out of tobacco or I'd offer a smoke."

Light looked up at the elm whose spreading branches seemed to cover the whole sky.

"Ain't it a wonder?" MacMillan said, his eyes following Light's to the top of the tree. "Ain't another 'round here to match it. Two hundred fifty feet if it's a inch." He patted the trunk.

"Gotta be eight feet thick."

Light nodded. It was hard for him to make talk unless there was something to discuss.

After a lengthy silence, MacMillan said, "Ya goin' to the Bluffs?"

"To the mountains to the west."

"I heared them mountains reaches to the sky. Feller with Clark said 'twas the prettiest sight he ever did see. Said beaver'd come right up to say howdy."

"How far to where the river turns northwest?"

"Not goin' to the Bluffs, eh?" MacMillan chuckled. "I was wonderin' how come ya tied up with that outfit. Figured ya knowed four men ain't goin' to get that cargo to the Bluffs." When Light remained silent, MacMillan added, "Up ahead there's towing and cordelling to be done. It'd take eight or ten men for that and ta fight off the riffraff on the river 'bove the turn. Where ever ya be goin' ya'd have the best chance to go by canoe and be rid a him and that German feller."

"I was told it was mostly Osage country between here and the mountains," Light said, ignoring MacMillan's words of advice.

" 'Tis. Ya be Osage?"

Light nodded.

"My woman's ma was Osage, her pa a Pittsburgh boatman. He was the orneriest bastard to come down the Ohio." After another silence MacMillan said, "Miz Mac bein' Osage helped me get a foothold here. Fine people, the Osage. Treat 'em fair and they'll do the same by ya," he added.

The sound of Maggie's laughter floated out the door. Both men looked toward the house.

"That bald-headed bastard's after yore woman," MacMillan said quietly. Light's dark eyes narrowed, but he didn't answer. "See one like him ever' once in a while. They don't give up once they get a woman on their mind. Not even a Indian woman'd suit after he seen what he wants. Guess ya know ya'll have to kill 'im sooner or later."

"I reckon so."

Maggie had seldom been in the company of women who accepted her as readily as the Mac-Millans did. They didn't seem to think it strange when she prowled the house, exclaiming over the clock, the pewter plates and the pieced quilt that covered the bed in the corner.

"This is nice," she exclaimed, rubbing her moccasined toe over the hard-packed clay floor. Do ya sleep in here, Aee?"

"Pa and Ma sleep in there. We sleep in there." She gestured toward the room separated by a half partition.

"Can I see?"

"I guess so," Aee said, after her mother nodded her approval.

Aee led the way into the other room. Her sisters, clearly fascinated by the visitor, followed.

"This is nice," Maggie exclaimed again. She moved to sit down on the wide shelf that served as a communal bed for the girls. "Do all of ya sleep on here?" Without waiting for an answer she said, "I slept on a pallet. Pa was goin' to build me a bed off the floor . . . someday."

The youngest girl, a child of three or four years, came to lean against Maggie's knees and gaze up at her. Maggie's smile was one of pure pleasure.

"Yore name's Eee, ain't it, little 'un?"

"Uh huh. I can stand on my head."

"Ya can?"

"Want me to show ya?"

"If ya want to."

"Not now, Eee. It's time for noonin'," Aee said, then to Maggie. "She's a hoyden. Ma said she should'a been a boy."

"What's a hoyden?"

Aee frowned and wondered if it were possible that she had more book learning than this woman.

"It means she acts like a boy . . . sometimes."

"And that's bad?" When Maggie stood, the little girl took her hand.

"I got a pet chicken. I'll show you, if ya won't go."

"They ain't goin' . . . yet," Bee blurted, then turned beet red when Maggie looked at her and exclaimed, "Ya can talk!"

" 'Course she can. She's bashful, is all," Aee said, and led the way to the door.

The MacMillan children were well-mannered even though they were excited about having visitors. Maggie found herself seated across the tres-

133

tle table from Light. There had been a quiet commotion when Eee had been told to sit in her usual place, which was not beside Maggie. The child had gone sullenly to the other end of the table. The meal of roasted buffalo hump, pigeon pie, hominy and soda bread was followed by vinegar pie.

Hungry for news, MacMillan asked about the latest happenings in St. Louis and St. Charles. He had not heard that Aaron Burr had been brought to trial and acquitted or that an Indian trail from Davidson County, Tennessee to Natchez on the Mississippi River had become known as the Natchez Trace, a road much used by traders and the military.

Mrs. MacMillan listened carefully to the conversation but did not participate. The younger children appeared to be too excited to eat. Aee waited on the table, pouring tea and removing empty serving platters.

Aee shyly asked if they knew Berry and Simon Witcher, who lived north of where the Missouri flowed into the Mississippi.

"Light does," Maggie said proudly. "Tell 'em, Light. Tell 'em how Berry saved Simon from the mad riverman, Linc Smith, and how you killed that man that was goin' to blow them up."

"You tell it, *chérie.*"

Maggie repeated the story that had become a legend up and down the rivers. While telling it her eyes went often to Light. He added a word or two when she asked him to confirm a fact.

He listened carefully, his dark eyes traveling from one face to the other and returning often to gaze proudly at his wife.

"Light threw his knife and killed the man just as he was goin' to shoot the barrel of gunpowder. He saved them all."

"Maggie," Light admonished gently. "Jeff and Will were there."

"But ya did it, Light. Berry tells ever'body ya did. Light went t' the weddin'," Maggie said, and looked around the table at the expectant faces. "Zeb Pike was there. He wanted Light t' go with him up the Mississippi."

All eyes turned to Light. "No, I didn't go," he said, and then, to Maggie, "*Chérie*, you talk too much." There was love and pride in his dark eyes when he spoke.

Maggie laughed. "And ya don't talk enough."

The girls gazed at Light with awe. They had heard the story many times but never expected the famous scout would be sitting at their table.

Later MacMillan showed Light his grindstone, root cellar and the pull-bucket well surrounded by a waist-high stone wall. He lowered a bucket on a rope, pulled it up and poured the water in the chicken trough.

"Spring-fed," he said proudly. "Clear and sweet."

They walked to a railed enclosure where a cow chewed contentedly on meadow grass that had been forked from the large pile outside the fence. Two hobbled oxen grazed in the open field beyond the cowpen.

"Don't keep horses," MacMillan explained. "Too big a temptation for the Delaware."

Light didn't reply. Men who lived in the woods did not speak when no answer was required.

In a shed beside the barn a Negro worked at making bowls out of burls from ash and maple trees.

"Got two Negroes and a couple of Osage on the place," MacMillan volunteered. "Them, my two oldest and Miz Mac are all crack shots."

Eight guns in a place like this would hold off a good-sized attack. Light was curious about the Negroes. It prompted him to ask a question, something he seldom did.

"You keep slaves?"

"Don't believe in tradin' in human flesh. Never did. The Negroes and the Osage are free to go anytime. Osage drift in and out from time to time. Howdy, Linus," he said to the Negro, who was bent over a bench where he was scraping the inside of a burl.

"Howdy, Mista." The small man smiled warmly, and his dark eyes flicked from MacMillan to the scout.

"Linus is the best woodworker I ever did see. Looky here at this. He can burn the inside of a burl to within a half-inch." MacMillan held a highly polished bowl for Light's inspection. "We send 'em downriver to a feller in St. Louie. He sends them on to New Orleans. Linus gets part of the money. He's goin' to have more than me if I ain't careful, and I'll be workin' for him."

Linus's grin widened, and his eyes glistened with unvoiced pleasure. He was still smiling when they left the shed.

The settler led the way to the larger building. The minute they entered, two Indians went out the back.

"My potash works," MacMillan said. "Know anythin' 'bout potash?"

"Nothing at all," Light said.

MacMillan chuckled. "Ya start with a pile of wood ashes," he said and continued on. "Got the idey when I cleared a spot a farmland. We downed the trees one year, burned 'em the next. I got to thinkin' them ashes'd make lye after a time and when the water is boiled out, ya get the potash." He showed Light an iron pot holding gray powder. "That's called pearl ash. Not easy work, but it sells good downriver. We boil some of it with animal fat to make soap.

"I'm figgerin' on having a settlement here. Folks comin' upriver all the time now: trappers and settlers. Good land for crops right here without goin' any farther. Only one drawback." His eyes twinkled. "Man has to run after he sows seed to keep ahead of the crops a jumpin' up behind him."

That brought a smile from Light and encouraged MacMillan to continue.

"Might even have a town on this bend someday, what with the salt works back in the cave and the potash. Miz Mac ain't fond of the idey. 'Course we won't see a full-blown town, but our

137

younguns will. Be mighty proud to have ya and yore woman a part of it. We'll give ya a hand settin' up if ya'd want to squat here and dig in."

"Thank you, but I'd not be much good as a farmer."

"Didn't think ya'd want to."

In the middle of the afternoon Light and Maggie prepared to leave the homestead. At the edge of the clearing Maggie looked back to see the MacMillan girls lined up beside their mother. All were waving good-bye.

"They liked me, Light." There was a kind of wonderment in Maggie's voice.

"They did, *ma petite*. It was no surprise to me." Light threw his arm across her shoulders.

"Will we be back?"

"*Oui*, you will see your friends again."

Several canoes, a raft and two flatboats were moored in the creek that ran alongside Mac-Millan's homestead. Light directed Maggie to the canoe he had purchased for two of his precious hoard of coins. After a few instructions from Light, Maggie proved to be an able hand with the paddle. By the time they reached the faster water of the river, they had settled into a rhythm, and the canoe slid smoothly through the water toward Eli's boat.

"What'll we do without horses, Light?"

"I want to talk to you about that, pet. It's gettin' late in the year for us to start across the plains. I'm thinkin' we will stay somewhere near here for the winter. It'll take time to build a shelter and lay in supplies for winter."

"Oh, could we? Will we be close enough so I can see Aee and Bee sometimes?"

"It is possible, *ma chère*."

Light's mind was forging ahead. The crickets were singing, which meant they would have a killing frost anytime. The tree limbs would soon be bare, and the cold north wind would sweep the dry, crisp leaves along the ground. He wanted to take a look at the country on the other side of the river and get some idea about the abundance of game so he'd know what he could count on when winter came. They would live off the land as much as possible. Other provisions he would buy from MacMillan.

He felt no obligation to be part of Nielson's crew. This was the place and the time to break with the Swede. Something about Nielson created a restlessness in him. It was not only the way he looked at Maggie, it was the way Eli looked at *him*.

When they reached the flatboat, they found Eli lying on a pallet. Paul was on his knees beside him trying to get him to drink tea.

Otto Kruger sat on the bank above the craft, his back to a tree, a keg of Eli's whiskey beside him.

Light tied the canoe to the boat and he and Maggie scrambled aboard.

"What's the matter with Eli?" Maggie went

139

immediately to where he lay.

"*Mon petit chou!* It's glad I am that you've come back. Eli is burning with a fever. He is sick. Very sick."

"He was a'right when we left."

Paul threw up his hands and sputtered in French.

"Speak English," Light said sharply when he saw the anxious look on Maggie's face. "She can't understand you."

"Forgive me, *madame.* I am so . . . worried."

Light knelt down and placed the back of his hand against Eli's forehead, then touched his arms and placed his hand inside his shirt.

"The fever will burn his brain. We wet him down."

Taking a bucket from a hook on the side of the shed, Light lowered it into the river and filled it. Starting with Eli's bare feet he poured the water over him, then went back for another bucketful.

"I wet his shirt, *m'sieur,* and wrap it about his head. No?" Paul's face was clouded with worry. He knelt beside the delirious man.

Eli thrashed around on the pallet, his hands flying up as if to ward off an attack. He muttered, his eyes opened suddenly and his hand lashed out, striking Maggie on the shoulder and knocking her back on her heels.

"*Madame!*" Paul hastened to explain. "He did not know . . . he did not mean to —"

"I know that. Hold his foot so that he'll not hurt it more."

"Fraulein!" Kruger's speech was whiskey-slurred. "He vill soon be det! Den who be boss?"

Maggie turned on him. "Hush yore nasty mouth, ya bald-headed . . . old . . . buzzard."

The German hooted with laughter. "I like voman vit' fire."

"Ignore him, pet," Light murmured. "Take the wet rag from around Eli's ankle and apply another poultice."

"I grind the *gonoshay* leaves between two stones as *madame* had done," Paul said.

Maggie took the slab of bark holding the pulverized herb and added enough water from the water barrel to make a sticky paste. She applied it carefully to the swollen angry flesh of Eli's ankle. She took one of the rags her mother had put in her pack to use when she had her monthly flow. While she was wrapping Eli's foot, it crossed her mind that she had finished her woman's time just before she left home and it had not come again.

Was there a child already growing in her belly?

Thinking of that secret part of her body, her eyes sought her husband. Just looking at him sent her heart to fluttering in remembrance of what they had done together. She tingled as she thought of the two of them warm and naked beneath the blankets: his being hard and deep inside her and his hot splash of seed awakening a soft explosion from her own body.

Maggie lowered her head to hide the blush that covered her face. Her mother had told her it

141

was a man's right to do as he wished in the marriage bed. She had not, however, mentioned how enjoyable it would be for the woman or that she had the privilege of pleasuring herself on her man's body. Light had whispered to her that she had a right as his wife to reach for him when she felt the need.

She remembered the first part of their journey as being the most wonderful time of her life. She longed to be alone with her man again. Light was the only person she had ever known who didn't seem to think her odd. He did not think it unnatural for her to travel the woods at night or to be unafraid of animals or sing and dance when the mood struck her.

She smoothed the hair back from Eli's fevered brow. They couldn't leave him while he was sick. The man who lay fever-bound on the pallet had become dear to her, but not in the way Light was dear to her. She liked Eli very much though. In just the few short days they had known him, she had come to trust him completely. She glanced at Light and found that he was looking at her as she stroked Eli's brow, his clearly defined features devoid of expression.

Maggie sat back on her heels. She wanted Light to *like* Eli. At times she thought he did, and at other times she thought he did not.

When she stood, she caught Light staring up-river and followed his gaze. Four paddlers dipped into the river rhythmically, sending a canoe speeding through the water. Maggie soon recognized

MacMillan and one of his girls in the front of the craft, an Indian and a Negro in the back.

From a few yards out MacMillan threw a rope to Light, who pulled the canoe close to the boat and secured it. After MacMillan boarded, he held a hand out to assist Aee.

"Heared ya got a sick man."

CHAPTER TEN

Neither Paul nor Maggie stopped to wonder how MacMillan knew Eli had taken a turn for the worse. Light, however, remembered the settler saying that nothing went on up or down this section of the river without his knowing about it. The scout filed the thought in the back of his mind and listened to what MacMillan was saying to Paul.

"The man be sick a'right. Take a look, Aee. If she don't figger it's a catchin' sickness," he said to Paul, "we'll help ya pole upriver to our landin' if ya wants. My woman is a smart hand at doctorin', but Miz Mac ain't in no shape right now to be traipsin' 'round. Her time's nigh to drop the babe."

Aee knelt down beside Eli and looked closely at his face and neck. She pulled down the neck of his shirt to look at his chest, then his upper arms.

"There's no spots on him, Pa."

MacMillan nodded and spoke to Paul. "What'll it be, man?"

"We be glad fer help, *mon ami*."

144

In response to a wave of MacMillan's hand, the two men in the canoe scrambled aboard and took up a pole. Paul slipped the mooring line holding the craft to the shore and the boat began to drift out from the bank.

Kruger jumped to his feet and shouted. Paul ignored him.

"*Verdammt!*" The German let out a bellow of rage and leaped to the deck of the boat, leaving the keg of whiskey beside the tree. "Sonabitch! Ya'd leaf me!"

"*Dieu!* Be glad to be rid of ya!" Paul shouted with more anger than Light had heard from him before.

"Ya vant I kill ya?" Kruger started for Paul, his ham-like fists clenched. He stopped suddenly when he felt the prick of Light's knife in his back.

"Pole or go over the side."

The whiskey Kruger had consumed made him brave. He moved to turn on Light but was stopped when the pressure of the knife increased.

"I cut yore t'roat den I take yore voman."

"Touch her *one* time and I'll cut your heart out." There was a deadly menace in Light's voice. He prodded Otto again with the tip of his knife.

"*Mein Gott!* I vill kill ya." Kruger's eyes met those of MacMillan, then drifted to the Negro and on to the stoic face of the Indian. They were both ready and waiting to jump him if MacMillan gave the nod. The German was not so drunk that he couldn't figure the odds.

"Vatch yore back, breed," he snarled and moved away to pull a pole from the slots.

The six men poled the craft, leaving Maggie to work the new steering oar and Aee the job of tending to Eli.

She dipped a cloth in the bucket of water and bathed Eli's head. She had never been this close to a young and handsome white man. This one was helpless as a babe, which both thrilled and scared her. As she bathed his head, she studied his face. His forehead was broad, his nose straight, his mouth thin and firm. Thick, light-brown hair grew back from his forehead and fell down over his ears. He looked younger than he had the day before — almost boyish.

Eli muttered a few unintelligible words, opened his eyes and looked directly into hers. Aee was so startled that she backed away before she realized that although his sky-blue eyes were clear, they were not seeing her.

"Pretty," he murmured and lifted a hand toward her face.

She grabbed his wrist and forced it back to his side. He groped for her hand and held it tight. She could barely speak for the excitement that crowded her lungs.

"Be . . . still, mister."

"Hoist the sail, Paul," Eli whispered hoarsely, then bitingly, "Goddamm bastard. A slutty savage! Got ta see — Got ta know —"

"Shhh . . . Be still."

"Bitch! Injun . . . bi . . . tch —" Eli's lids

146

closed, and his voice faded.

Aee was taken aback by the cruel words and blinked moisture from her eyes. The hurt was there even though she knew that he was out of his head. Fever did that to a person.

"Ya'll be a'right." Aee spoke without a trace of sympathy in her voice. "Go t' sleep," she said when his eyes flew open and he continued to look at her.

"Mag . . . gie," he murmured. "Mag . . . gie," he said again as his lids fluttered down over his eyes.

He wanted Maggie! Aee tried to pull her hand from his, but his fingers tightened. She decided to leave it there until he was completely asleep lest she rouse him again. It was exciting to have her hand held even though she knew that he didn't realize it was *her* hand he was holding.

Aee remembered how his eyes had passed over her and rested on Maggie the day before, when she had come with her father to invite the travelers to the homestead. He had haughtily refused the invitation, saying he had to stay near his boat and guard his goods.

"He wants *her!*" The words came from under Aee's breath. She couldn't blame him. Maggie was so beautiful. Did he want her badly enough to fight her husband for her?

She had really wanted this handsome young man to come to their home. Pa had said their place was as nice as any along the river. Her mother's father had been a rich merchant who had had his daughter tutored to live in the white man's world. She had taught her daughters proper manners.

Zee would have watched his goods. But . . . she reasoned, looking down at him . . . Mr. Nielson didn't know about Zee.

With six men at the poles the craft moved upriver, and soon MacMillan was directing them to a bank below his homestead where thick willows hung out over the water, partially concealing the mouth of a creek that flowed into the river. The flatboat glided smoothly into the opening. Inland a quarter of a mile, completely hidden from river traffic, was MacMillan's mooring site.

"Ya want Caleb to tote the man to the sickroom?" MacMillan asked as soon as the boat was secured to the dock.

"Tote him?" Paul echoed.

"It won't be no chore fer Caleb."

"Then we'd . . . be obliged."

The huge man moved lightly up onto the wooden platform. Light judged him to be close to six and a half feet tall. He was one of the biggest men Light had ever seen, but rawboned big, without an extra ounce of flesh on his body. A doeskin sleeveless shirt stretched smoothly across his broad chest. Around his bare upper arms, as big and as muscled as an ordinary man's thigh, were tied bands of red cloth. He stood on legs as sturdy as tree trunks. His face was ebony black, smooth-skinned and shiny as hard coal.

Caleb's large golden eyes swept the area, taking

in everything. Light had the impression that he was making a thoughtful evaluation of what he was seeing, especially in regard to Kruger. After the two women had walked past him up the path to the homestead, he stepped back onto the boat and picked Eli up in his arms, carrying him as easily as if he were a child.

Paul hesitated. Although he was anxious about his friend, he didn't want to leave Light alone on the boat with Kruger.

"Mr. Deschanel," MacMillan said, "ye and Mr. Lightbody be welcome in my home." He ignored Kruger as if he were not there. Then, after he had received a nod from Paul, he spoke in Osage to the Indian. Paul didn't understand what he was saying, but Light remembered well the language of his mother.

"Watch the bald one. If he starts up the path, kill him."

The Indian made no sign that he had heard, but when they left the boat, he followed them for a few yards, then turned off into the brush and disappeared.

A bed for Eli had been prepared in a small room attached to the side of the house where Mrs. MacMillan treated anyone who came to the homestead seeking help. The narrow bunk attached to the wall was several feet off the ground. The mattress of heavy duck cloth filled with straw was clean, as was the feather pillow placed beneath his head.

149

The Osage often brought their sick and were taken in if it were determined the sickness was not catching. Occasionally a trapper or an injured riverman occupied the room. A small cemetery on a nearby rise was the resting place for a half-dozen strangers.

"Miz Mac and the girls'll tend him," MacMillan said to Paul. "We take off his wet britches."

After that was done and his private parts were covered with a sheet, Mrs. MacMillan came into the shed. Although her belly was huge with the unborn child, she walked with her shoulders squared and her back straight. Aee followed her with a basket and a pitcher of water.

"Leave us," Mrs. MacMillan said to the men in a tone that left no room for argument. Paul was reluctant, but he followed MacMillan to the well, where the homesteader drew up a fresh bucket of water.

"If anythin' can be done, Miz Mac'll do it," he said matter-of-factly to Paul while handing him the dipper. "Have a drink a this and tell me if it ain't the best gol-durn water to go down yore gullet."

The younger children were delighted to see Maggie again so soon. Their faces were flushed with excitement. The two smallest, Dee and Eee, hung onto her hands. Cee and Bee lingered at the entrance of the shed ready to run and fetch when their mother gave an order.

Light leaned against the trunk of the giant elm tree and watched his wife play a game of squat-tag with the little girls. At times, he thought, she was like a child. But only at times. It was not a child who had killed the Delaware in the cave. She was not a child when they were in their blankets. Light felt a stirring beneath his buckskins at the thought of how quickly her passion could be aroused. He wanted to be alone with her, longed for the time when they would be free to continue their journey to their mountain.

He also felt a nagging unease about Maggie's interest in the Swede. Had her feelings for *him* changed now that she had met this white man? Light had never been uncomfortable living between the Indian and white world. He had not stopped to consider what Maggie's feelings might be in the years to come.

After he had killed the man attempting to rape her, he had wanted to take her with him, keep her with him, protect her. It had not occurred to him that he would come to love her so desperately, love her with every fibre of his being. She was truly his life, his treasure.

When morning came, he would look for a place along the river and build a winter shelter. He would trap, then sell his furs to MacMillan for enough money to buy horses from the Osage to take them across the plains in the spring. He had hoped to winter with the Osage across the river, but it was time to stop. They would be safer near MacMillan should the Delaware or a raiding party of river pirates attack.

He watched Maggie frolicking with the children. No man would take her from him. No man would understand her free spirit as he did. She was his woods sprite, his pretty butterfly. He would kill the Swede before he let him have her.

Bee went to the well for a bucket of water and hurried back to the sickroom. Light realized that Nielson was very sick, but he felt that Eli was strong enough to weather the fever. Paul had told him something of the man's background. Eli's Swedish mother had been in this country only a year when she had given birth to him. At age eleven he had been left to fend for himself. Nothing was said of his father.

Paul had explained that he and Eli had spent the last few years on the Ohio, so unlike the great Missouri with its turbulent currents, strings of small islands and the sudden surges of muddy water. He admitted that they were ill-prepared to tackle the savage river and the untamed wilderness. It had been foolish of them to come up-river with only six men to pole or man the oars. The two crewmen who had deserted the flatboat a week from St. Charles had had a chance of making it back. The other two had more than likely provided entertainment for the Delaware.

Light liked the Frenchman and admired his devotion to his friend, but he felt no obligation to stay with Paul until Nielson was well again. Light hoped that MacMillan could furnish the Swede with a crew of Osage to enable them to continue on up the river. He would be willing to bet, however, that after the settler sized up

152

the two rivermen, he would dangle his older girls under their noses in an effort to persuade them to settle here.

MacMillan was a hard man. Hadn't he ordered the Osage to kill Kruger if he came toward the house? With river pirates on one side, the Delaware on the other and bands of restless Indians prowling the land, the settler did what he had to do to survive and protect his family.

In the deepening dusk the fireflies had come out. The croaking of peeper frogs down at the creek was joined by a choir of crickets. Birds flitted restlessly in the treetops as they settled for the night. Downriver an owl hooted. It was a lonely sound that reminded Light of his life after his family had been killed and before Maggie had come into it.

Caleb came up from the dock with Light's packs, crossed the yard and dropped them at his feet.

"Mista say Caleb fetch 'em." The voice was exceptionally soft considering that it came from such a large man.

"My thanks." Light had to tilt his head to look into the man's face.

"Caleb! Caleb!" MacMillan's youngest child, Eee, ran across the yard. "Swing, Caleb." Maggie and Dee trailed behind her.

With a delighted grin, the giant held out two large hands. Eee ran to him with arms raised. He grasped the child's wrists and swung her off the ground. Around and around they turned

. . . Eee's merry laughter rang out confidently; this was a game they had played before.

"My turn, Caleb!" Dee screeched and ran to him when he stopped and Eee stood upright once again.

It was difficult to decide who most enjoyed the game, the huge man or the children. Eee was jumping up and down by the time Caleb finished swinging Dee.

"Maggie's turn! Swing Maggie's turn!"

"No! No!" Maggie ran behind Light, wrapped her arms about his waist and buried her face between his shoulder blades.

"Caleb won't let ya fall, Maggie."

Mrs. MacMillan came out of the shed. "Don't ya be pesterin' Mrs. Lightbody."

"We ain't, Ma."

"You're spoilin' them again, Caleb." Mrs. Mac-Millan clicked her tongue and shook her head in mock anger.

"Yass, Miz Mac. I guess I is."

"It's time to come in, girls. Say goodnight to Mr. and Mrs. Lightbody."

"Ma—"

"Caleb was goin' to catch us a firefly. We was goin' to show Maggie."

"Come. You'll see Maggie tomorrow."

The girls went reluctantly to the house and Caleb loped back toward the dock.

When they were alone beneath the tree, Maggie threw her arms around Light's neck and snuggled her mouth against his in a long deep kiss.

154

"Where will we sleep, Light?"

"I've already picked out a place where I'll have you all to myself." He kissed her again, then held her away so he could look at her.

"I've got that hurty feelin' I get when we kiss. I'm all wet between my legs too. Will ya give me lovin' t'night?" Maggie asked, wrapping her arms around his waist and wiggling closer to him.

"As much as you want, *chérie*." He chucked her beneath the chin with his fist, then held her tightly to him for a long moment.

Maggie moved out of his arms. "I'll see 'bout Eli, then we go."

"No! Stay with me." Light held tightly to her hand when she would have left him.

"Light?" She moved back to him, tilted her face to his, her eyes questioning.

He shook his head. "He doesn't need you, *chérie*. He has others to tend him."

"I want t' see how he is, Light."

"It's been a while since we've been alone. I want you to come to our bed."

"Why ya saying this? Why don't ya like Eli?"

"It's not important, my pet. We go from here in the morning."

"Ya said we'd stay."

"Not here, *ma petite*. We'll make a place for ourselves and stay the winter."

"We can't stay here?"

"Not in another man's home, *chérie*. I'll make a place for us. It will not be so far away that we can't return here if trouble comes."

155

"But . . . Eli and Paul —"

"— will go their own way. Come, my treasure. I've been longing to have you alone."

"Ya liked Eli. Ya saved him —"

"I would have done the same for any man."

"Even Kruger?"

"*Oui,* sweet pet, I would have tried. Even knowing that later I might need to kill him."

Maggie's face wore a puzzled frown. "I don't understand, Light, but I'm yore woman an' I do what ya say."

She *was* his woman. Light experienced a queer stab of fear. He had not wanted to love her. He had not wanted to expose his heart to the pain of loving and losing ever again. He pulled Maggie to him, held her tightly, and rocked her in his arms.

Aee lifted Eli's head and held the cup to his lips. In his fevered state he craved water and obediently drank cup after cup of the tea her mother had brewed from willow bark. After examining his ankle, Mrs. MacMillan proclaimed that it was not the cause of the fever. The *gonoshay* poultice was working. Nevertheless, she had given her husband orders to kill several squirrels in the morning so that she could make a poultice of squirrel brains and crushed ginseng leaves to apply to the wound.

His illness, she believed, was due to swallowing so much river water.

The homestead was quiet. Aee would be relieved of her duty in an hour or two. In the flickering light from the candle, she studied Eli's face. What would it look like without the whiskers? Hesitantly, she lifted her fingers to touch his beard. It was as soft as her hair after she had washed it in the rain barrel. She fingered the hair that lay on his shoulders. It was fine and silky too. Never had she seen such a handsome man. Hearing a sound, she quickly jerked her hand away and looked guiltily toward the door.

Eli moved his arms to the top of the blanket, baring his shoulders and chest. Aee wasn't sure what to do. Her mother had said to keep him covered and warm. The fall night air had a bite in it. She had thrown a shawl about her own shoulders. She stood, leaned over him, gently lifted an arm and put it back under the blanket.

"Who'er you?"

The whispered words startled Aee. She straightened. His eyes were open. A bead of sweat was on his forehead. She gaped at him in surprise.

"I'm hot," he said before she could answer.

"All the more reason to keep covered."

"You're that . . . girl."

"Aee MacMillan."

"Where am I?"

"At our place. Ma has been doctorin' ya."

"The boat?"

"Tied up at Pa's dock. Mr. Deschanel and the Lightbodys are here."

He closed his eyes wearily. Aee sat down, thinking he had gone to sleep. When she looked at him again, he was watching her.

"I could use a drink of water. My mouth tastes like I've been gnawing on a polecat."

"It ain't no wonder. Ya been drinkin' willow bark tea. It's broke yore fever."

He lifted his head when she held a cup of water to his mouth.

"Where's Maggie and . . . Paul?" he asked after he had sank back down.

"Mr. Deschanel bedded down in the barn. He'll sit with you later. Maggie is with her husband." Aee felt a little stab of delight in telling him that.

"He's not her hus—" Eli cut off the words. "Is Kruger with the boat?"

Aee shrugged. "Pa told him t' stay there."

"Get Paul," he commanded curtly and closed his eyes, dismissing her. A full minute of silence passed. His lids lifted. He tilted his head and stabbed her with hard blue eyes. "Did you hear me? Get Paul." His tone of voice didn't suggest she argue, but she did.

"No. I was told t' stay here."

"Who told you that?"

"Ma."

"Jesus, my arse! I'm not a babe to be watched over. If I have to shout for Paul, I will."

"Open yore mouth an' I'll poke a rag in it." Aee's brown eyes sparkled with anger. "Ya'll not wake up ever'body on the place cause ya've a hair crossways."

"Have you lost the few brains you have, girl?

Are you deaf as well as stupid? I said I want Paul."

"Wantin' ain't gettin', Mister Smart-mouth Nielson. Mr. Deschanel needs t' sleep now. He'll be comin' t' sit with ya later."

Eli's blue eyes glittered angrily. "Why you draggled-tailed, hard-headed little snippet!"

"Snippet? I don't know what that is, but it don't sound as bad as a sour-mouthed, brayin' jackass. That's what ya are! I'm sorry t' be missin' my sleep tendin' ya! Ma ort to a let ya lay wallerin' in yore sweat. She didn't 'cause she's got a soft spot for dumb animals." Aee's voice quivered with anger.

"Deliver me from a know-it-all, bull-headed, spiteful woman who can't take orders," he murmured and, in frustration, rolled his head back and forth on the pillow.

Aee sat down, her mouth tightly crimped. She folded her arms over her chest and focused her mind fully on the fact that the big muddy river would run backward before she'd take for her man this stupid pisspot who lusted for another man's wife.

CHAPTER ELEVEN

Light awoke instantly alert. There were no me-
anderings in his world between sleep and sen-
sibility. His hand grasped the hilt of his knife.
Almost simultaneously he was on his feet and
standing protectively over Maggie.

Overhead the diamond glitter of stars scattered
across the heavens was fading. Along the east
horizon a line of pearl-gray light gave the first
indication of impending dawn. A flight of geese
coming down from the north were on their way
to a feeding ground; their constant honking was
the only sound he heard.

In the gloom of the clearing, a shadow moved.
Every muscle and nerve in Light's body was
on guard. A man in Indian dress emerged from
the darkness. He stood stolidly, arms crossed over
his chest.

"Your ears are keen, Sharp Knife. I snapped
one twig."

"It was enough." Light answered in Osage.

The Indian nodded in agreement. "It is said
that Sharp Knife has the eye of the hawk, the
nose of the weasel, and that he can hear a

cloud pass overhead."

"Who calls me Sharp Knife?" Light had not been called by his Indian name in a long while.

"Many Spots, kin of Mac's woman."

"How is it you know my name?"

The Indian shrugged. "All know Sharp Knife, son of Willow Wind, kin of Nowatha the healer. Your mother sent word that Sharp Knife was bringing Singing Bird to the land of his ancestors."

"You came in the night to tell me this?"

"Morning is only a whisper away. I came to tell you No Hair take canoe downriver."

"It is good that he is gone. If he is taken by the Delaware, he will give them much sport."

"He take two kegs gunpowder."

"For the Delaware?"

"Not know. Maybe for keelboat one day downriver."

"Keelboat? Who comes this way?"

"Not friend."

"Does MacMillan know this?"

"Mac knows. Said wake the man called Sharp Knife by the Osage. Said No Hair may come back for Sharp Knife's woman. Said bring Singing Bird to strong cabin. Thick walls." The Indian spread his hands to indicate how thick.

"My thanks to you and Mac. Is anyone watching No Hair?"

"Zee will watch."

"Zee? That is good?"

"Very good."

Without a sound or a farewell the Indian backed

into the shadows and was gone.

Light listened for a long moment and, hearing nothing unusual, looked down at Maggie, who had slept through the exchange with Many Spots.

They had made love throughout most of the night. He could not seem to sate his appetite for her, nor she for him. Their loving had at first been a quick, ecstatic and irreversible tempo toward an all-absorbing fulfillment. Later they had lain side by side, her intimate down teased by his hardening flesh, until with a groan and a hungry forward motion he had again embedded himself in her sweet softness.

Time and again he had surfaced from the pleasure-tide and pulled away from her, only to be enticed back by her gasping, almost sobbing breath on his chest as her hand moved down to his flat belly. Her small hands wildly caressed him, soothed him, cradled him, driving him to that devastating, exquisite explosion. The stamina and passion of this small woods sprite astounded him.

"*My* man! My sweet man! My Light! My life!" She had whispered the words over and over.

Light realized then that this mysterious, unexplainable attachment that bound them together was stronger than all the uncertainties that had lately overwhelmed him. As they soared in fevered flight, their bodies locked together, the small resentments, anxieties, and his fear of losing her to the Swede faded into nothingness.

Now, in the early dawn, the love of his life

162

was tired from their hours of vigorous activity. Last night, as they had lain beneath the stars, it had been possible to believe that they were the only human beings on earth. But morning had come and it was time to face reality.

Reluctant to wake her, he knelt down on the bed of soft pine boughs and pulled the blanket up over her bare shoulder. After she had fallen asleep, he had pulled on his buckskin britches should he have the need to rise quickly. Beneath the covers Maggie was still as naked as a newborn babe.

"What'd the Indian say, Light?"

"*Chérie*, you pretend sleep," he chided gently, his eyes loving her.

"I woke up when ya left me," she purred in a soft slurry voice.

"I think you're tired. We romped most of the night."

"Ya love me, Light?"

"Can't you tell that, my sweet pet?"

"I like t' hear ya say it."

"I love you. You are my life, my soul."

"That's pretty, Light." She raised her hand and stroked his bare chest. "I feel cold bumps." She lifted the blanket in invitation. "I'll get ya warm."

Believing that the danger from Kruger was not immediate and the temptation to hold her was great, Light lay down beside her and pulled her to lie on his chest. She sighed like a contented kitten, snuggled against him, and waited for him to tell her about the Indian's visit.

163

"Kruger took a canoe and went downriver."

"I'm glad he's gone."

"MacMillan said you should come to the cabin."

"I stay with you, Light."

"MacMillan thinks the German wants you and may come back."

"I know he wants me. The first day I knew it. The fever was in his eyes." She shivered and moved her cheek against his lips. "I'll cut him with my knife if he touches me."

"He will never have you, *ma petite*."

His lips moved from her cheek and slowly, deliberately, covered hers, pressing gently at first. Then he deepened his kiss as she hovered against his masculine strength. The tip of his tongue caressing the corner of her mouth was persuasive. She parted her lips in invitation. The soft utterance that came from her throat was a purr of pure pleasure.

"*Mon trésor!* My treasure!" he whispered, his hunger growing to an ache. His body demanded more than a kiss, no matter how wonderful the kiss might be. But this was not the time to satisfy that hunger.

Resisting the pressure of her arms around his neck, he moved his head and looked at her face, pale and beautiful, still and waiting.

"You're the most vexing woman, and . . . the sweetest," he said in a raspy whisper. Her breath came quickly and was cool on his lips, made wet by their kiss.

"Vexing? What's that, Light?"

"When applied to you, *ma chérie*, it is good."

"Light" — she stroked his chest with her fingertips — "are ya glad yo're takin' me with ya t' yore mountain?"

"Why do you ask?"

"Ya don't smile, Light. I like t' see ya smile."

"I'll try to smile more —" His words melted on her lips.

Daylight was seeping through the trees when Light threw back the blankets, exposing Maggie's warm naked body to the cool fall air.

"Get dressed, Madame Lightbody." He grasped her wrists, pulled her to her feet and playfully slapped her bare bottom.

"In a minute. Oh . . . I feel good!"

Maggie threw out her arms and began to whirl away from him. Around and around she whirled, her bare feet seeming to float above the ground. She sped around the clearing, skipping, dipping and swaying. As she frolicked, her tangle of dark curls whipped about her shoulders and back, at times covering her perky bare breasts.

> Down came an ol' man
> A hummin' like a bee,
> An' found a hat a-hangin'
> Where his hat ort t'be.

His face creased with smiles, Light watched his bride. It was such a pleasure to see her dancing so uninhibitedly and singing her merry tune that he was reluctant to stop her, but he did so when she twirled near him. He caught her up in his arms.

"Yo're smilin', Light," she said happily and kissed his mouth. "If ya'll smile, I'll dance for ya ever'day when we get t' our mountain."

From the upper branches of a giant oak, the unblinking eye peered down through the dense crop of leaves. When the woman came out of the blankets and began to dance and sing, the creature clapped a hand over its mouth in order to stifle the giggles that bubbled up. He had never seen anything like this beautiful nymph dancing in the woods, and he doubted if anyone else had, other than himself and Sharp Knife. Her nakedness was nothing new. He had seen many naked Indian women, but this woman was like the damsel in the story told of wee fairies who danced in the glens on the Emerald Isle.

Many Spots had told him of the legend of Sharp Knife and of his many feats. He was a worthy mate for this rare lassie with exceptional beauty as well as exceptional skill with the knife and the whip.

Scarcely blinking or breathing for fear Sharp Knife would hear the sound or see the movement, the creature stood as still as a stone, muscular arms wrapped around a branch, his strong heart throbbing with painful memories of times long past. The clothing that covered his body blended with the thick grapevines that twisted and clung to the oak in an attempt to reach the sun.

The breathtaking performance was over all too soon. Sharp Knife had enjoyed it too. His usually somber face was alight with smiles. The creature waited until Singing Bird was dressed in her buckskin britches and long belted shirt and the couple had picked up their packs and walked toward the homestead before he swung himself hand-over-hand down the vine until his thin, wiry legs touched the ground.

MacMillan, carrying his rifle and with a pistol stuck in his belt, came out into the yard to meet Light and Maggie as they approached the house.

"The women's got vittles ready," he said briskly without further greeting.

"We'll make our own cookfire," Light answered in the same tone of voice. "We came to thank you for sending Many Spots with the news about Kruger."

"Yo're refusin' my invite?"

"We thank you for it, but we didn't come here to eat your food and give nothing back."

"Ya'll be givin' back if ya help me protect my family."

"That goes without saying, *m'sieur*."

"On that keelboat coming upriver is a feller named Ramon de la Vega, as black-hearted a rogue as ever was born. He be a pirate, murderer, a spoiler of womenfolk."

"Many Spots said as much."

"This is his third trip upriver that I know of. Ever' trip Osage women have come up missin'.

Favors 'em 'cause they be comelier than most. Takes white women if he can bargain 'em from the Delaware."

"The Delaware would have used them cruelly."

"No more so than Vega." MacMillan's eyes constantly searched the area as if he expected someone. "Know fer a fact he's taken trappers aboard, unloaded their furs and broke up their canoes."

Paul came from the sickroom and was greeted by Maggie.

"Paul," she called. "Is Eli still sick?"

"Better today, *madame*. Much better," Paul said cheerfully.

"Light —" Maggie shook her husband's arm. "A'right if I go see Eli?"

"Go, my sprite. But don't go from the house. Stay with the women." After she left them, Light asked, "Will Vega stop here?"

"It's likely. Miz Mac's gettin' thin's ready. She and the three little gals'll take to the caves. Aee and Bee is as good shots as I ever did see. Many Spots has gone t' the Osage. They won't just stand by if we be attacked."

"Has Vega enough men for that?"

"He don't need many. He's got a cannon."

"If Vega connects with Otto, *m'sieur*," Paul said, "he will know women are here."

"An' he'll have two more kegs of gunpowder," MacMillan said with a heavy sigh.

"Where does he take the women?" Light asked quietly.

"Caleb says he takes 'em to a place south of Natchez. Uses some there in a pleasure house an' sells others t' ship out t' heathen lands."

"How does Caleb know this?"

"Vega bought 'im t' use as a stud. They sold off his offsprin's, an' he had a passel of 'em, for breedin'. He ran off four or five years back. Don't know how he managed t' get through the Delaware, but he did."

"If Vega knows Caleb is here, he's sure to demand his property?" Paul asked.

"Far as I know he don't know it. Vega thinks Negroes is dumb two-legged animals, too dumb t' come all this way all by their own self."

"*M'sieur,* Kruger will tell him," Paul said quietly.

"God bless! That's right!" MacMillan said flatly, his eyes full of anguish. "I'll hide Caleb away. Ain't goin' t' let that bastard get his hands on 'im. By the time he got done, poor Caleb'd not be fit t' shoot."

"I talked about this to Eli," Paul said. "He says take what you need from his cargo to protect your home and family. There are eight more kegs of gunpowder, and ten rifles, if Kruger didn't take them."

"Many Spots says Kruger slipped over the side and pulled the canoe t' the river a'fore he climbed in. I had counted the kegs, thinkin' t' trade Nielson for all. That's how I know two are gone."

"What do you suggest, *m'sieur?*"

"Caleb is fetching the ox carts to take what

cargo we don't need to the salt cave."

"I go to lend a hand," Paul bowed and hurried away.

"Put your packs in the sickroom, Lightbody. Miz Mac'll dish out some grub. Might be a while 'fore ya eat again."

Eli was sitting on the side of the bed eating from a bowl of gruel when Maggie entered the sickroom. A blanket was wrapped about his middle. He was scowling at Bee, who stood as far from him as possible, her back to the wall, her head bowed.

"Mornin', Eli. Mornin', Bee."

Silence.

Maggie looked from Eli's set, angry features to Bee's rosy face and quivering lips. She put her hands on her hips and frowned.

"Eli!" she demanded. "Are ya bein' out of sorts with Bee?"

"Out of sorts?" he echoed as if she had spoken in a language he couldn't understand. "I'm damn mad!" he blurted. "She won't give me my britches."

"Maybe they're lost." Maggie giggled.

Eli glared.

"Ma'll come tell him when he can get up," Bee said, her voice scarcely above a whisper.

"Hell an' high water! When's she comin'? I ate every damn thing she sent in. I want to get out a here!" Eli set the empty bowl down on the dirt floor. "She'll bring them quick enough

170

if I walk out of here bare-assed naked."

Maggie giggled again. "Was only yesterday ya was out of yore head with fever. Are ya still?"

Eli's glower deepened. "I got to see about my boat. Kruger ran off with some of my cargo and, by God, I'll get it back. I'm not caving in to that block-headed German."

"Yo're too weak, Eli," Maggie argued.

"Confound it, Maggie! If I sit here I'll just get weaker. Get my britches. MacMillan's going to need all the help he can get if that feller Vega turns in here."

"They won't be needin' ya, Eli. Light will know what to do. He'll help Mr. MacMillan."

"Light this! Light that! I'm sick a hearing that *Light* can do everything!"

"Well, he can, Eli. And don't ya say no different or ya'll get my back up."

"Maggie," Eli said with forced patience, "I'm telling you, MacMillan will need all the help he can get. The pirate has a *cannon.*"

"Light's not 'fraid of a cannon." Maggie insisted. "Ya just wait an' see."

Eli threw up his hands in mock surrender. "I suppose he'll catch the ball in his teeth."

Maggie's laughter rang out. "Yo're bein' silly."

"Get my britches!" Eli roared.

Mrs. MacMillan appeared in the doorway.

"You needn't shout, Mr. Nielson. Here are your clothes, dried and patched, I might add."

At the calm, cultured voice coming from this tall, dignified woman in Indian dress, Eli's mouth

171

sagged open. Her black hair, streaked with fine threads of silver, was parted in the center and two long, fat braids hung down past her waist. That she was heavy with child oddly seemed to enhance her beauty. Her face was unlined, her eyes large and an usual shade of blue. She's proud and beautiful, he thought. Crowded in behind that thought was another. *Light's mother had been Osage.*

"I beg your pardon, ma'am. It's just that . . . well, I can't be lying here when . . . I should be helping. I do thank you for tending me."

"You are welcome. Your fever was short-lived." She turned to her daughter. "Bee, help Aee fill the water barrels should water be needed. Cee and Dee are penning the chickens. Mr. Lightbody is eating breakfast, Maggie. You should join him. We'll leave Mr. Nielson to dress." She made to follow the girls out, then turned back. "You shouldn't try to wear a boot on that foot. If you don't have moccasins, I'll find a pair."

"I'd be obliged, ma'am."

CHAPTER TWELVE

Ramon de la Vega steadied himself against the rail and held the spyglass to his eye. The canoe coming downriver was keeping close to the bank in an attempt to avoid the swift flood water and debris washing down from the north. The white man with the slick bald head was paddling furiously as he angled and tacked and sought out minor currents.

De la Vega removed the glass from his eye and sucked in his lower lip. It would take a full day of going against the current for him to reach MacMillan's. The canoe, however, was hours away from the homestead, considering it was coming downriver with the fast water. The man in it would, perhaps, have useful information.

Slender fingers stroked a dark pointed goatee and the silky hair that surrounded his thin red lips. He had not planned to stop at MacMillan's. James MacMillan was too crude for his taste; and if he discovered that furs were not the only cargo on the Vega boat, he would, no doubt, report the fact to Daniel Boone, who had considerable influence in the territory.

Vega had been careful, very careful, to do his raiding as far from Natchez as possible. His family had no idea that he was a white slaver, or that the bundles of furs he brought back were not purchased as he claimed.

On his first trip up the Missouri he had been looking for Caleb, a runaway slave. Then he had discovered how easy it was to relieve a lone trapper of his winter's work. Over the next two years he had perfected his technique of luring the trappers, hungry for human contact, to his boat. Although the pickings were easy, the Indian women had proven to be more profitable. Now he had hopes of picking up a couple of Osage and heading back home. He had two Delaware, a white woman, a Shawnee, and enough opium to keep them docile until he got them back to the Pleasure Place.

The white woman was a slut that one of his men had brought back after a foray into St. Louis. He allowed her on board not only to service the crew, but to wash his clothes and empty his slop jar. She had proved useful in other ways too. She washed up the youngest of the Indian girls for his use because he never went where other men had gone.

The younger Delaware girl he would keep, he mused, unless he found a younger more comely Osage girl. The others he would ship to Spain, including the white woman if she were still alive and not out of her mind by the time they reached Natchez. American Indian women were far more valuable. They had become a novelty in the brothels of Spain.

"Julio!" Vega shouted.

A short shaggy-haired man came from the cabin, tying the cord that held up his duck britches. A foolish smile split his swarthy face, revealing large white protruding teeth with wide gaps between them.

"Have you been banging that slut again?" Vega asked in amusement.

"*Si, señor*. It is a temptation I cannot resist."

Ramon de la Vega shrugged. Well-serviced men were contented men unless they quarreled over the woman. He had divided the men into two groups. Each group had a day from dawn to dawn with a day of rest in between for the woman. At first there had been some grumbling, but the men soon settled into the routine when they discovered they could use her as many times as they wished on their regular shift. No man dared to break into one of the virgin Indian girls. He knew the penalty. His private parts would be lopped off.

"On your way, Julio. A canoe is coming downriver with a white man in it. I want him. Alive."

As agile as a monkey, Julio leaped aft to the top of the cabin and shouted an order. Minutes later, with eight men at the oars, the keelboat moved out into the river. The canoe must pass between it and the shore or risk the rapid current.

Within an hour the canoe was tied to the keelboat and Kruger was hauled aboard to face a dark slim man dressed in a shirt of fine lawn with ruffled sleeves and a lace stock. The top of his dark head came to Kruger's shoulder. In his high boots of superbly worked leather, Vega stepped back a bit so that he could look up into Kruger's face.

"Who are you?"

"Otto Kruger."

"German, aren't you? I've not much use for Germans." Vega pulled a knife from his belt and slapped the blade against the palm of his hand again and again while he stared at Kruger. "Well. Open up, or I'll open *you* up."

Until now Kruger had thought Vega nothing more than a fop. Now he revised his opinion. The little dandy was like a coiled viper with bright snake-like eyes that followed Kruger's every move. He began to sweat.

"V'at you vant to know?"

"You're dumber than you look if you have to ask."

Kruger looked around him. The men were all dark and swarthy and armed with knives and cutlasses. They were river pirates; he had known that from the first. He also knew that he was at their mercy. His mind worked frantically for information to offer in exchange for his life.

A woman with blond hair hanging limply around a pockmarked face came to stand in the doorway of the cabin. The neck of her dress was cut so low that her breasts were in danger of spilling out. Her lips were smiling; her eyes were vacant.

"You want her?" Vega's eyes had followed Kruger's.

Kruger licked his thick lips. "*Ja*. I ain't had a voman for a vhile."

"My men share her. After our . . . visit, you can have her for as long and in as many ways as you want. Get the man a cup of ale, Julio. We have some talking to do before he relieves himself of that load he's carrying around."

Ramon de la Vega congratulated himself. Persuasion was better than force when you found a man's weakness. This big, dumb ox was drooling over the slut. In less than an hour he'd know everything the man knew and some of what he had thought he had forgotten.

Light was impressed with the way MacMillan organized. By noon the homestead appeared, from a distance, to be deserted. Heavy shutters barred the windows and doors of the cabin. The livestock had been moved back into the woods. The middle of the afternoon saw the boats hidden away upstream and Eli's cargo stored in one of the salt caves. MacMillan pointed out a large willow tree that, when felled, would block the stream to prevent Ramon de la Vega from getting close enough to damage the homestead with his cannon. He and Caleb would do the chopping should it become necessary.

Aee, her braids tucked up under her old hat,

built a small fire beneath an oak tree behind the house. The thin smoke would scatter in the branches overhead. She placed a bar of lead in a small iron pot with a pouring spout. When it melted, she would pour it into the bullet mold. Although they had a good supply, there was no way of knowing how long a siege would last.

Calmly and efficiently, Mrs. MacMillan packed food and bedding for herself and the younger children. Bee would go with her to the caves above the homestead and stay until the Osage women arrived, then return to the homestead and take up her rifle. Mrs. MacMillan assured her husband that the babe would not come for a day or two, and he could put his mind on protecting their home.

Light urged Maggie to go with Mrs. MacMillan, but she refused.

"I stay with you, Light."

"*Chérie*, it would ease my mind a great deal if you went with the lady —"

"Ya say we stay t'gether . . . always." Maggie's beautiful eyes never wavered.

"That is so. I said that. But, my pet, it is sure that Kruger has told the pirate there are women here. He has told about Caleb. Vega will attack to get his property back and to capture women for his brothel." He didn't put it into words, but he sensed that after hearing about Maggie, the pirate would be hell-bent to get her.

"I won't go. We stay t'gether, Light." Seldom did Maggie insist on having her way, but she did so now. Her face was set in stubborn lines; her hand clutched his arm. She did not beg; she merely stated what she intended to do.

"I want you safe, my treasure."

"Give me a gun. I will shoot it."

"You cannot fire a gun," Light said firmly. For the first time since leaving St. Charles, he was impatient with her.

"Why can't she?" Eli asked, moving away from the tree trunk where he had been leaning and listening. "MacMillan's girls shoot."

Light turned to the Swede with a look of such intense rage that a lesser man would have cringed and stepped back. Eli refused to lower his gaze.

"The rifle comes near to equaling half of her weight. There is a chance it would break her shoulder should she fire it, that is if she could lift it and hold it steady." Light's lips scarcely moved as he spoke. "I tell you this even though it is no business of yours."

"I'll give her a pistol."

"You will give her nothing, *m'sieur*. This is between me and my wife." Light's words were as cold as a frozen pond.

"That is a thing we need to discuss."

Light's arm swept Maggie behind him. His hand went to the knife in his belt. His body was rigidly alert. His crisp words fell into a deathly quiet.

"Not now. Not ever. We go our own way from here when this is over."

"We'll see about that."

Paul thought it time to interfere. He wedged

himself between Eli and Light.

"Eli, *mon ami,* come. The man is right. This is not your concern, eh? Mademoiselle Aee is pouring lead. She needs our help to make the bullets."

The Swede yanked his elbow from Paul's hand, and his eyes sent sparks of venom toward the scout. Slowly he followed Paul to the fire where Aee squatted beside the small blaze. When she looked up at him, her lips curled in sneering contempt. She rose, turned her back to him, and waved to her mother and sisters as they rode away in the ox cart led by Linus. *The fool was lusting after another man's woman.* How stupid she had been to have fancied him.

Aee continued to ladle the silver liquid into the bullet mold, her thoughts well concealed. She couldn't blame the Swede, she conceded. Any man would adore Maggie and want to protect her. She was as small and as perfect as a doll.

Aee had always been proud of her size and her strength, but beside Maggie she felt big and clumsy and . . . ugly.

"What needs to be done, *chérie?*" Paul asked.

With her foot she nudged a bucket half-filled with rough bullets.

"Do ya reckon he's got gumption enough t' smooth them bullets with his knife?" Her voice was loaded with sarcasm. "Ya don't have t' be very smart t' do it."

"You're a flitter-headed, loose-mouthed woman!" Eli snarled, flopping down on the

180

ground and digging into the bucket. He was as limp as a wet rag and glad to sit down, but he would never admit it to this smart-mouthed female.

"Yo're full a sass now that ya don't need tendin' to no more. I don't give a dram a powder or lead what ya think I am."

"It ain't much," he retorted, hoping to shut her up.

Aee saw him glance at Light and Maggie standing a distance away. Light was talking earnestly to Maggie. Then with an arm around her he led her into the woods.

"If ya had any sense ya'd stop makin' them cow-eyes at Miz Lightbody. Her man'll cut yore throat a'fore ya can say pee-doodle-dee-squat."

"I guess you think I'd just lay back and let him. I'll tell you one thing, Miss Smart-mouth MacMillan, I'll not be sitting on my hands if he jumps me."

"I heared tell he ain't got no quit a'tall once he's riled and don't hold with no rules 'bout what's fair in a fight neither if a man needs killin'." Aee felt a surge of glee when she saw Eli's face redden with anger. She gave him a sassy grin. "Reckon I'd back off if I was you."

"Well, you're not me, so *you* back off and mind your own dad-blasted business." Eli clenched his teeth and spoke through them in a flat monotone.

"Ain't ya got enough smarts to know she ain't wantin' ya? She ain't needin' ya t' butt in. It jist riles her man."

"Haven't you been taught any manners? Hasn't anyone ever told you a *lady* keeps her opinions to herself unless she's asked for them?" Eli murmured, after glancing up to see that Paul had moved out of earshot.

"Fiddle-faddle! I ain't knowin' nothin' 'bout *ladies* and ain't wantin' to. I'm thinkin' the closest ya ever got t' one was in a picture book."

"You need the flat of my hand on your behind."

"Try it an' yo're sartain t' get a hole right a'tween yore eyes." She threw a leather pouch that hit him in the chest. "Put the finished bullets in that — that's if ya finish any."

"Are ya mad at me 'cause I didn't go, Light?" Maggie asked the question as soon as they were alone.

"You promised to obey me."

"I did promise. But if somebody's tryin' to hurt ya I can't stand off an' wait t' see it. I got t' be with ya, Light. If ya die, I want t' die too."

Light leaned his rifle against a tree, grabbed her hand and pulled her to him.

"Do not forget this, *chérie*. There are worse things than dying one time. If you were captured and taken from me, I would die a thousand times."

"I won't get taken from ya. I don't want ya to be sad," she said quickly, moving her hands up and down his arms. "Don't be thinkin' we'll die. We won't for a long time after we get to our mountain."

"Ah . . . *mon trésor,* how can you be so sure?"

"I just know. We got to have our babies yet, Light," she said so earnestly that he had to smile.

"You will listen and obey me?"

"Yes, Light."

"You will not butt into my fight?"

"No, Light."

"You will stay where I can see you?"

"Yes, Light."

Above them a blue jay chattered angrily. A crow, daring in his hunger, landed on a nearby bush and added his croaking comments to those of the blue jay before flying away to a more productive bush.

Maggie was so intent on what Light was saying that she was oblivious to these sounds she loved. She stared into his dark eyes.

"Why didn't ya let Eli give me a pistol?"

"If you have a pistol, it will be one that I provide for you." His hands closed on her shoulders. "I don't want you to take anything from him."

"Why? He likes you. He likes me."

"He does *not* like me, Maggie. He'd like nothing better than for me to be out of the way so he could have you."

"No, Light." Maggie shook her head. "He's not like other men."

"I suppose you just *know* that too."

"Yes, Light."

Light shrugged off his backpack, placed it on the ground and opened it. He took out two knives.

183

He stuck one of them in a pocket on the side of his knee-high moccasins. The other he showed to Maggie.

"You need an extra weapon. Carry this knife in the back of your belt." He turned her around and fitted it so that it lay with the tip resting on her hip. "See if you can get it out quickly and easily."

After several attempts she was able to draw the knife in one swift motion.

MacMillan came through the trees, followed by Paul carrying two extra rifles.

"It's my thought that Vega'll let part of his crew off downriver t' come through the woods."

"It'd be a foolish move," Light said.

"How so?"

"A couple of bowman could pick them off one by one."

MacMillan scratched his head, then laughed. "Many Spots will be back in a few hours."

"Any news of Kruger?"

"Vega took him aboard. He'll wring ever'thin' the German knows 'bout this place out a him."

"Did Zee tell ya?" Maggie asked. "Aee said not t' worry. Someone called Zee'd watch."

"Yes, ma'am. I got his signal 'bout a hour ago."

"Is Zee one of yore younguns, Mr. Mac?" Maggie asked in her wide-eyed, unabashed fashion.

"No, ma'am. I named him that 'cause I didn't think I'd live to get enough younguns to get through the alphabet. Zee forgot what his name was long ago an' it ain't no wonder a'tall. He don't take to folks right away. He'll show hisself when he's ready."

"What's the . . . alphabet?"

"Wal . . . now." MacMillan took off his hat and scratched his wooly head again while he tried to figure out a way to explain the alphabet. He looked first to Light for help. Light said nothing and his dark eyes were alight with amusement. Paul lifted his hands palms up in a futile gesture. Finally MacMillan said, "It's the letters ya read by. A, b, c, d, e, an' f an' lots more."

Maggie clapped her hands. "I heard of them. Ya named yore younguns for readin' letters. They ought t' be right proud."

"Yes'm. Miz Mac was learnin' them t' me when Aee was born. We thought it fittin'."

"I never learned readin'. But Light has. He can read ever'thin'." Maggie gazed up at her husband with fierce pride.

"That's mighty . . . fine." MacMillan couldn't think of anything else to say.

Light took a dozen arrow shafts from his pack, along with an equal number of metal tips and a ball of strong cord.

"*Chérie,* put the tips on the split end of the shaft in the way I showed you. We will need many more arrows than we have." He left Maggie sitting on a log and walked a distance away. Paul and MacMillan followed. "*M'sieurs,* I do not like to sit like a waiting duck."

"I ain't likin' it none either," MacMillan said. "But there ain't much ya can do till ya know

185

what he's goin' t' do. Might be he don't do nothin'."

"That's not likely, *m'sieur*. Kruger will have told him about your womenfolk and Mrs. Lightbody. If he's what you say —" Paul left his words hanging.

"— And Caleb. Pride will goad him t' kill 'im. Them Vegas ain't wantin' t' be outdone by no slave. Caleb's had him a taste a bein' a free man earnin' pay. He'll fight till he drops 'fore he goes back to Vega."

"Will the Negroes run off when fightin' starts, *m'sieur?*" Paul asked.

"Stake my life on Caleb an' Linus standin' with us. Many Spots will bring back warriors. They be the best woods fighters I know, but they ain't worth much with firearms. They like to shoot 'em, but don't come in a mile a hittin' what they shoot at. All they do is make a racket."

"Many Spots is an old man," Light said, thinking back to MacMillan's saying he had no horses. "Much too old to run many miles."

MacMillan remembered and grinned sheepishly. "Figgered ya'd catch me on that. Truth is, I got a couple a ponies hid up in the hills where the Delaware can't find 'em. Few more up with the Osage —"

He stopped speaking, cocked his head and listened. The repeated whistle of the redbird was followed by the call of a squalling hawk. A minute later they heard the call of the hawk and then the redbird.

"That's Zee. Got to go." MacMillan trotted to the edge of the dense woods and disappeared.

Light was uneasy with the situation. It was not his way to wait to be attacked, nor had it been Jefferson Merrick's, or Will Murdock's. In his opinion it would be better to attack while all were on the boat. A barrage of flame arrows would set the craft afire and the gunpowder would do the rest.

"*M'sieur*, I would speak to you of my friend, Eli." Paul edged close to Light and lowered his voice after glancing at Maggie.

"Cannot your friend speak for himself?"

"My friend, Eli, has a devil on his back, *m'sieur*," Paul said, ignoring the question. "He is much, much troubled. I ask for your understanding."

"I will kill him if he continues to come between me and my wife." Light's voice was clipped and hard. In his anger, his French accent was more pronounced.

"He is an honorable man." Paul's voice wavered. "He realizes that he owes you for saving his life. The burden is heavy."

"He owes me nothing," Light spat out angrily. "Had it been a dog caught in the sawyer I would have done the same."

"He would not dishonor your wife."

On hearing the words, Light spun around. His head was thrown back, and his lips were parted in a snarl like that of a cornered animal.

"He even thinks it . . . I will kill him!" His

187

voice was laced with icy rage.

Paul lifted both hands, palms out. "*M'sieur* Light, please — In time all will be . . . clear."

"Light?" Maggie was beside him, holding his arm. "Are ya and Paul fussin', Light?"

Light put his hand behind her head. His face softened when he looked down into her anxious green eyes. She had such keen perception where he was concerned. It was as if she could read his every thought.

"No, *ma chérie*. Men can have differences without being angry."

"Ya was angry, Light," she insisted. "Ya was frownin' and yore brows came down like this." Maggie beetled her eyebrows.

Light smiled. Paul laughed.

"Don't ya laugh at me." Maggie turned an angry face to the Frenchman. "I don't want ya and Light t' be mad at each other."

"*Madame.*" Paul's voice was hushed, almost reverent. "I laughed only because you make such a charming face. Please forgive if I offend."

"It's all right." Her frown instantly changed to smiles. She hugged Light's arm and asked, "Where'd Mr. Mac go?"

"I'm not sure, *chérie*." Light heard a sound and lifted his head to see MacMillan coming out of the woods.

"I ain't sure what it means," MacMillan said as he came toward them, "but the bastard tied up off a island a mile back. Aee calls it Berry Island cause it's got berries all over. It's closer to the other side than to this'n."

Light glanced at the darkening sky. "He may have already unloaded some of his men."

"They might a'ready got 'round Zee if they come in far enough from the river."

"I will go see. How many game trails are there coming upriver?" Light asked.

"Two main ones. One near the river. The other'n a quarter of a mile or so north."

Light took Maggie's hand. "Stay with Paul, *chérie.*"

"Light . . ."

"You promised, *mon amour.*"

"Yes, Light. I stay with Paul." Her worried eyes roamed over his face.

Light cupped her cheeks with his hands and placed a soft kiss on her lips before he turned away to slide his tomahawk in his belt and loop the bow and quiver of arrows over his shoulder. Leaving his rifle with Paul, he trotted into the woods.

CHAPTER THIRTEEN

Running cautiously, Light made his way through the tall gloomy forest. His ears were alert for the faintest sound, his eyes searching for the slightest movement. The solitude of the forest closed around him and he felt its familiar soothing influence. He paused often, stepping off the path to turn his head slowly, listening first in one direction and then in another, striving to catch and identify any alien sound.

As the gloom deepened and nighttime approached, he concentrated solely on his mission, dismissing all else from his mind, especially the distracting thoughts of Eli Nielson's interest in his wife and Maggie's interest in him.

Before long Light could hear the sound of distant voices and knew that he was now opposite the island where the keelboat had been tied up for the night. Inching slowly toward the river, careful to make no sudden moves that might frighten the waterfowl, Light found a safe spot behind a rock and crouched there, hidden from the river pirate should he be scanning the shore with a spyglass.

Across the fast water that rushed to reach the Mississippi and on to the sea, a campfire burned brightly on the island. It glowed against the darkening sky and gleamed ever so faintly on the water. Several men moved around the fire.

Light scanned the whole area for several minutes. The campfire was large enough to be seen up and down the river and across. From the camp came a man's laughter and the muffled screech of a woman. The men from the keelboat were clearly enjoying the evening. There could be only one reason for the huge campfire and the sounds of raucous merriment — to draw MacMillan's attention and convince him that the keelboat crew had settled for the night.

Light moved back into the forest, slowly at first, then rapidly when he reached an animal path leading away from the water. The rivermen, not wanting to risk getting lost among the dense growth, would follow a path, Light reasoned. When Vega let his raiding crew of cutthroats off downriver, they probably would have gone inland and stumbled onto the north trail MacMillan spoke about.

A half-mile back from the river Light found what he was searching for. Bending low so he could see in the dim light, he discovered the print of a heavy boot.

The forest now was cloaked in semi-darkness. Head up, Light moved like a shadow among the trees. Knowing the rivermen were ahead, between him and the homestead, he stopped often to listen.

He was reasonably sure they would not attack until the dead of night; they would hide themselves and wait.

Light lifted his nose, sniffed the air, and caught a faint whiff of wood smoke. After a few more steps, he heard the low murmur of voices. He moved slowly from tree to tree until he came to a dense thicket. Dropping to his hands and knees, he parted the bushes ever so gently and silently crept forward behind the cover of brush.

Four men squatted beneath the branches of a large tree. A small fire burned brightly, the smoke scattering in the branches overhead. In front of the men was something that resembled a small animal. It squatted, too, so low its rump touched the ground. Long buckskin-clad arms were wrapped around its head as it tried to protect itself. One of the men prodded the small creature with a stick and it jumped sideways. Light saw that it was tethered to a tree by a leather thong tied about one of its legs. Another man tormented it with the tip of a long stiletto, making it jump this way and that.

"Vat ve do vith it?" The voice was Kruger's.

"Keep it. Folks'd pay to see it."

"Keel it." The man who spoke had a heavy mustache and a Spanish accent.

"It's mine. I ain't killin' it yet."

"I hooked it out of the tree with a fish line. I got some say."

"Ya hooked it but I catched it when it'd run off."

192

The two men continued to bicker until the Spaniard became impatient.

"Hush your caterwaulin'. Señor de la Vega didn't send us here to catch little beasties."

"How'er ya goin' t' get it t' the boat, ya dumb ass?" The man who spoke wore a knit cap.

"Are ya goin' to carry it when we go to get the gal?" the man who hooked it out of the tree asked.

"I'll truss it up an' come back fer it."

"Cain't it talk?"

"Don't guess so. Ain't made no sound."

"Vega'll split yore gullet if ya keep us from gettin' that gal."

"I ain't goin' to keep ya from doin' what the dandy wants, Rico. I wager he'll want this thin'." He prodded the creature with the stick again. "He'll be wantin' to show it off down at Natchez." The man's laugh was as dry as a corn shuck. "He jist might dress it all up like a little dandy, put a jewel collar on it, an' lead it 'round."

"Sh . . . eet!" Rico spat. "He'll keel it. We be havin' our hands full a totin' the woman without a messin' with this here thin'."

"If she be anythin' like the German said, I'll tote her clear back to Natchez."

"Ya vait. Ya see. She be like a picture. I tote 'er," Kruger said firmly. "Brings up yore pecker just lookin' at 'er."

"Reckon that don't take much. Brought yores up lookin' at the slut." The man in the cap pointed a finger at Kruger's crotch and the men snickered.

"Ya was randy as a billy goat," Rico said to Kruger. "Ya used her four times one after the other. Ya rocked the boat so hard we thought we'd hit a swell."

"An' the hole he put it in was big as a water bucket." Rico made a circle of his arms.

The men laughed. Kruger snarled, but kept quiet.

After a brief silence, Rico again urged the man with the stiletto to kill the cowering creature.

"I ain't killin' it."

"If ya vant to keep it from runnin'," Kruger said, "ya better cut the cords in its feet."

All eyes turned to the big German.

"What ya talkin' 'bout?"

"The cords in back vat holds its feet up." Kruger ran his finger behind his ankle. "Cut 'em. It cain't run — feet jist flops."

"That's a idey."

"Looky! It knows what ya said. It's shakin' like a dog pissin' peach seeds."

Light had heard enough. An intense hatred for the rivermen welled up in him. Men like these had raped and killed his young wife, his child, his mother.

The small deformed creature must be no other than MacMillan's friend, Zee. If Light waited, they would cripple the little man even more.

Light analyzed the situation. He had two knives, the bow and the tomahawk. To succeed against four men, his attack must be swift and deadly. The man with the stiletto was the one to take out first. Rivermen were slow, clumsy fighters, more at home in a barroom brawl than in the forest. If Light struck fast, before they realized he was alone, he could get three. The other one would break and run, or stand and fight. Light was confident he could hold his own with any man on a one-to-one basis.

Having made the decision, Light pulled the knife from his boot and slipped it into his belt, adjusted the scabbard that lay on his thigh so that he could reach it easily, fitted an arrow into the bow, stood, and moved out of the brush. The men were too busy talking to hear the scratching sound made by the stiff brush rubbing against his buckskins.

The arrow zinged and went through the neck of the man with the stiletto. He made a gurgling sound and fell back. The others, stupefied by the sudden happening, paused, giving Light time to sink his knife into the chest of the Spaniard. Two men turned to run. One fell like a pole-axed steer when Light's flying tomahawk split his skull. The fourth man kept going. Light could hear him crashing through the brush like a wounded buffalo.

The entire encounter had taken less than a minute. Knife in hand, Light sprang forward to retrieve his tomahawk. He pulled his other knife from the chest of the Spaniard, who thrashed on the ground. With a quick flick of his wrist, and without the slightest hesitation, he brought the bloody blade across the man's throat.

After a glance at the man he had killed with the arrow, he turned his attention to the creature cowering with its arms over its head. Light sliced through the thong that tethered it to the tree.

"Come. We must leave here."

An unblinking eye peered up at him.

"Sharp Knife."

The words were guttural, as if they came from deep inside the man. The face that turned toward Light was covered with a dense brown beard. The hair on his head was thick and long. Only the nose, the eyes, and the forehead were visible. The large head, without a neck, seemed to sit on shoulders too broad to belong with the rest of the small body.

"Can you walk?" Light asked.

"Not far."

Light squatted down and looped his bow and the quiver of arrows over Zee's shoulder.

"Climb on my back. We must go."

Thin bowed legs wrapped around Light's slender body, and heavy muscular hands clamped his shoulders. When he stood, Light discovered that the man weighed less than Maggie did. As he clasped the dwarf's legs, his hand encountered wetness, and Zee grunted in pain.

"You hurt bad?" Light asked.

"Not bad."

As they traveled swiftly up the animal path toward MacMillan's, Light's mind replayed the scene. Kruger was the one who had got away. Would he return to the keelboat in defeat? If

Vega were the kind of man MacMillan said he was, he would not welcome the messenger who brought bad news.

It was possible that when Kruger had described Maggie to Vega, he had also told him about her spending the nights with her husband on bedrolls separated from the others. Probably the men Light had attacked had been sent to jump him and steal Maggie. Vega would not have been so foolish as to send just four men to attack a fortified homestead. Light reasoned that the pirate boat had come close enough to this side of the river for the men to wade ashore and was to meet them well below the homestead after they had completed their mission.

Occasionally, Light heard a small grunt of pain from the small man who rode his back. As they approached MacMillan's place, Many Spots appeared on the path ahead. He looked at Light and Zee and, after giving the call of the nightbird, turned and led the way to the homestead.

Eli hated his weakness and was careful to rise slowly to his feet and not to bend over lest he become dizzy. It was a serious blow to his pride to have Aee MacMillan doing work that he was unable to attempt because he was weak from the fever. Now he sat on a bench behind the cabin cleaning the guns Kruger had thought to render useless by dropping them over the side into the river before taking off in the canoe. When Many Spots had reported seeing the action, MacMillan had had the guns brought up out of the muddy water.

Eli watched Aee work alongside her father, Caleb and Paul to do what they could to protect their home. She filled the water barrels Caleb had brought from the barn in case the cabin should be fired and she cut and pulled all brush and flowers back from the cabin walls. Eli found himself gazing at her rounded bottom in the duck britches as she bent to pick up anything that would carry fire to the cabin.

Since their bickering exchange earlier, Aee had ignored him. When her father told her to pass out bread and meat for a midday meal, she gave Eli's portion to Paul to take to him. Somehow this irritated Eli. He might have been harsh with her, but she hadn't been a bit shy about giving it back. She had no business sticking her nose into his affairs.

Aee was capable; there was no doubting that. No task seemed to be too hard for her to tackle. She kept her Kentucky rifle close by, taking it with her as she moved from task to task.

"How fast can you reload?" Eli asked as she passed him, carrying the long Kentucky rifle, its length of four inches over five feet equaling her height.

"Fast as ya can, I wager."

"Twelve seconds?"

"Ten."

He gave a derisive snort that he knew would rile her. It did.

"I suppose a smart-mouth, know-it-all like ya can do it in eight."

"Around there. How do you know you can do it in ten? You carry a clock?"

"I count 'donkey carts' an' can come within a half a second of the best time clock ya ever saw."

"Donkey carts?" He snorted again.

"It's what I said. Are yore ears stopped up?"

"I heard you," Eli said irritably. "I don't see what 'donkey carts' has got to do with how fast you can load that rifle."

"Donkey carts, donkey carts, donkey carts. Three seconds, ya dumb Swede."

Eli's laugh was low and rumbling. "We'll count your way and have us a little wager when this is over. I can beat you whether you count donkey carts or donkey wagons."

"When this is over, I'm hopin' ya take yore high-'n'-mighty self back downriver to a town where ya'll find plenty a married women t' put yore cow-eyes on. Ya ain't got the gumption t' find yore own woman."

Aee walked calmly away, leaving Eli sputtering. As soon as she was out of sight around the cabin, she stopped, stomped her foot and uttered a swear word she had heard her pa use on occasion. The dang-blasted polecat made her *so* mad! He had turned down the invite to eat at their table, but when he needed doctoring, he had come fast enough.

She wished now that when he was drinking

the willow bark tea, she had given him a few cups of "hockey tea." Aee and her sisters called the brew her mother made from Culver roots "hockey tea" because of what it made a body do. After drinking a cup, they stayed close to the woods lest they mess their drawers before they got there.

Glory be! Why hadn't she thought of that?

Laughter burst from her lips before she could clamp her hand over her mouth. She leaned her forehead against the side of the cabin and pictured in her mind the big-mouthed, cock-a-hoop Swede running to the woods as if chased by a swarm of yellow jackets. Her shoulders shook with muffled laughter.

When she was reasonably sure her giggles were under control, she straightened. Her face was flushed, her eyes wet with tears of laughter. Sweat plastered loose hair to her cheeks. She took off her hat to run the sleeve of her shirt over her wet face. Still giggling, she flipped her braids over her shoulders and dropped her hat. When she stooped to pick it up, she saw Eli standing at the corner of the cabin, his shoulder against the wall.

Seeing the frown on his face and with the thought of the "hockey tea" still fresh in her mind, she could not control the giggles that bubbled up and out of her. She couldn't have stopped them if her life had depended on it.

"Somebody tickle your funnybone?"

"Co . . . ck-a-ho . . . op —" The words were

200

strangled by her laughter. "Oh . . . oh . . . I wish I'd . . . a thought of it —"

"Thought of what?"

"Ah . . . hockey tea!" she blurted, then, amid peals of girlish laughter, she grabbed her rifle and ran toward the barn.

Eli watched her until she disappeared inside.

"What's she talking about?" he muttered. "What the hell is hockey tea?"

It was that golden time of evening. Eli watched Paul and Maggie, followed by MacMillan, emerge from the woods and approach the cabin. Maggie walked with her head down, clearly unhappy about something. She passed him without a glance and went into the small room attached to the cabin where Light had left their packs. MacMillan veered off toward the barn.

"What's happened?" Eli asked when Paul sank wearily down on the bench.

"Vega's tied up to that brushy island downriver. Mac and Light think it likely that he put his raiding party ashore a mile or so back and they'll come up through the woods. Light's gone scoutin'."

"What's Maggie down in the mouth about?"

"She wanted to go with Light. He told her to stay."

"I'm surprised he didn't take her." Eli's voice was heavy with sarcasm.

"*Mon Dieu*, Eli. I do not like what's going on a 'tween you and Lightbody."

"I don't either."

"What you mean?"

"I mean, goddammit, Maggie deserves more than to be dragged through the wilderness by a half-breed heading for some godforsaken mountain he's never seen."

"The devil!" Paul hissed. "Have you forgot who he is? Have you forgot she is *his* wife?"

"She's *not* his wife." Eli gave a derisive snort. "They didn't stand before a preacher or a magistrate."

"How you know this?"

"She told me they wed each other on a bluff above the river. What kind of a poppycock marriage is that?"

"It appears to be good enough for them. *Mon ami,* stay away. She love him."

"Horse piss. She depends on him."

"She is with him 'cause she want to be with him. You must accept it."

"She has not had a chance to choose."

"Ho! She could have any man she want. She want him." Paul raked his fingers through his tight dark curls. "I wish that we had not come looking for Lightbody. I wish we were back makin' good coin on the Ohio."

"I could not go through life not knowing."

"And now?"

Eli shrugged. "He's a man, a breed."

"But a civilized breed, *mon ami.* He saved your life."

"He was showing off for Maggie."

Paul drew in a deep breath. "How you say that? When he give you life."

"I thanked him. What do you want me to do? Kiss his feet?"

"Leave his woman be."

"You think I want her because he's got her, don't you?"

"Yes, I think that. You want to take something from him."

"And if I do?"

"You cause only trouble for yourself and him."

"What about Maggie? She should be in a comfortable house, with nice things."

"She's got what she wants, *mon ami*." Paul spoke tiredly. "Leave her be." He got up and looked down at his friend. "I have known you since we was striplings. I was never disappointed in you till now."

Eli sat alone watching the fireflies and thought of the years he and Paul had been together. When they were boys working on the river docks for food and a place to sleep, Paul had been the one to keep them out of trouble. Although he was scarcely five years older, Paul seemed, and was, more mature. As Eli looked back, he could not remember a time when he and his friend had been so at odds with each other.

The bastard had come between them.

CHAPTER FOURTEEN

Many Spots returned from the Osage camp with eight braves; all were mounted on spotted ponies. They eyed Eli and Paul with stoic expressions, then ignored them and listened carefully to Mac-Millan as he moved among them. One of the ponies carried double. A small figure slipped down. Eli heard Bee telling her father that her mother had walked most of the way to the cave rather than ride in the cart.

"No sign of the babe comin'?"

"She says not. Yellow Corn come down with Many Spots to say her piece when the babe gets here."

The warriors were all young and extremely muscular. Each carried, besides his bow and quiver of arrows, a war club rendered more lethal by a metal blade protruding several inches from the end. Their leggings were decorated down the sides with beads and fringe. Small, colorful feathers adorned their hair, and metal amulets hung around their necks.

The ponies were picketed and a brave sank down on his haunches to guard them. The rest of the braves and Many Spots melted into the darkness. MacMillan came back to where Eli and Paul waited.

Suddenly remembering that Maggie had not come out of the room, he went to the door.

"Maggie?"

In the dim light he could see her standing beside the low bench where Light had placed their packs. She was looking toward the door, yet she didn't answer him.

"Do you need to get something from your pack? I'll get a candle."

"Go 'way, Eli. I want t' be here with Light."

Eli was startled not only by her words, but by the dreamy way she said them. Had something happened to frighten her out of her mind?

"Maggie," he said gently. "Light isn't here."

"Don't say that. He is too here." She moved her fingers back and forth, lovingly caressing the pack Light had carried since they left St. Louis.

"Paul said Light went downriver."

"Go 'way, Eli. I want to be here with Light," she said again.

Confused, Eli moved away from the door.

Maggie hardly noticed that he was gone. Dropping to her knees, she wrapped her arms around the pack and pressed her cheek to the deerskin wrapping. She closed her eyes tightly and saw Light's thin serious face. She felt his gentle hands stroking her hair.

Come back, Light. Come back, come back.

205

I will never leave you, mon amour.
Ya left me here. I love ya, Light.
You're my treasure, chérie.
I'm yores, Light. Come back —

"The Osage will take the north and east. Caleb, Linus, Aee and Bee will watch down by the river in case Vega tries to slip in by canoe. There's not much chance they'll come from the west because of the bluff and the creek."

"It was my understanding, *m'sieur,* that Indians would not fight at night."

"Believe about half a what ya hear 'bout Indians, Mr. Deschanel," MacMillan said and chuckled. "Osage be the best night fighters I ever did see. They ain't nothin' gettin' past 'em out there. I'd stake my life on 'em — and have more'n once. They see in the dark like owls. Ain't no cowards 'mong 'em, either. Tol' ya I'd not a got a foothold here if not for 'em. If they like ya, they like ya. If they don't, they be meaner than a pissed-on polecat."

"Will Light be back afore morn, *m'sieur?*"

"Depends on what he finds. Where's Miz Lightbody?"

"In there," Eli jerked his head toward the open door of the room.

"She took it hard when her man went. Had misery all o'er her pretty little face."

"*M'sieur,* what is it you wish that I do now?" Paul asked, wanting to change the subject.

"Sit tight. If a leaf stirs we'll get a signal. Don't

reckon ya ort t' be roamin' 'round. Ya might get took for a Vega man an' get shot . . . or axed."

"You seem to think Lightbody knows enough not to get shot or . . . axed," Eli said irritably.

" 'Pears to me he's knowin' what he's doin'. He ain't no slouch at trackin' or fightin' either. I knew it right off when I heared his name. Ain't a Indian or a white man between here an' the mountains ain't heared 'bout Sharp Knife."

"— And we're a couple a pilgrims who need to be looked after. Is that the way you see it?" Eli's tone was hardly civil.

"That's it. Ya may be good on the river, but ya don't know beans 'bout Indians or ya'd not come up the river with a two-man crew," Mac-Millan answered in a tone equally cool.

"We made it, didn't we?"

MacMillan snorted. "Ya was lucky t' get by them Delaware. They can slip up on ya silent as a snake. Ya can't guess what they'll do no more than ya can guess when ya'll get yore next fit of the ague."

"*M'sieur,*" Paul inserted quickly, "the guns are cleaned and loaded should they be needed."

"I thank ya for it. I'll not be lettin' the Osage have 'em till —" MacMillan stopped speaking when the sound of a nightbird reached them. He stood. "Many Spots is comin' in."

It was a dark night. The quarter moon was barely visible through the drifting clouds. The three men sent searching looks out to the edge of the woods. Silence hung like a cloak over the homestead until MacMillan cupped his mouth with his hands and imitated the soft call of a very young hoot owl. The answer came from close by, and two shadows emerged from the woods and trotted toward the cabin.

"Light!" Maggie ran out the door and past the men waiting beside the house. "Light . . . Light —"

"*Oui, chérie,*" Light called.

"Ya come back!"

"Of course, *chérie.*"

"What ya got there?" MacMillan asked, then, "Jehoshaphat! It's Zee!"

"Careful, *m'sieur.* His leg is hurt where they hooked him out of a tree with a casting line."

"Sonsabitches!"

MacMillan removed the bow and quiver from Zee's shoulder and carefully lifted the little man from Light's back.

"Sonsabitches," he swore again when a muffled groan came from Zee. "Many Spots, get Aee. She's somewhere along the river."

As soon as Light was relieved of his burden, Maggie wrapped her arms around him.

"Yo're a'right, ain't ya, Light?"

"I'm all right, *ma petite.* The blood is from the small man." Over her head he spoke to Mac-Millan. "Four men came ashore. One of them got away. It was Kruger. He headed east."

"There was four and ya killed three of 'em?" MacMillan questioned.

"Come morning you'll find them on the north path. Zee can give you the exact location." Light walked away with Maggie still clinging to him. "I must wash, *chérie*." After he had washed the blood off his hands in the hollow log trough beside the well, he put his arms around his wife and held her tightly to him.

"I stayed by our thin's, Light, just like you tol' me. I don't want ya to go away again." She raised her lips for his kiss. "My . . . my heart was gone."

"*Mon amour, mon trésor*. My mind was at ease knowing you were safe." He dotted her face with kisses. "There will be other times when we must part for a while. I will always come back to you."

She looked toward the sickroom, where candles were being lit.

"What did ya do, Light? Did ya kill somebody? Was they hurtin' Zee?"

"Yes, my pet. I found him being tormented by four rivermen. One of them was Kruger."

"Ah! That man is not good. I think he is mad, Light. Someday ya'll kill him."

"*Oui*. He is a bad man. It will be good to be rid of him."

"It was mean what they did to Zee. I'm proud, Light. Proud ya saved him."

"I'd have killed Kruger if I could have pulled out my other knife in time."

She took Light's hand, brought it to her lips and kissed it.

"I love ya, Light."

"I love you, my treasure."

"I should go see if I can help with Zee."

"*Oui, chérie*. Go give words of comfort to the little man."

Zee lay on the bunk where Eli had lain the night before. The leg of his britches had been split to expose the gaping wound in his thigh where the hook had opened the flesh to the bone.

MacMillan tried to block Maggie's way into the room, but she slipped past him, went directly to the bunk and looked sorrowfully down on the grotesque face of the little man.

"Tch-tch-tch." Maggie shook her head and clicked her tongue as her friend Biedy used to do back home. "It was mean what they did t' ya, Zee," she said, and smoothed the bushy thick hair back from the grossly distorted face. "I'm glad Light killed 'em."

The unblinking eye looked at her with alarm; the lid of the other eye drooped, almost covering it. The nose was merely two nostrils in a face covered by thick brown beard. The man's head, large in comparison to his small body, looked as if it had been placed in a vise and squeezed. One eye, one nostril and one side of his mouth were higher than the other.

Maggie seemed to take no notice of the deformity. She continued to stroke the lopsided forehead and speak soft smoothing words.

"Aee'll come an' fix yore leg. Me an' Light's got *gonoshay* we picked for Eli's foot. There be plenty left. We'll put it on if Aee ain't got nothin' better. The *gonoshay* healed Eli's foot jist fine."

MacMillan, Paul and Eli gaped at her in amazement. Light was amused by their expressions. He was exceedingly proud of his young and beautiful wife and was not at all surprised by her reaction to the deformed little man.

"Get rags outta our pack, Light. He's bleedin' somethin' awful."

"Aee'll have t' stitch up the hole, ma'am," MacMillan said. "Many Spots has gone t' fetch her. Guess she's comin'. I can hear her mouth goin'."

Aee's voice, speaking in Osage, preceded her. She came in hatless and wearing an old black wool coat. She went right to the bunk.

"Oh, Zee! Name of a cow! What happened to ya?" Aee looked down at the wound, ignoring Maggie.

"I . . . be a bit careless, lass." The voice was deep, a man's voice.

Aee quickly took off her coat and dropped it on the end of the bunk.

"Them pissants! Many Spots said Mr. Lightbody killed 'em. Good. I hope they hurt like hell 'fore they died."

"He didn't kill Kruger," Maggie said. "But he will."

"Zee, it's a big hole. I'll have to sew it." Aee looked closely at the wound and dabbed at the blood that still oozed. "Shoot! I wish Ma was here."

"Don't fret, lassie. Ye'll be doin' fine," Zee assured her.

"Pa, we'll need vinegar t' wash it. And get Zee some milk. Ya know how he likes it. I'll go get Ma's basket of doctorin' thin's."

Eli picked up a candle. "I'll help you."

Aee's head turned so quickly that her braids whipped around.

"Ya reckon yo're up t' doin' it, town-man? Ma's basket's loaded with herbs an' cloth an' thread an' such. It'd be a mite hefty fer ya t' carry."

Eli's jaws clenched. "Hush your back-talk and get on with it," he growled, following Aee out the door.

Paul looked quickly to see if Aee's father had taken exception to what Eli had said. He was surprised to see that MacMillan was grinning.

"Strike sparks off each other like flint hittin' rock. Ain't it the dad-gummest thin' ya ever saw? Aee ain't never give a feller the time a day before. 'Course the ones that come by warn't much. Says she cain't abide the Swede. Wants me t' give him the boot. Not Mr. and Mrs. Lightbody," he hastily added. "Just the Swede. 'Course, she knows ya'd go, too," he said to Paul. "Thick as the two of ya are."

Paul's shoulders squared. "For a certainty, *m'sieur*. My friend and I will not stay if the welcome is gone. We'll be goin' when this is past, you can be sure of it."

"Don't get yore back up, Frenchman. The

womenfolk don't rule the roost here. 'Course I live with 'em an' listen t' their wants. Ya an' yore friend be welcome here fer as long as ya want t' stay."

"We owe you for Eli's doctoring. He will pay in coin or goods."

"Aye. T' have ya standin' by till Vega leaves — that be all the pay I be needin'."

"That we'd do regardless of the welcome, *m'sieur*."

When Aee and Eli returned, he carried the basket and Aee held a lamp. Eli set the basket on the end of the bunk. He turned the cloth back from Zee's thigh to look at the wound.

"I've mended a few sailors in my time. Do you want me to do it?" he said to Aee.

"No. Yo're apt t' get thin's bassackwards an' sew up his mouth."

This brought laugher from MacMillan and a snicker from the little man on the table, who grimaced afterward.

"Then you do it, sour-mouth," Eli growled, and stalked out.

Aee ignored his parting shot, slipped a doeskin under Zee's thigh and prepared to wash the wound with the vinegar.

"This'll hurt like yo're bein' poked with a hot pitchfork, Zee. I'm hatin' t' do it, but I got to. Ma says it'll get pus in it if we don't. She learned that someplace. If we don't have vinegar we can use whiskey, but vinegar's best."

Aee kept up a constant line of chatter while

213

she sewed and bandaged Zee's leg. When she finished, she covered him with a blanket and then brought him biscuits filled with berry jam and insisted that he eat.

"Tomorrow I'll get a reed from the river an' fix it so ya can suck up the water. My ma did that once when I was sick." Maggie lifted his head and held the cup while he drank water. Losing so much blood had made him thirsty.

Although the pain was agonizing, Zee had not let out even a groan while Aee stitched his leg, smoothed the jimson-leaf salve over it and wrapped it in clean cloth. With Singing Bird there fussing over him, he would have died before he showed a sign of weakness.

Aee made a strong toddy of whiskey and honey and again Maggie held the cup so he could drink.

"Go ta sleep, Zee. Ya'll feel better in the mornin'."

It was the most wonderful night in Zee's life. Two young women were treating him as if he were a normal man. They had touched him, spoken to him, tended him, without even a hint that he was so grossly ugly that even he avoided looking at his reflection in a clear pond. Their attention was far more than he had ever expected. His crooked mouth smiled beneath the heavy beard. Before he went to sleep he silently thanked the rivermen for hooking him out on the tree.

Light squatted on his heels and explained to the three men what he had overheard being said

214

by Vega's men and Kruger. He was careful to keep his voice low when he spoke of their plans to capture Maggie.

Eli swore.

"They have women aboard. They talked of Kruger using one."

Light told in as few words as possible about Zee and what the boatmen had planned for him. He did not, however, go into the details of how he had killed the three men. MacMillan didn't question, knowing he would get the full story from Zee.

" 'Pears we won't be attacked this night, but the warriors an' Caleb an' Linus will keep watch. They'd be disappointed t' be called off so soon," MacMillan said. After a short silence he said, "I guess yo're curious 'bout Zee now ya got a look at him."

"It is so, *m'sieur*," Paul agreed. "You do not see such a one every day."

"He's a sight if yo're not used t' seein' 'im. Years back he was with the Delaware. He's not sure how he got there or fer how long. He don't recall much 'fore that. I'm stumped why they didn't kill 'im, mean as they be. But it 'pears they was scared he'd come back an' bring a plague or somethin'. When a Osage raidin' party took him from an old woman who took care of 'im, they never tried to get him back. They mighta been glad t' be rid a him, thinkin' he was bad medicine. Not the Osage. They think he's magic. He gets credit when game is plentiful, crops is good, and their women fertile."

"If he's good medicine, why'd they give him up?" Eli, still in a sour mood, asked.

"They ain't give him up. Few years back, Many Spots brought him down. He'd almost forgot how t' talk English. Said he talked it to hisself some. After talkin' it a while with us, some come back to 'im. He ain't no dummy, I can swear to that. Somehow he kept hisself alive. In the shape he's in, that took some doin'.

"His legs is terrible bowed fer walkin' so he learned t' climb. Climbs like a squirrel. Goes up a grapevine lickety-split and scampers 'round in the trees. Dangedest thin' ya ever did see. Ain't much good on the ground though. Lately he stays here most of the time. Many Spots takes him up t' the Osage now and then. They'd not let him stay if it wasn't for Miz Mac. The chief's the son of her ma's brother."

MacMillan waited for that to soak in before he continued.

"Me and Zee worked out some signals. I knowed when ya tied up on that bar before the storm. I knowed when ya was tryin' to get the boat off the sawyer. Knowed ya had a hurt man so we come down."

"What would you have done if we'd jumped you?" Eli asked.

"First one t' make a move woulda got a arrow. Zee ain't big, but he can put a arrow anywhere he wants." MacMillan turned to Light. "Stories will be told an' told in the lodges of how Sharp

216

Knife saved Zee from the rivermen."

"The Osage did not give him his name."

"Ya knew that, did ya?"

"They would wait until he chose one."

"He did not choose. We had to call him somethin', so we named him Zee. He likes the name. Makes him feel part of the family." Mac-Millan explained. "The Osage thought it all right for me to put a name on him 'cause we're both white. Now they call him Zee too.

"It pure-dee took me back," MacMillan continued, "when Miz Lightbody didn't blink a eye when she saw him. Men've come off the river what couldn't look at him. My younguns is used t' him. We don't pay no mind what he looks like no more. He's Zee. He looks after us. We look after him."

Aee and Bee alternated sitting with Zee throughout the long cold night. The little man slept fretfully and called out in his sleep. Aee, wrapped in a blanket, talked soothingly to him, and when he quieted, she dozed.

MacMillan invited Light and Maggie to spend the night inside the house. Maggie tugged at Light's hand and Light politely refused. Now, not wanting to fall completely asleep, Light sat in the yard, his back to the elm tree, and held Maggie across his lap.

For a long while they had whispered, saying the private things lovers say to each other after being apart and sharing long clinging kisses. Maggie told him that when she sat near their things she felt him to be with her. She explained that when she closed her eyes she could see and talk to him. She shifted so that her heart and his were pressed closely together and beat in unison. He was truly her heart, and she was his.

After Maggie had fallen asleep, Light's mind forged ahead to the time they could continue their journey to their mountain. He longed to leave this place, leave the sulking Swede before he had to kill him, leave the anxious Frenchman, leave the burden of helping to protect MacMillan and his family from the river pirate.

He tucked the blanket snugly around his sleeping wife to protect her from the cold. Until tonight, they had not been apart more than a few minutes at a time. He had not realized that parting from her for a few hours would cause her such anguish. Her love for him was as deep and abiding as his for her.

Light listened to the night sounds and wondered now at the advisability of the two of them striking out across the plains alone. What if something happened to him? He could not bear the thought of her wandering alone and lost. She was his sunlight. She was the wind. She was the moon and the stars.

He pressed his lips to her forehead. When he raised his head, he sniffed the frosty air. The smell of drying leaves wafted on the night breeze. He should be preparing for winter, but first Ramon de la Vega had to be dealt with.

Light thought of something Will Murdock had said two years before when they had been attacked by Pittsburgh boatmen. He and Will had been taking their winter catch of furs to St. Louis to trade. Jefferson had come along to buy supplies.

"Split 'em up an' we can whip 'em," Will had said, after they had been pinned down for an hour.

The plan had worked well. Being more fleet of foot than his friends, Light had been the one to show himself and run. Four of the pirates had followed him. He had led them into the woods knowing that he could lose them there. He had spied a huge hornet's nest and knocked it from the tree with the barrel of his rifle as he ran by. The swarm of hornets attacked the boatmen that followed him. To escape the vicious stings, they had scrambled back to the river to immerse themselves in the water. Meanwhile, Jeff and Will had easily dispatched the other four with a few flaming arrows.

Light reasoned that Vega was already short three crewmen. To weaken him further, more of his men must be lured from the boat. But how?

Light pondered the question until the clouds drifted away and the quarter moon shone brightly. Finally, an idea took form in his mind.

In the morning he would seek out Caleb and tell him his plan. He had liked the Negro immediately and was sure he would cooperate. The man had been loyal to MacMillan and had much the same relationship to him as the free Negro men who lived and worked on Jefferson Merrick's place had had with him.

His mind more at ease, Light dozed, his cheek resting against his wife's hair.

CHAPTER FIFTEEN

Ramon de la Vega was angry. He scanned the shoreline with his glass and saw nothing of the men who were to meet him at first light. Before daylight, risking damage to his craft, he had drifted a mile downriver to the meeting place.

Having been convinced the woman he sought was of rare beauty, he had sent three of his most reliable men with the German. The man she was with was a breed. Kruger had said that he insisted on bedding down with her away from the others, no doubt to satisfy his sexual perversions.

Four men should surely be able to handle one half-breed. But if the German had led the other men into a trap, and if he came out alive, he would wish he were dead long before he drew his last breath!

"Julio!"

"*Si, señor.*"

"Send Dixon ashore to look around."

Julio hesitated, then asked, "Alone?"

"*Si*, you fool. How many men does it take to look around? Tell him to look for a sign they've been there and had to go on downriver."

Julio turned away and kicked at one of the oarsmen sleeping on the deck. He sat up and turned on Julio with a clenched fist.

"Get up," Julio said loudly and then hissed in a low voice. "Move or he'll cut yore throat." Loudly again, he said, "The *señor* want you to go ashore."

"What for?"

"Look for sign. See if ya can see anything of the men sent to the homesteader's. The *señor's* workin' hisself into a fit," he added in a whisper.

Noah Dixon rose hurriedly to his feet, casting fearful glances at Vega. A few days after they left Natchez he had learned how cruel the man could be. Because Noah had grumbled about being at the oars for a twelve-hour stretch, the Spaniard had had the men hold him while he lopped off the end of Noah's forefinger. The pain had sent him into a faint. He had come to only when Julio had held a hot iron to the end of his finger to stop the bleeding.

Dixon was slight, agile and young, still in his teens. He went over the side, into the canoe Kruger had brought downriver, and grabbed a paddle. He angled and tacked as he crossed the river, wishing to God he had the nerve to beach the canoe and head off through the woods to the homesteader's place. He had heard Vega telling Julio they would not attack the homestead at this time, that he planned to return sometime later with a larger crew. The German had told Vega that there were two Negroes at MacMillan's but

222

could not recall their names. Vega thought one of them might be his runaway, Caleb.

The idea of deserting became more and more appealing to Dixon. He'd more than likely never make it back to Natchez anyway. If he was going to be killed, he would as soon it be by the homesteader as by the crazy, puffed-up little dandy who was so free with the whip and sword.

Vega had whipped one poor bastard nearly to death for grabbing at the Indian maid he'd set aside for his own personal use. In a fit of rage he had run another man through with his sword when the man had fallen asleep at the oars. Dixon had been ordered to help throw the body over the side and had watched it twisting and turning as it went downriver.

Noah freely admitted that he had committed his share of sins. He'd taken his turn with the white woman because he was horny as a two-peckered goat, and she had been willing. But more than that, he hadn't wanted the men to tease him if he didn't.

He tried to close his mind to the Indian maids who sat in an opium stupor in the cabin because there was nothing he could do. The trip downriver would take at least three weeks — less if they could use the sail. Would the women be alive when they reached Natchez?

He beached the canoe on a sandbar, looked back toward the keelboat and lifted his hand before he turned into the woods. He had no weapon; Vega kept them locked up, allowing the crew to carry only their eating knives unless the boat were attacked. Dixon had been so eager for a little time to himself that he had forgotten to ask Julio for a gun or a knife.

The woods were dim, cool and quiet. The wave of waterfowl that had flown up when he approached the bank had settled farther downriver. Well out of sight of the Spaniard's spyglass, Dixon stopped and leaned against the trunk of a towering oak. His boots, stirring the dry leaves, made the only sound. What to do? This was the first time he had been alone since he had signed on to crew this hell-boat.

His eyes roamed the woods around him. Nothing moved except a squirrel busy packing away acorns for winter. He wondered what was keeping the men from returning to the boat. Had they failed to capture the woman? It was unlikely that four men would be unable to overpower one, if the German had told the straight of it. Dixon's stomach churned at the thought of killing a man and stealing his wife to be used by that sorry piece of cow dung who was considered "quality" by the folks back home.

He thought of his ma and his sisters back on the bayou. Admittedly, he had traveled far from his ma's teachings, had done things he hoped and prayed she would never find out about, but he had not dishonored a woman or killed a man except for a Delaware who was trying to kill him.

Having unconsciously made his decision, Dixon

started off through the woods, stopping occasionally to listen for voices. What would he do if he met Rico and the men on their way back to the meeting place? They would be sure to kill him if they thought he was going to desert, and the homesteader would kill him on sight if the boatmen had taken the woman.

The thought caused Dixon to pause. Life was good back home. He didn't want to die here in this lonely place. If he returned to the keelboat and told the Spaniard he had seen nothing and the man didn't believe him, he would think no more of running him through with his sword than of swatting a fly.

Standing with his back to a large tree, with only the sounds of fluttering birds to break the silence, Noah felt a sudden chill of apprehension. Fear raised the hair on the back of his neck and on his arms. He tilted his head to listen and heard a slight rasping sound behind him. Before he could turn, a blow to the back of his head knocked him off his feet. His eyes crossed, his vision blurred and he sank into blackness.

After a morning meal of bread, hot gruel and tea, Light left Maggie and Aee fussing over Zee in the sickroom and walked down to the creek, where MacMillan said he would find Caleb. The huge Negro was skinning a large catfish. In his belt was a knife and a tomahawk. A strong bow and a quiver of arrows lay nearby. He grinned at Light as he approached.

Light found Caleb to be a strange blend of brawn and sharp native intelligence. His body, hardened by a lifetime of backbreaking labor, was all interlocking muscles, yet his hands were remarkably deft as he handled the fish-skinning knife. The large golden eyes had a soft sadness in their depths. He appeared to be cheerful by nature rather than bitter over his hard and degrading years as a slave.

Light nodded a greeting.

Caleb responded.

"You've got a good bow," Light said, and lifted the five-foot-long shaft of carefully selected ash strung with two buffalo sinews twisted together for extra strength.

"Yas'sah." Caleb chuckled. "Many Spots learn me how to make it an' shoot it. Mista Mac show me how to shoot the gun, but I load the bow faster an' I hits what I shoots at. It don't make no racket an' don't let out no smoke." He flourished his skinning knife. "An' I ain't havin' to tote no lead balls, waddin', firin' pins, an' gunpowder."

A rare smile flashed across Light's face, then lightning-fast, it disappeared as if it had no right to be there.

"Many Spots says that Vega moved downriver before daylight and tied up again. He's waiting to rendezvous with the men he sent to kill me and take my wife."

"That devil man ain't goin' t' like it none a'tall if he be countin' on gettin' the little missy."

"I'm not sure Kruger will return to the boat. He'll take off downriver by himself, which means he'll have to steal another canoe."

"Devil man maybe kill him, he go back. If he don't, he sure t' cut off ears or nose."

"What's Vega's next move? Do you think he will go back downriver when he finds out he lost three men?"

Caleb's eyes went round with astonishment. No man other than Mr. Mac had ever asked his opinion on anything.

"No, sah. If that No-Hair man tell 'im Caleb here, he not go . . . yet. Them folks take it hard when a nigga run. He wants t' get me back an' cut me t' pieces with dat whip. Dat'd make 'im feel good."

"I understand he's been here two other times and, each time, he asked about you."

"Mis-put him a plenty dat I run an' he ain't found me yet."

"If he started out with eight crewmen, he has five men left, four to row and one at the steering oar. I have an idea how we can make him even more short-handed than he is, if you and Many Spots will help me."

"I ain't talkin' for Many Spots, Mista Light, but yo sho' got my he'p."

Light squatted down on his haunches and told Caleb his plan while he drew a map of the river in the dirt with a stick.

"If he's tied up here" — Light poked the stick in the ground — "and Many Spots says he is,

227

there is a sandbar that stretches out about twenty feet. Behind it is a thick stand of bushes and trees."

"Yo kin get out a sight fast."

"That's the idea. We'll be using you for bait, Caleb. I'm counting on Vega seeing you and sending some of his men to get you. Many Spots and I will be waiting for them."

Caleb's eyes danced with laughter. "I can sho be the drunkest nigga yo ever did see, Mista Light. An' I can run like a scalded cat."

Light smiled again. He liked the man more and more.

When they left the homestead, Light set a fast pace through the woods. Maggie was behind him; Many Spots and MacMillan brought up the rear. Paul, Eli and Linus were digging graves for the rivermen Linus and Caleb had brought in at daylight. Many Spots had been contemptuous of the burial, but MacMillan had insisted.

Aee was tending to Zee, who had developed a fever during the night, and was keeping an eye on the disgruntled Osage warriors who prowled about the homestead. They were disappointed that there had been no fighting, and they were eager to be on their ponies and away.

With Kruger roaming the woods, Light insisted on keeping Maggie with him, even though MacMillan questioned the decision.

"My wife goes where I go." Light said the words with such finality that the homesteader said

228

nothing further on the matter.

In her buckskin britches, her hair pushed up under her old hat, Maggie looked like a slim boy. Carrying her bow, her quiver of arrows on her shoulder, she easily kept pace with Light. She was happy. Light had explained to her what they planned to do. He was including her. She would stand beside him and make him proud. The woods were quiet and restful after the activity at the homestead. Maggie loved the woods, longed to let her feet take wings and run, run, run —

They walked steadily for half an hour, hearing only the sounds of birds, squirrels and pack rats scurrying through the mat of leaves. Many Spots veered off the trail to check on Caleb's progress rowing downriver in a canoe with two jugs that, to Vega watching with the spyglass, would appear to be whiskey.

Abruptly, Light's arm shot out to stop Maggie and push her into the thick undergrowth alongside the trail. MacMillan followed.

A long silent moment passed, then Light cautiously raised himself to a kneeling position so that nothing of him was visible from the trail. He waited a moment before motioning to Maggie and MacMillan.

"Something ahead. No birds."

"Animal?"

"No."

When he heard the chirping of birds again, Light beckoned and they moved silently once more along the trail. Maggie remembered to stay calm as she followed Light, her bow in her hand. Light had said nerves were a worse enemy than the meanest Delaware alive.

They had come around a thick stand of sumac and not a dozen yards ahead was a man lying on the ground. Once again they sidled off the trail and into the undergrowth and waited until Light motioned. Then they cautiously approached the still figure. MacMillan knelt down beside the man on the ground while Light's sharp eyes searched for movement and his ears for the slightest sound.

"He ain't dead. Gol-durnit, he ain't no more'n a boy with peach fuzz on his jaws. Why ya reckon somebody hit 'im for?" MacMillan turned Dixon over. "Hellfire! If he had a gun or a knife, he ain't got it now. He's got nothin' on him but a eatin' knife."

"I just betcha it was that mean old Kruger," Maggie said.

"Wasn't no tomahawk what done it. He'd a been dead."

Many Spots trotted toward them from the river. "Caleb comin'. What this here?" He touched Dixon with his foot. "Want me kill 'im?"

"No, he be just a boy."

"We must go," Light said urgently. "We can tend him on the way back . . . if he's here."

"Whoever hit 'im heard us comin'."

Before they came out of the woods above the river where Caleb was to beach his canoe, Light motioned the others to stay behind. He crept forward to peer through the bushes. Now he could hear Caleb coming along just outside the reeds. He appeared to be drunk and was singing what he called a "moaning" song.

Light melted back into the forest where the others waited.

"Caleb is almost there. If they send a boat out, he will pretend not to notice until they are almost ready to beach it, then he'll run toward that tree." Light pointed to a tree that had been uprooted during the last storm.

"We kill?" Many Spots asked.

"Depends," Light said. "We'll see what they do. Use only the bows. No gunfire. We want to keep Vega guessing for as long as we can."

"What you want captives for?" Many Spots asked MacMillan.

MacMillan shrugged. "If they be like the German, I kill 'em. I can't have that sort 'round my womenfolk."

"Kill 'em now," Many Spots said.

"Ya can see he ain't got much use for rivermen," MacMillan explained to Light. "It was rivermen who killed his two boys last year. He thinks it was men from Vega's boat. The younguns was jist playin' along the riverbank. Bastards used 'em t' practice on."

Light positioned Maggie well back behind a tree with some branches low enough to reach so that she could scramble into the upper ones should the need arise.

"*Chérie,* you watch all around. Kruger may be

231

close by. Give our call if you see anything."

"Be careful, Light."

He tucked a stray curl under her hat, his eyes telling her how precious she was to him.

"You will obey me?"

"Yes, Light."

"Stay here. I will see about Caleb. It is his life that is in danger now."

When Light parted the bushes to view Caleb's performance, he could almost believe that the big Negro was drunk. He pulled the canoe up onto the sandbar, falling twice as he did so. He lay laughing each time, then got up to go look at the canoe Dixon had left there. He staggered about for a time, taking drinks from the jug. He began to sing loudly, mournfully, and off-key.

"I'se jist a po trav . . . ler,
A-goin' through dis world a sin
an' woe.
Wanderin' on . . . a' creakin' on . . .
through dis world a sin an' woe —"

Caleb fell to his knees, hung there for a minute, then flopped on his back and poured the liquid from the jug into his mouth.

Light made the sound of a bullfrog to let Caleb know he was there, then watched as a canoe was lowered into the river from the keelboat. Two men, one with a long gun, stepped into the canoe and took up paddles. The man with the gun had a black bushy beard and wore a red knit cap

232

low over his eyes. A richly dressed dandy on the keelboat held a spyglass, and waved a hand for them to hurry. When the canoe was no more than a dozen or so yards from the sandbar, Light made the sound again.

Caleb sat up, wiping his mouth with the back of his hand. He looked at the men in the boat, then leisurely got to his feet.

Run, Caleb. Now!

The big man staggered a few feet, picked up his jug, and turned to look at the men, who had run the canoe up onto the sandbar and were getting out. Light's heart jumped in his throat when Caleb took a step toward the men. Then, quick as a flash, he whirled around and ran for the woods.

"Shoot him! Shoot him!" The words came over the water from the keelboat.

The man who toted the long gun hesitated and pushed back his cap; he didn't dare waste his shot until he had a clear view of the fleeing man zigzagging through the trees. He lowered the gun and crashed through the bushes after Caleb. The other man followed at a slower pace. Caleb led them toward the downed tree, keeping just far enough ahead so they could catch a glimpse of him from time to time.

Several hundred yards inland, the pirates paused. The man with the red cap kept the rifle at ready. He turned a half-circle, scanning the trees, looking for movement. It was then Mac-Millan called out.

"We got ya in our sights. Put down the gun —"

The red-capped man spun and aimed the gun in the direction from which the voice had come. He never fired. A silent arrow, which seemed to come from nowhere, pierced his chest with a dull thud. The other man looked down in horror, then lifted his clasped hands high over his head. Sure that he was about to die, he waited, trembling. A white man and an Indian came out from behind the fallen tree, then the Negro they had been sent to capture emerged.

He wasn't drunk! It was a trap!

The thought crowded into the boatman's mind amid all the others as Light and Maggie filed silently from the woods. Maggie's hat had come off. She had slammed it back on her head without taking the time to poke the mass of heavy ringlets up into the crown. The riverman gaped. *This was the beautiful woman the German had described.* His eyes went to the man beside her. *And the half-breed Kruger had said would be so easy to kill.*

They stood looking at him, then turned their attention to his fallen companion when the Indian reached down and yanked the red cap from the man's head.

"He be the one. Had red cap, black hair on head, black hair on face."

"If he be the one, 'twas yore right t' kill him. How about this other feller? Was he there too?"

"Not there," Many Spots stated emphatically. "Rivermen had black hair. That'n too skinny. Hair not black." With a few deft movements of his knife, Many Spots made a circle on the top of the dead man's head. With his foot on the man's face, he twisted his hand in the dark hair and yanked. He held up the bloody scalp. "Take to Chattering Tongue. She no grieve. She give me more sons."

After a glance at his mutilated companion, the riverman blurted:

"I ain't never kilt nobody. Not even . . . not even a Inj—" He cut off his words and looked fearfully at Many Spots. "Vega don't let us have guns or knives on board."

"What did Vega tell ya t' do?"

"Get the nigga. Said cripple 'im if we had to, but get 'im. Mister, this be my first trip up-river. I didn't know he was a river pirate, waylayin' trappers and takin' their furs and Indian women. I swear to God."

"Did the German come back to the boat?" Until now Light had said nothing.

"Nobody come back . . . yet. That's why Vega's worked up an' sent Dixon to look around."

"How many Indian women does he have."

"Three. Got a white woman too, but she's not a captive. He don't tie up the women no more. They kiss his feet t' get the dope he lets 'em smoke. Then they sits like they ain't even knowin' where they're at."

"It be what he get off that ship in Orleans,"

Caleb said with disgust, then bent over to go through the dead man's pockets. "Didn't have nothin' but the gun."

"He had his eatin' knife, like the other'n had." MacMillan said.

"The other'n? Mister, he sent Dixon ashore a couple hours ago to look around for the German an' Rico an' the others. He ain't come back. He's not much more'n a youngun, ain't shaved yet, an' mighty scared Vega'll kill him 'fore he gets back home. Did ya see anythin' of him?"

"Why'er ya carin'?" MacMillan asked bluntly. "Ya best be lookin' 'bout yore own hide."

"Wal . . . me an' him was tryin' to stay alive to get back to St. Louie. We was goin' to jump off —"

"Desert?"

The man's eyes scanned the expressionless faces of the men and the beautiful young woman who watched him. To admit planning to desert was like admitting to plotting a mutiny in the eyes of a riverman.

He hesitated, then said, "I . . . guess we was — but we wasn't sartin we'd live to get back. Vega killed two of the rowers, lopped Dixon's finger off — and two more don't have ears no more. One ain't got no nose to speak of."

"What's yore name?"

"Bodkin. Linton Bodkin."

"What'd ya do afore ya signed on with Vega?"

"Worked for a cooper."

"Why'd ya quit makin' barrels an' tubs?"

236

"To see . . . what was upriver, I guess," he finished lamely.

"Want me kill 'im?" Many Spots asked.

Bodkin's frightened eyes went first to MacMillan and then to Light.

"Naw," MacMillan said with a twinkle in his eye, after he let the man sweat for a while. "He's got a good strong back. We'll let him tote his friend Dixon back to the homestead if he ain't already dead."

"Ya got Dixon?"

"If that's his name. We found him with a lump on his head. What weapons was he carryin'?"

"I don't reckon he had any."

"Vega sent a man off without weapons?"

"Nobody's got weapons but him and Julio. He's scared somebody'll slip up on him an' cut his throat. He's been crazy mean lately. He give him the gun" — he jerked his head toward the dead man — " 'cause he wanted him to get the nigga or kill him. He can't stand thin's not goin' his way." His eyes slid over Maggie and away — glad she had escaped the debasement she would have suffered at the hands of the Spaniard.

MacMillan picked up the dead man's rifle and handed it to Many Spots.

"Me no want. Too heavy."

"Yore plan worked, Light." MacMillan tossed the gun to Caleb, who caught it with one huge fist. "Vega's short two more men, three counting the one with the bashed head. That leaves two beside himself." He looked at Bodkin. "What'll he do?"

"Put the women to the oars."

"It'll take a strong wind, a good steersman and luck to get a boat that size back downriver without running aground."

"Julio is as good a steersman as they come. My guess is he'll make it."

CHAPTER SIXTEEN

MacMillan and Many Spots, with their prisoner in tow, went back to pick up Dixon and take him to the homestead.

"We go to watch Vega." As Light spoke to Caleb, he moved to put his body between Maggie and the dead man. Flies had begun to swarm around his bloody head.

"Yas'sah. What we do with this?" Caleb's head jerked toward the dead man.

"In the river, when Vega leaves."

"Light —" Maggie placed her hand on his arm. "Would be decent t' put him in the ground."

"He was the worst kind of man, *chérie*. He doesn't deserve a decent burial."

"Hee, hee, hee." Deep chuckles came rolling up out of Caleb's massive chest. "Missy 'fraid he make dem catfish plumb sick, Masta Light."

"I didn't mean that an' ya know it." Maggie put her hand on her hips and glared at the big man.

Caleb sobered immediately. "Yas'm. I put him in the hole where them tree roots was." Grasping the body by the feet, he dragged it toward the tree toppled by the storm. "An' I ain't carin' if the wolves gets at 'im," he added under his breath.

"Keep an eye out for Kruger. He has no gun or knife — that we know of. But he'll be desperate now."

"I watch."

"What'll Kruger do, Light?"

"There are only two places he can go, *chérie*. To Vega or to MacMillan's. Let's go watch and see if he goes to Vega."

Maggie and Light moved upriver through the woods until they came to a place where they could part the bushes and see Vega's boat. With his spyglass, the pirate was searching the area where his men had followed Caleb into the woods. His movements were jerky, and the voice that came over the water was high-pitched and angry. He was speaking in rapid Spanish.

If there were no women aboard, Light thought, he would shoot fire arrows and try to blow up the boat.

As they watched, two men and a blond-haired woman took up poles and strained to turn the keelboat around. With the bow pointed toward the shore where the canoes were beached, the poles were stuck in the river bottom to hold the craft in place.

"*Mon Dieu!* He's going to use the cannon." Light got to his feet. "*Chérie*. Come. We must warn Caleb."

"You go on. I hold you back —"

"Obey me! I've not got time to argue," Light said sternly.

"Yes, Light."

He pushed her ahead of him until they came to the path, then ran ahead, shouting for her to keep up. He didn't dare send her toward MacMillan's with Kruger somewhere nearby.

They ran zigzagging through the woods. Light had no idea how long it would take to load and fire the cannon. That fool Vega was going to fire into the woods in the hope of getting Caleb even though his own men were there. Bodkin was right; the man had lost his reason.

"Caleb!" Light did not care if the pirate heard his shout. "Caleb!" he bellowed. The Negro had heard him and was halfway across the clearing when Light reached it. "Hurry! He's firing the cannon."

Light turned and raced back up the path behind Maggie. She picked up speed and ran lightly and swiftly. On a short sprint Light was sure she could outrun him. He could hear the heavy footsteps and the labored breathing of the huge man behind him.

Boom!

It seemed only seconds after they left the clearing that the sound reached them. Another second later they heard the ball tearing through the trees behind them.

"Run!" Light shouted when Maggie slowed down. He knew the principal danger lay not in being hit by the ball, but by tree limbs it shattered.

241

Minutes passed. They reached the place where they had camped when the storm struck. Light called out to Maggie and they veered off the trail toward the river. They stood on the high bank and looked back downriver. The swift current had caught the front end of the keelboat and turned it downriver before Vega could fire the second shot. Any activity taking place aboard the boat was no longer visible.

"Maybe he'll go now," Maggie said.

"But he be back," Caleb said with resignation and a slump of his massive shoulders.

"Ah . . . Caleb. Ya always have t' be worryin' 'bout gettin' took back an' bein' a slave again." Maggie placed her hand on the huge arm.

Caleb flinched as if her hand were a red-hot iron. His eyes, full of alarm, went to Light. *Touched by a white woman! Would the scout send his knife through his heart?*

"Many things in the world are not right, *chérie,*" Light said. "Slavery is only one of them." He turned and looked back downriver.

Caleb looked at Light with naked gratitude in his eyes.

"Caleb will have t' come with us to our mountain, Light." Maggie moved up beside her husband. "That mean old man'd not find 'im there."

Light said nothing, but Maggie's suggestion sank into his mind. He wanted to leave this place — leave MacMillan, the Swede and the Frenchman to deal with the crazy German running amok

242

in the woods. After all, the Swede had brought him here.

His original idea of wintering with the Osage was no longer practical. He realized now that Maggie would not be able to adjust to their way of life; but, more than that, the Osage would not understand why Sharp Knife's woman did not skin the animals after a hunt, or cook, or make moccasins, or mate with him while others were in the lodge. She would not be subservient to the males of the tribe. The first time one hit her with a switch for not moving to serve him, she would take her whip to him. The brave would fight, and Light would be forced to kill him. It would cause chaos.

They would not winter with the Osage. Light would not see her humiliated and disgraced for not understanding the Osage way of life.

As they watched, the polers on the keelboat struggled to keep the craft behind the island and out of the river's swift current. More than an hour passed before they gave up the fight, and the bow turned with the current. Then the sail was hoisted, and the steersman took his place at the steering oar. The sail filled with the westward wind and the craft moved downriver.

"He's not waitin' t' see if his men is comin' back." Maggie held tightly to Light's hand.

"He doesn't care about them, *chérie*."

"He be back," Caleb said again.

"Not for a while. He doesn't have enough crew to buck the current. We'll take the canoes back to MacMillan's so Kruger can't use them."

Light led the way back to the sandbar where the canoes were beached. Maggie followed and Caleb brought up the rear, his bow on his shoulder and the rifle in his hand. It eased Light's mind to know he was there.

At dawn that day, Caleb, Linus and four of the Osage warriors had taken the two-wheel cart to fetch the bodies of the rivermen who had come ashore with Kruger. The German had not gone back during the night, as they had feared, to get the slain men's weapons. MacMillan took the two pistols and the saber, leaving the eating knives, boots and clothing for anyone who wanted them. The warriors stripped the bodies, and the three naked men were buried in one grave.

The homestead was quiet with the Osage warriors gone. They had mounted their ponies, and with much "yipping" and showing off of their riding skills had ridden toward their encampment beyond the salt caves. Many Spots had gone with them, proudly waving the scalp he would present to his woman.

Dixon had been struggling to sit up when Bodkin, emerging from the trees with the Indian and the homesteader, had arrived at the site of his ambush. His head felt as if it had been kicked by a mule, and his vision was so blurred that he thought he was dreaming when he saw his friend. With Bodkin's help Dixon had made it to MacMillan's homestead, although at times, he would have just as soon lain down and died.

The treatment he and Bodkin received at the homestead was totally unexpected. He had thought they would be locked up or shackled. Instead Aee MacMillan had taken charge, shaved the hair from the back of Dixon's head and applied the jimson-leaf salve. She then had urged him to lie down and rest.

Seeing the ugly little dwarf for the first time had been a shock to both Dixon and Bodkin. That the MacMillans treated him as one of the family was a bigger shock yet. It was a strange group at the homestead: the dwarf, the Indians, the Negroes, and the dark, quiet breed and his beautiful woman. Dixon was grateful now that the crazy Spaniard had ordered him to go ashore to look for his men.

Light, Maggie and Caleb returned with the birch-bark canoe from Vega's boat and the more sturdy cottonwood dugout canoe Kruger had stolen. The news that Vega had set the sail and headed back downriver was welcomed. None of them believed he was gone for good. If he didn't come back before the winter freeze, he would be back in the spring.

After talking at length with Bodkin, MacMillan was convinced that he and Dixon were no more than what they appeared to be — young men who had sought adventure and were relieved to be off the Spaniard's boat.

Anxious about his wife and confident the home-stead was in safe hands, MacMillan took his second daughter, Bee, and went to bring his family home. If at all possible, MacMillan wanted his sixth child to be born in the place where he had been conceived.

Eli was sick of hearing the praise heaped upon "Sharp Knife." He had to admit rescuing the little man was a heroic act, but he was tired of hearing about it. Zee had recounted every detail to Mac-Millan, and the settler had repeated it to the others. Many Spots had embellished the tale in repeating it to the warriors, and they looked at Lightbody as if he were God himself.

"Yo're thinkin' ya can hire them two Vega men t' help ya get to the Bluffs, ain't ya?" Aee came from the barn and paused when she saw Eli sharpening an axe on the whetstone.

"What if I am? The sooner we're away from here the better I'll like it."

"The sooner yo're gone the better we'll like it too. We be jist poor wilderness folk," she said with heavy sarcasm. "But our *eats* is good enough for ya."

"Don't worry, I'll pay before we leave."

"I'm glad to hear it. I can mark *cadger* off as one of yore faults."

Eli put down the axe and looked at her for so long that her face reddened. She really was pretty. She had a lithe, supple form, and the shirt she was wearing was snug over her firm high breasts. Her nose was straight, her mouth soft. Her teeth were white, and she had all of them.

246

Her thick dark-brown hair was parted in the middle and loose braids began beneath her small ears and hung to her waist.

"Gettin' yore eyes full, riverman?" she asked scornfully, flushing angrily beneath his intense scrutiny.

"I was just thinking that, cleaned up, in a *dress*, and with your hair put up the way a woman ought to wear it, you'd be almost pretty . . . that is, as long as you kept your mouth shut." Eli turned his head to grin.

Wham! She hit him a stinging blow alongside the head with her old felt hat. He was stunned for the time it took to take several deep breaths.

After the impulsive act, Aee ran for the house.

"Damn you, you little flitter-head! I'll whop yore hind!"

Eli ran after her. He rounded the corner and saw her dart behind Caleb's massive figure. The Negro stood with hands on his hips, his teeth bared. He was ready to do battle!

"Yo gwine t' do what, mista?"

Aee peeked around from behind Caleb and grinned at him.

Eli stalked off so angry that he didn't see Maggie until he was almost up against her.

"Why'er ya chasin' Aee for, Eli? Ya playin' a game?"

"No, I'm not playing a game," he growled.

"Then why'er ya mad?"

"I'm not mad!"

"Yes, ya are too, Eli. Don't story to me."

"Don't you have anything to do but stick your nose in my business?"

"See there? Ya are too mad. I ain't goin' t' like ya if yo're mean to Aee."

"Lord help me! All women should be put in a sack and thrown in the river!" Eli threw up his hands and walked away.

Maggie laughed. "Now yo're bein' a flitter-head," she called after him.

Aee came out from behind Caleb.

"What yo teasin' that man for, Miss Aee?"

"I wasn't. He jist made me so mad I hit him."

"Lawsy mercy me. Yore mamma'll have to take ya in hand when she come back." Caleb went away grinning and shaking his head.

"I come t' see 'bout Zee. Did his fever go down?" Maggie headed for the sickroom, and Aee walked along beside her.

"He's better. Wants to get outside. Can't hardly stand on his hurt leg yet."

"Somebody can carry him. I'll get Eli."

"No!" Aee said quickly. "Don't get that . . . pissant. I ain't wantin' to have nothin' to do with him a'tall."

"I thought ya liked Eli."

"Well, I don't! Here comes Mr. Deschanel. I'll ask him."

Aee brought a chair from the house and lined it with a blanket. Paul carried Zee out and carefully lowered him into the chair.

"Anythin' I can get ya, Zee?" Maggie asked.

"Ah . . . no, ma'am."

"I'll get ya a swatter to keep off the flies. My, they're pesky this time a year. I guess they be knowin' they're 'bout done for." Maggie brought him a narrow flat strip of board with a floppy square of leather nailed to one end. "Here ya are. Are ya warm enough, Zee?"

"I . . . be fine, lass."

The ugly little man watched her run lightly toward the open door of the cabin.

Guard your treasure well, Sharp Knife.

"Pa's comin'."

The sun had set and Aee had begun to be anxious because her parents had not returned. She stood out near the cow lot and watched them approach. Her father led the oxen. Bee, the younger girls, and an Indian woman walked behind the cart.

"Is Ma all right?" Aee called.

"It won't be long. Is thin's ready?"

"Yes, Pa."

MacMillan stopped the oxen beside the door and went around to help his wife out of the cart.

"Stop fussing, Mr. Mac. I'm perfectly able to get out by myself. Land sakes, you'd think this was our first youngun the way you carry on."

She got out of the cart and stood for a moment holding her huge abdomen. She took several deep breaths.

"Is it time, Ma?" Aee asked.

"It is time. Say hello to your aunt."

Aee spoke a few words in the Osage language

to the woman. The only words that Maggie, who was standing nearby, understood were "Yellow Corn." The woman's hair was completely gray and her face was heavily lined. Her clothes, however, were richly decorated with beads and feathers and the blanket wrapped around her shoulders was colorful and new.

Maggie gazed in fascination at Mrs. MacMillan's large belly. How was that large lump going to pass out through such a small opening between the woman's legs? Each time her aunt back home had given birth, Maggie had run off into the woods so she would not hear the screams. She wasn't sure now if she should leave or stay. She wanted to know what this birthing was about. Someday she would be having Light's babes.

The younger girls had gone immediately to Zee, happy to see him, and bombarded him with questions. Linus stepped out of the gloom to take the oxen and the cart to the barnyard.

When Aee led the way into the house where the lamps were lit and water was heating in a large iron pot, Maggie followed behind the Indian woman. Mrs. Mac walked up and down the room, after her critical eye had checked on the preparations for the birth. She smiled at her older daughter, then turned to Mr. MacMillan, who stood nervously on first one foot and then the other.

"Mr. Mac, you should be out setting up a watch for that German fellow if he is as bad as you said he was. The girls will tend me. We'll let you know if you are needed."

MacMillan, with a worried look on his face, went to his wife, took her hand, raised it to his lips, and went quickly out the door.

"Pa's always antsy like this," Aee said aside to Maggie. "Bee an' I helped Ma through the last two babes. Pa acted like he had been settin' on a hill a red ants. He ain't ort t' worry like that. The last one was four years ago. We're older now and Ma has told us what t' do. If ya want t' stay, ya can."

"What can I do?"

"Nothin'."

"What's she goin' t' do?" Maggie gestured toward the Indian woman.

"Her name's Yellow Corn. She's one of the oldest in the tribe. As soon as the babe is born, she'll start tellin' it how the world was started and the history of the Osage."

"Why is she doin' that?"

"It's somethin' they do."

"It'll understand?"

" 'Course not, but she thinks it will. It's the Osage way and Ma don't want them to think she's turned her back on the old ways."

Suddenly Mrs. MacMillan went to the corner of the room, lifted her skirt and stood straddling a china pot. Aee hurried to her and took her arm to steady her. A stream of bloody water gushed out. It came and it came until Maggie grew alarmed.

"Oh, is she . . . is she peein'?" she asked Bee.

"No. The sack of water holding the baby broke. It'll be comin' soon."

Maggie looked at Aee and Bee with new respect. They knew so much about many things. Their flushed faces were the only sign of worry and excitement. Mrs. MacMillan and the Indian woman were as calm as if bringing forth a new life were an everyday occurrence.

The girls helped Mrs. MacMillan remove her dress. Beneath it she wore only a white shift that hung loosely from her shoulders. Lifting it to around her waist, she knelt down on a blanket-covered pile of straw at the foot of the bed and held on to the support post that went from the floor to the roof.

Bee checked and rechecked the supplies they would need: sharp clean knife, linen thread, dishpan with warm water, grease for the newborn's skin and a roll of white cotton cloth to wrap it in.

It was quiet in the room, except for the mumbles of Yellow Corn. Mrs. MacMillan's hands moved up and down the pole as she pulled and strained. Occasionally a grunt escaped her. When the pain passed, her gasps for air were loud and labored. Her face and neck became wet with sweat. Aee and Bee stood beside her.

It seemed to Maggie this went on for a very long time. It could not have been more than half an hour when Mrs. MacMillan strained and half stood.

"It's coming!" she gasped. "Oh . . . oh —"

Aee knelt in front of her mother and caught her new sibling in her two hands when it slid from Mrs. MacMillan's body. The babe was wet and bloody and wrinkled.

"A boy! Pa got his boy!" Aee made room for Bee, who quickly cut and tied the cord.

Aee stood with the baby in her arms. She dug into the baby's mouth with her finger to remove the mucus and lifted his tiny arms over his head. He gasped for breath and let out a loud wail of protest.

"He's all right, Ma." Aee laughed happily.

Bee had placed a shallow pan between her mother's legs. A moment or two went by. Maggie was amazed to see Bee take a feather and tickle her mother's nose. Mrs. Mac strained once again, and the afterbirth slid into the pan. When that was done, Bee handed her a rolled cloth to catch the bloody flux. Mrs. MacMillan stood and moved around to the side of the bed.

"He's got ever'thin', Ma. All his little fingers and toes. Two ears. Two eyes. Ever'thin'." Aee held the baby so her mother could see him. "Look at the hair, Ma. He's fat as a little pig. Pa'll be fit t' be tied when he sees 'im. I'll wash 'im up before we call him."

Yellow Corn's mumbles had become louder with the baby's birth. The women ignored her. Bee helped her mother to slip into a clean nightdress and get into the bed. Then she tenderly washed her face and neck with a wet cloth.

"You done good. Both of you."

Maggie was unable to take her eyes off the baby. It was red as a beet and had a head of thick black hair. It reminded her of a newborn cat or rabbit. She thought it the ugliest thing she had ever seen, but she kept her opinion to herself when she saw how proud Aee and Bee were of their new brother.

"What will you name him?" Maggie asked.

"Eff, of course." Aee laughed. "But we'll call him Frank." Aee finished greasing the baby, wrapped him in the cotton cloth and carried him to their mother. "He looks like a boy, don't he, Ma?"

"He sure does. My, he has big hands. Just like Mr. Mac. You'd better call him, Aee. You know what a worrier he is when it comes to the family."

Aee opened the door. "Pa," she called. "Ma said t' come see Frank."

A whoop went up. Then it seemed to Aee that a swarm of men were at the door. Paul was slapping her Pa on the back. Everyone was smiling: Light, the Vega men, Paul and even Eli Nielson. Behind them, Linus's and Caleb's faces shove with happiness. Caleb held Zee up so he could see. The younger girls crowded into the room.

"Ya can't all come in. Just Pa for now."

"Can we come?" Cee, Dee and Eee yelled in chorus.

"If yo're quiet. Somebody better be watchin' out for that German." She looked directly at Eli.

"He might come bustin' in while yo're lollygaggin' 'round doin' nothin'." She tilted her chin and turned her back.

Eli swore under his breath.

CHAPTER SEVENTEEN

The birth of MacMillan's son was cause for a celebration. The morning after the birth, the happy homesteader announced that there would be no work this day and that they would have a feast the following day.

Immediately after the announcement Light and Maggie slipped away from the homestead. When they returned several hours later, a small deer was draped across Light's shoulders. He hung it to a tree limb behind the house and carefully skinned it. The soft pelt, when cured, would go to line the newborn's crib, and the meat would be roasted for the feast.

Caleb brought in a goose all plucked, dressed, singed and ready for the spit. Not to be outdone, Linus caught a mud turtle the size of a washtub. He dressed it out and laid aside large chunks of white meat to boil for meat pies.

Before noon, Many Spots arrived to take Yellow Corn home. Later he returned with a wild turkey for the feast and the pelt from a young raccoon and a cradleboard for the new son. He dropped them on the ground in front of the door and, with a wild whoop that woke the sleeping babe, rode away.

Eli and Paul brought from their cargo a sack of milled flour, a sack of coffee beans, and a length of printed cloth for Mrs. MacMillan.

Pumpkin was cooked, pies were made, onions, potatoes and turnips readied for meat pies. Mrs. MacMillan, holding her new son, directed the girls. Even the youngest one had something to do. Zee was brought into the house. The bandage was taken from his leg so Mrs. Mac could inspect the wound. She praised Aee for the job she had done, and Zee was allowed to sit at the table and crack nuts for the pumpkin cake.

Bodkin and Dixon, eager to participate, chopped wood and kept the fires going, glad to be a part of the celebration, but aware that they were constantly being watched. They could not blame the homesteader for being cautious.

During the afternoon, Bodkin showed MacMillan how his pa in the Tennessee hill country made an outdoor oven by poking strong but limber willow sticks in the ground in a circle the size of a washtub. He brought the other ends together at the top and tied them to form a small dome-shaped hut. Leaving a small hole in the top, he covered the frame with several inches of mud brought up from the river in buckets. A slow fire inside dried the mud to brick hardness. By morning the oven would be ready to roast the turkey or the goose.

In spite of the festive mood, watchful eyes

scanned the edge of the woods for a sign of Otto Kruger. MacMillan had considered speaking to Many Spots about him. He and the Osage warriors would search the woods until they found him or a sign that he had gone on downriver, where they hoped the Delaware would take him. After what had been done to Zee, MacMillan was certain the Osage would not merely kill Kruger but would torture him to death, and the sound of his screams and the smell of burning flesh would mar the celebration. He decided to wait another day.

It was Eli who encountered the crazed German in an unexpected place.

Since Aee had referred to Eli as a cadger, resentment had gnawed at him. He had paid his way since he had been twelve years old and had never begged a crumb from anyone. He had intended to leave a bag of tobacco with MacMillan when they left but decided to give it to him now after first shoving it in the face of his mouthy daughter.

When it was thought that Vega would attack the homestead, Eli's keelboat had been poled up the creek, where it was anchored amid thick willows. The instant Eli stepped on the boat he knew someone else was there. He pulled the pistol from his belt.

Kruger came from inside the shed. He stood with his back to the door, his balled fists on his hips. He was dirty, his shirt ragged. His bald head had deep bloody scratches, Eli presumed from going through the blackberry briars when he ran from Light. The eyes that stared out of the whiskered face were hate-filled and feverish.

"What are you doing here, Otto?"

" 'Tis *mein* boat."

"You sold it to me to pay your debts in St. Louis."

"*Mein* boat!"

"You'll find no weapons here."

"Viskey —"

"No whiskey or gunpowder. You stole two kegs of my gunpowder and took them to the pirate."

Kruger shrugged. "He iss gone."

"Why didn't you go with him?"

"He leaf me. I come back to *mein* boat."

"You're no longer a member of my crew. You deserted. I could shoot you for that. If MacMillan sees you, he *will* shoot you for what you did to the little fellow."

"Baa!" Kruger snorted. "I did not do it."

"You stood by and let others do it. It's the same thing."

"I kill no one! The breed kill!"

"You were bringing those river rats to kill him and take his wife."

"She *mein* voman!" Kruger pounded his chest with his fist.

"You stupid son of a bitch! You've lost your senses."

"He vill gif me *mein* voman or I kill him."

"You had your chance. Four of you came to kill him. You didn't even get to the homestead." Eli had a sudden, unwelcome feeling of pride

259

in Baptiste Lightbody.

As Kruger took a step toward him, Eli could almost feel the heat of his hatred. Waiting for the next move, he knew he had one shot to stop Kruger if he attacked him. Still weakened from the fever, he was aware that he would be no match for the crazed German should it come to a hand-to-hand fight.

Otto had been irritable since leaving St. Louis. He had been unable to cope with the fact that he'd had to sell his boat to meet his debts or else be killed. That he should blame Eli and Paul for his troubles showed his unreasonable state of mind. His irrational behavior had escalated after they had met up with Light and Maggie, and Otto had focused his anger on them.

"Take a canoe and go on back downriver, Otto. I don't want to see you killed."

"I stay here on *mein* boat."

"Gawddammit! You can't stay here. If Mac-Millan doesn't kill you, Lightbody will."

"Vat you care? You vid them."

"Hell yes, I'm with them. What did you expect?"

"I vant food."

"Take the Vega canoe. It's at the dock. Also the one you stole when you deserted."

"Ya tink I don' know dat?"

"There's a bag of dried meat and one of raisins in the shed. Take what you'll need. You can catch fish and find duck eggs along the riverbanks. You'll not starve."

Kruger said nothing. Eli held the pistol steady.

A smile tilted Kruger's full lips as he backed into the shed. Out of sight, he reached behind him and removed the large blade he had tucked in the back of his belt when he heard Eli step onto the boat. He had hidden the knife in the shed weeks ago when he began to realize the Swede and the Frenchman were plotting against him.

A crafty gleam lit Kruger's eyes. He smiled as he hurriedly stuffed a bag with food, then took what tools he wanted: a hammer/hatchet, a saw, a handful of square nails and a length of rope. He wrapped them and the knife in a blanket. That done, he hid a prying tool behind the loose board where he had hidden the knife just in case the Swede decided to take all the tools off the boat before he could come back.

Kruger came out of the shed, walked past Eli without a look or a word, and jumped off the boat. Eli stepped into the shed, hoisted the bag of tobacco to his shoulder and followed Otto to the docks. He watched him throw his bundle into the canoe, step in and take up a paddle.

Eli walked along the bank until Kruger reached the river and disappeared behind the high bank before he stuck his pistol in his belt and turned back toward the homestead.

Kruger lingered behind the bank for a short while, then turned the canoe around and paddled furiously upriver.

Toward evening Eli took Paul aside and told

him about the encounter with Otto.

"*Mon Dieu,* Eli. He's lost his wits. You shouldn't have let him go."

"Do you think I should have shot him? He's killed no one that I know of."

"He was bringing Vega's men to get Maggie. Not only did Light hear them say that, Zee told MacMillan."

"They didn't succeed."

"If Light hadn't found them they would have killed Zee and come here thinkin' to sneak up on Light. Maggie could have been killed."

"I couldn't just shoot him down, Paul. I would've if he had made a move toward me, but he didn't."

"Is he gone for good?"

"Your guess is as good as mine. Strong as he is, and in the birch-bark canoe with a strong current, he should make forty or fifty miles a day going downriver if he really wants to get back to St. Louis. He may be able to get past the Delaware."

"He might catch up with Vega."

"Hellfire! He should know by now that the man can't be trusted." Eli's eyes strayed past Paul and followed Aee as she carried a bucket from the house to the barn.

Paul saw the interest in his friend's eyes as he looked at the MacMillan girl, and an idea began to form.

Eli looked back at his friend. "It worries me that Otto speaks of Maggie as his woman. That proves that he's crazy in the head."

"Ho!" Paul took the pipe from his mouth and knocked the ashes out of the bowl by hitting it on the sole of his boot. "Can you blame him for wanting the lass, *mon ami?* Are you not sweet on her yourself?"

Eli's mouth snapped shut and his eyes hardened. He was quiet for a minute before he spoke.

"I *like* her. I don't believe she should traipse off into the wilderness with Lightbody. His life could be snuffed out with a shot, an arrow, a snake bite. She'd be alone."

"Do you have it in your mind to *traipse* after them?" Paul asked in a voice flat with disapproval. When Eli didn't answer, he said, "Hire Dixon and Bodkin and let's go on up to the Bluffs. Another couple of months and they'll be iced in up there."

"MacMillan said we'd have no trouble getting back downriver. In the spring trappers want to bring down their furs."

"We've still got to get *up* there, *mon ami.*"

"Light plans to go a hundred miles upriver and cut across the plains to the mountains."

"Have you not seen all of Lightbody you want to see?" Paul asked gently.

"I don't know," Eli answered honestly.

"His life is separate from yours, Eli. He has his values and you have yours."

"His is a savage way of life. Not fit for —"
Paul held his hand up. "What has he done

that you would not have done under the same circumstances? He has killed, yes. He has strong instincts of self-preservation. Can you blame him for that?"

"Why are you always defending him?"

"Why are you so against him? He has done nothing to you, taken nothing from you."

"I say he has."

"Eli, be reasonable —"

The conversation was abruptly halted when MacMillan approached with a jug of whiskey and a tin cup, but it had given Paul a further cause to worry about his friend and his fascination with Baptiste Lightbody's wife.

"It is rare that we have cause to celebrate or good friends to celebrate with." MacMillan was in high spirits. "Let's drink a toast to F. Frank MacMillan."

The night was cool. A full moon shone brightly amid a sea of stars. Everyone at the homestead, with the exception of Mrs. MacMillan and the newborn, sat in the yard around a small fire. Caleb, Linus and Zee were as eager as the children, who sat wide-eyed with excitement and listened avidly to the stories told by Paul, Eli and Bodkin. Dixon was so bashful in the presence of the girls that he said not a word, but his eyes strayed often to Bee.

Eli presented MacMillan with the sack of tobacco. The homesteader was overjoyed.

"By jinks damn, Eli, it be too much fer mere

doctorin'. There be enough tobaccy to last till next year."

Eli smirked at Aee. "I hope I'll be back with another sack by then."

In the shelter of Light's arms, Maggie watched Aee cast fleeting glances at Eli; and when Paul was telling the story about Eli being chased down the street in a river town by a barmaid and having to jump on his boat and pole it out from the bank so she couldn't reach him, Aee tossed her head, curled her lips and snorted in disgust.

"The maid was goin' to bang his head with a skillet. She say to me, 'He has billy-goat in his blood.' " Everyone laughed at the story, but Eli had a special interest in Aee's reaction to it. She gave him a caustic look, turned, and smiled sweetly at Bodkin.

Five miles downriver, Ramon de la Vega's steady drinking had transformed his frustration into rage. He walked the deck and shouted abuses at the diminished crew. A sudden gust of southern wind had propelled the keelboat onto a sandbar. The two crewmen and the women had strained at the poles for hours and had been unable to budge the craft.

Vega had vented his anger by using the young Delaware girl cruelly, then forcing her to bare her body and touch herself intimately. In her drugged state she had groggily obeyed him. Afterward he had whipped her. Using the lash on the girl was more sexually satisfying to him than the act he had performed on her body. He then applied the whip to all the women, laying it especially hard on the white woman known as the slut.

The other men on board were disgusted by the performance of the Indian girl and shocked by the cruel whipping of the women, but they were too afraid of the Spaniard to object.

Born to a whore in a brothel, sired by one of the hundreds of Pittsburgh boatmen she serviced, the white woman had been named Betsy by her mother. Betsy was twelve years old and already wise in the ways of pleasing men when her mother died of the pox. A life of depravity was all she had known. Now six years after her mother's death, she thought nothing of spreading her legs for any man who wanted her as long as she received something in return.

On Vega's boat she had been given food and a place to sleep, and until now she had not been whipped but rather ignored by the richly dressed little dandy. She had whored for his crew, washed his clothes, emptied his piss-pot, and washed the Indian girl for his use. For this she had been given a small pinch of the white powder that gave her forgetfulness.

Deep inside Betsy resentment began to rise. Not only was her back afire from the lash, but the fierce pain in her head and belly had intensified. She had eaten little for days, and when she used the pot, she had found streaks of blood. She knew she would die soon. She had begun to welcome the idea of death as a release from the pain.

After his tantrum, Vega permitted a half hour of rest. As she huddled in the darkness next to the cabin, Betsy's dazed mind suddenly became alert. Beside her were the two kegs of gunpowder the German had had in his canoe when they had brought him aboard. The top of one keg had been pried open when the cannon was fired. The lid had not been nailed shut again. Betsy moved it aside far enough for her hand to dip inside.

Slowly and cautiously she brought out handful after handful of the black powder, spreading it around the kegs and along the wall of the cabin. She was amazingly calm. Soon her torment and that of the Indian women would be over.

When the Spaniard yelled for Julio a half hour later, the trail of black gunpowder had reached the cabin door.

"Go over the side and see how bad we are stuck."

Julio gaped. "*Señor*, I cannot see. Do you not think we should wait for morning —"

"In the morning we'll be sitting ducks." The Spaniard's voice rose to a shriek. "Get over the side or I'll run you through like the filthy swine you are," he shouted.

"I . . . will need a . . . light, *señor*." Julio trembled so violently that he could hardly speak.

"Get him a light!"

Betsy got to her feet as quickly as her aching, trembling body allowed. Inside the cabin she struck a spark and first lit a candle, then held the flame to the wick in the lantern. Shielding the candle flame from the thin night breeze with her body, she handed the lantern to Julio when he came to the door. Betsy waited until the candle flame was strong. Then she went out, bent, and dipped the flame into the narrow trail of gunpowder.

With a smile on her face, the woman known as the slut looked straight into Vega's horrified eyes as he watched the hissing blue-green fire race along the cabin wall. The lantern, held by a paralyzed Julio, cast an eerie light for the few seconds it took the flame to reach the gunpowder kegs. The last thing Betsy saw before the brilliant light was the terrified face of Ramon de la Vega.

The explosion was heard for miles.

At the homestead the children were sent to bed. The men sat beside the small fire and talked of many things. MacMillan believed that with the number of people coming into the territory Missouri would soon be admitted to the Union.

"Then watch out. The land grabbers will come a rollin' up the river. Man'd be smart to get hisself a place staked out a'fore the rush."

Light smiled behind his hand. It was the same forecast MacMillan had offered to tempt him into staying and helping start a village.

"Indians is friendly here," MacMillan continued. "Osage people mighty fine people. Treat 'em right an' don't try t' change their ways. Hell!

Some a their ways is better'n ours."

"Careful, Mac," Eli teased. "You'll get you a town started here before ya know it. You've got two young bucks here and two pretty daughters."

"Well, now . . . I ain't aimin' for that."

Eli watched Aee squirm and with a half-smirk on his face, continued on.

"Yessiree. Wouldn't take long to throw up a couple a cabins. Right here on this bend is a good place for a town. You could call it Mac-Millanville."

"That's a good name," Bodkin said. Then when all heads turned to look at him, he turned a fiery red.

"See there, Mac. You've got you a cooper. Now get him a wife and you've got MacMillanville's first businessman."

Paul watched the glances Eli cast toward Mac's eldest daughter. When Aee got up abruptly and went into the house, Eli leaned back with his hands behind his head and said no more. Bee followed her sister after a while.

The men drank sparingly; all but Light took a swallow when the jug was passed. They were taking turns patrolling the woods surrounding the cabin. When the moon was straight overhead it was time for Light's shift. Maggie went with him, holding onto his hand, walking quietly.

Maggie loved to walk in the woods at night with Light. She liked the night sounds; the rustle of the leaves stirred by a pack rat, the hoot of an owl, the cry of a nightbird. Most of all she loved the sound of a wolf howling at the moon or calling to his mate. In the soft darkness she could almost believe that she and Light were the only people in all the world.

They didn't speak. There was no need for words between them.

When Caleb came to relieve them, they talked quietly with him for a moment, then sought their blankets. Maggie snuggled close to Light, seeking the warmth of his body and the security of his arms.

"Aee an' I was goin' t' take us a bath tomorrow, but now I can't. I got my woman's time today. Ma says not t' get in the water when I'm bleedin'."

"Why is that?"

"It would stop it an' I'd be sick."

"I've not heard of that, love. Indian women bathe more at that time than at any other."

"I've not got a babe growin', Light," Maggie announced matter-of-factly.

"I realize that. Have you been hoping one was started, *ma petite?*"

Maggie was thoughtful for a moment before she spoke.

"No. I want us t' get t' our mountain first."

"Would you rather we didn't mate until then? It's the only way to be sure."

"Then I don't want t' be sure." Maggie leaned up, placed her nose next to his and spoke against his lips. "If a babe starts t' grow, it'll just have t' put up with us."

Light laughed and hugged her. "My jewel, I treasure each day with you."

"I'm not afraid t' have the babies, Light."

"Were you afraid before, *mon amour?*" He stroked the hair from her face.

"I was . . . dreadin' it. My aunt used to holler somethin' awful when she was havin' her younguns. Mrs. Mac didn't holler a'tall. She just squatted down, held onto a post an' in a little while the babe slid out. It was wet an' bloody . . . an' ugly lookin'. I didn't say it was ugly, 'cause Aee kept sayin' how pretty it was."

"You'd never before seen a woman give birth?"

"I saw a deer. I rubbed her head while the babe came out."

"*Mon Dieu!* She let you?"

"Uh-huh. Animals aren't scared of me. Ya know that."

Maggie laid her head on Light's chest and placed her hand over his heart. She liked to feel it beat. When she heard a sound that resembled a loud crack of thunder, she lifted her head.

Light had heard it too. He turned his head to listen.

"Is it goin' t' rain, Light?"

"There are no clouds, *chérie.*"

A feeling that he could not quite understand drew him to his feet. He looked and he listened. The moon shone, the stars were bright, the night was quiet . . . but somehow eerie.

And to the east the sky was aglow with a rosy light.

CHAPTER EIGHTEEN

Daylight came and the smell of woodsmoke mingled with the aroma of roasting meat. Linus began cooking a hindquarter of the deer before dawn. The other parts of the deer were curing in the smokehouse.

Bodkin's oven became the center of attention for a while. Aee exclaimed over it. Mrs. MacMillan came from the house to look at it and see how it worked. Beneath an iron grate set on river stones a slow fire of hickory chips burned. The oven was roomy enough to hold both the turkey and the goose. Fat falling from the birds hissed and burned and smoked. Bodkin basked in the women's praise.

Over the morning coffee the men talked about the loud noise they had heard during the early part of the night.

"There warn't a cloud in the sky," MacMillan said. "Maybe there was a storm far off, an' lightnin' set the woods afire."

"If it did, *m'sieur,* it soon burned itself out."

"Sounded to me more like something blew up."
When he heard the *boom-boom,* Eli had thought

of the two kegs of gunpowder Kruger had stolen. He was crazy enough and knew enough about explosives to set the charges.

"Might be the German blew one of his kegs of gunpowder."

"Otto wouldn't waste the powder unless he had a good reason. It would take more than one keg to make a noise like that." It was clear to Eli that MacMillan didn't know much about explosives.

"The German left the gunpowder on Vega's boat, isn't that right, Noah?" Bodkin squatted by the oven making hickory chips with a hatchet.

"They was sittin' by the cannon when I left. Vega had three more kegs he kept locked up," Dixon said shyly. He wasn't comfortable enough with these men yet to venture an opinion, and when the girls were around he was more tongue-tied than ever.

"What do you think, Light?" Paul asked.

Light shrugged. Whatever had happened didn't appear to be a threat to him or Maggie nor to the homestead. Light's mind was on other things.

Everyone was ready to celebrate. The weather was perfect, no wind and pleasantly warm as a sweet-smelling fall day can be. The men carried the long trestle table from the house to the yard to hold the food. Afterward they shaved and combed their hair, and those who had them put on clean shirts.

The women changed into their best dresses after

the food had been prepared to Mrs. Mac's satisfaction. The MacMillan girls wore the same dresses they had worn the day Light and Maggie came to dinner, blue linsey with white collars. Aee brought out a dress for Maggie that eleven-year-old Cee had outgrown. It had been put away for Dee to grow into. It was like the others except that the color was a deeper blue and was faded from many washings. For this very special occasion, each of the girls wore a blue ribbon in her hair.

Maggie had never had the companionship of women near her own age. She laughed and giggled with them over the tangles in Dee's hair and the fact that Cee at eleven years was as tall as Maggie. At Cee's age it was all right for her ankles to show, but when she reached Bee's age it would no longer be proper.

Aee didn't think she had ever seen anyone as pretty as Maggie. She could not yet understand why Maggie was so oblivious to the Swede's interest in her. Aee brushed Maggie's hair until it was a mass of shimmering ringlets, then slipped the ribbon under her hair at the back of her neck, brought it up behind her ears and tied the bow at the top of her head. When Maggie saw her reflection in the mirror, her delight was with the ribbon.

"Take yore hair out of the braids, Aee. Fix yore ribbon like mine."

"Ma says that in town grown women don't let their hair hang down," Aee said, forgetting she had never seen Maggie's done up.

Maggie looked stricken. "I do. I'm a grown woman —"

"Of course, Maggie. But yo're different."

"How am I different? I don't want t' be different."

"Well . . . I mean that yo're so . . . pretty."

"Ya are too. I don't want to be prettier'n ya are," Maggie said in a small sad voice.

"A'right. Bee, let's let our hair hang down too."

"What'll Ma say?"

"I don't think she'll mind . . . this one time."

When the girls came out of the room and lined up for inspection, Maggie stood beside Aee. Mrs. MacMillan looked at each one carefully, then smiled.

"My, my, my. I don't know when I've seen prettier girls. Cee's dress fits you perfectly, Maggie."

"I had a dress like this a long time ago when we lived in Kaintuck. A lady there showed me how to do this." She spread the skirt with her hands and bent her knees in a quick bow.

"That's very nice."

"Let's go show Light and Eli and Paul." Maggie took Eee's small hand in hers and pulled her toward the door.

That damn Swede's eyes will pop right out when he sees her! The thought leaped into Aee's mind as she heard the sound of galloping horses come into the yard.

Neither MacMillan nor his wife had been able

to persuade their Osage friends to leave their ponies in the corral behind the barn. Owning a horse was an indication of a man's importance. They wanted to show off for the white men. Many Spots and his warriors left their horses beside the door of the cabin.

"We come to eat."

"You are always welcome."

"We hear big noise. Zee make big magic for Mac's son."

MacMillan scratched his chin to hide his smile when he looked down at Zee.

"My son is fortunate that Zee is our friend."

"He will need much magic to grow strong," Zee said solemnly, his unblinking eye on Many Spots.

Light's dark, serious eyes went from the little man to the homesteader. The two of them knew better than to scoff at the beliefs of the Osage. Light was aware that he was a long way removed from his mother's people. His father, Pierre Baptiste, had loved his mother fiercely and he, like MacMillan, had been tolerant of her people's primitive beliefs.

When Light was born, his mother had told him, he was so small that he could be held in one of his father's hands. His grandmother had been alarmed that he had such a light body and worried that he might not live. She had placed the afterbirth in a bag and hung it in the branches of an oak tree to ensure that the frail babe would grow strong. The infant thrived. His mother had named him Baptiste Lightbody.

It was a good name for a man, Light thought now. His father had lived to see his son grow into a man and had taken pride in him even though they were vastly different. Pierre Baptiste had been a big, burly man with a golden beard; his son was slim and dark.

Light's wandering thoughts came back to the present when MacMillan, speaking in Osage, asked Many Spots and his warriors to tie their ponies to the trees at the edge of the woods because Mrs. Mac was going to bring the newborn to the table and the horses drew flies.

Very diplomatic, Light thought. MacMillan was a good man. He liked the way he treated the Negroes and the little deformed Zee. MacMillan respected the Osage and they him.

If not for his burning desire to live on his mountain, Light thought now, he would be tempted to find a place a few miles from here and build his home. But, no. Using the river as a road to the west, people would soon fill the country and he would become restless as he had back in St. Charles.

Maggie and the girls came out of the cabin, each carrying a dish to the table. Maggie set hers down and hurried to Light. She grabbed her skirt in her two hands and curtsied as she had for Mrs. MacMillan. A happy smile covered her beautiful face.

"*Ma petite!* You are magnificent!" Light's eyes were alight with love. He had never seen her with a ribbon in her hair or in a dress with a white collar. She was lovely, but to him she was never more beautiful than when she was striding along beside him in the woods wearing her buckskin britches with her bow and whip on her shoulders.

"See my ribbon." She whirled around with a happy laugh. "Look at Aee, Light. Ain't she pretty?" Maggie grasped Aee's hand and pulled her to where Light stood with his back to the cabin wall.

Aee's face turned a rosy red and she tried to pull her hand away. The Swede had stopped talking — for once — and was leering at Maggie.

"*Mademoiselle.*" Light made a courtly bow, and Maggie giggled.

"Bee," she called. "Come show Light."

Bee acted as if she hadn't heard Maggie call and hurried into the house.

Watching, Eli wondered once again at Maggie's naiveté. It was so rare for a woman to be so beautiful, rarer yet for one to be so open and honest. The women he had known, including Orah Delle Carroll, Sloan's daughter, kept their feelings carefully concealed. Such open pleasure as Maggie was exhibiting would be unthinkable among women who had been tutored to behave in ways considered proper.

Eli's eyes rested on Aee. It pleased him that she knew he was looking at her and was bothered by it. She stood a head taller than Maggie yet her body was slender and strong as a willow

278

switch. She was plainly uncomfortable, but she had not scurried away as her sister had done. Her eyes had passed over *him* as if he weren't there.

Since she had hit him with her hat, Aee had completely ignored him except for the one scathing remark she had made after her brother was born. Eli chuckled. She was a woman who would be able to take care of herself in most situations and would stand shoulder to shoulder with her man. She was also a mouthy, opinionated *brat*. But with her hair hanging in heavy brown waves down to her waist, she was a mighty pretty one.

Maggie left Light's side and went to the Indian ponies. Alarmed, Eli stood. He darted a glance at Light, thinking the man would surely go to her, but Light was calmly watching her rub the noses and whisper in the ears of the half-wild ponies. She patted the sides of their heads, her nose next to their noses. The braves squatting beside the cabin wall watched and muttered to each other.

"What the hell!" Eli started to cross the yard toward her. Light stepped into his path.

"Leave her be."

"For crissake! They'd take half her face with one bite!"

"Leave her be!" Light commanded in a low, icy voice.

"I . . . don't understand you!"

Light looked at him then. His black eyes were hard.

279

"No, you don't understand me . . . or my wife. Keep your distance."

The two men glared at each other, then Light felt a small hand in his and looked down at Maggie. She had not heard the words that passed between them. She was smiling.

Squatting on his heels beside Zee's chair, Paul watched the exchange between Eli and Light and held his breath. It was important that his friend's interest be directed away from Maggie Lightbody, or her husband would kill him.

MacMillan's oldest daughter Aee was pretty — in a way different from Maggie and far more suitable for Eli. Mac had figured it right when he said they struck sparks off each other. It was a heck of a lot better that they go head-to-head than be indifferent. The idea Paul had been mulling over in his mind began to take form.

The table looked as if it were set for a Thanksgiving feast. The women stood by while the men heaped their plates and retired to the woodpile to sit on stumps and eat. Aee made up a plate for Zee. MacMillan carried Zee, chair and all, to where the men were eating. Many Spots and his braves, not at all bashful about helping themselves, took large helpings of meat, but little else. Aee and Bee filled plates for the younger girls and then for their mother, who sat at the end of the table with Frank in her lap.

Caleb and Linus were hanging back pretending to cut meat from the haunch over the fire.

"Caleb, what'er ya and Linus lollygaggin' around for? Ya'll not get any a that goose if ya don't come on. My goodness, ya know better'n to hold back when the Osage are here. They'll clean this table down to the boards in no time a'tall."

"Yass'm, Missy Aee. We comin'." Caleb pushed Linus ahead of him and they came to the table.

"Take plenty, but save room for the pumpkin cake."

Aee went to the fire to pour tea into a mug from a large pot.

Linton Bodkin set his plate down and hurried to her.

"Ma'am, can I hep ya do that?"

"Thank ya, Mr. Bodkin. If ya take this t' Zee" — she looked directly at Eli — "ever'body else can wait on themselves."

Plates were filled and filled again. Aee cut the pumpkin and suet cake and covered the remaining food with a cloth to protect it from the flies.

To Maggie's delight, MacMillan went into the cabin and came out with a fiddle. He tucked it beneath his chin and played a merry tune.

"A'right, girls. Show 'em how ya can dance."

"Ah . . . Pa —" Bee protested, but Cee took her hand and pulled her into the yard. The two youngest MacMillans joined hands, and when the music started, they galloped around the yard. Bee and Cee began to dance, their full skirts swishing about their ankles, long dark hair swaying on their backs.

281

Zee clapped his hands in time with the music. First Bodkin, then Paul, Eli and Dixon joined. Maggie stood and clapped with the others.

When MacMillan finished the tune, he beamed at his daughters.

"Ain't they the beatin'est? Been dancin' since they could walk. Come dance with 'em."

Bodkin reached for Cee. "I got a sister back home 'bout yore age."

Dixon stepped shyly toward Bee. She took his hand, but didn't look at him.

"Want t' dance?" Four-year-old Eee asked Paul.

Paul made a courtly bow. "*Mademoiselle*, I would be honored."

"Ya get t' dance with me, Mr. Nielson." Dee gave Eli a smile that showed two missing front teeth.

"I was just about to ask."

MacMillan began to fiddle. The song was "Yankee Doodle." As the couples whirled around the yard, Maggie stood beside Light, clapping her hands. Light knew she wanted to dance, but he couldn't bring himself to take her hand and join the others. He had never danced, never wanted to, and would feel foolish doing so. But he wanted Maggie to enjoy herself.

"Dance with Paul, *chérie*," Light said when the music ended and the couples changed partners.

"Ya ain't carin' if I dance?"

"No, my pet."

Light stood by quietly while Maggie danced

with Paul. To him her laughter was sweeter than the sound of the fiddle. Her head was thrown back, her mouth open as she gasped for breath. He loved her so much that he was tempted to reach out and snatch her back to him.

The dance was long; and when it was over, the exhausted dancers sank down to rest. Maggie came to Light. He put his arm around her and pulled her down to sit beside him on the ground.

The merriment went on. Bodkin asked Light's permission to dance with Maggie. She danced with Paul again. Eli did not come near, nor did he dance again. After a while Aee played the fiddle and MacMillan danced with his daughters.

In late afternoon when Many Spots and his warriors left to return to their encampment, MacMillan sent the chief a small sack of the tobacco Eli had given him. After they mounted their ponies, each warrior rode past Maggie and dropped the feathers that had been entwined in his pony's forelock.

Maggie picked up each feather and stuck it in her hair, then looked at Light with a question in her eyes.

"They honor you, pet."

"Why?"

"They think you're magic, as I do."

After the table was cleared and carried back into the cabin, MacMillan took Bodkin and Dixon to the shed to show them his potash works. As soon as the men disappeared around the corner of the house, Paul turned to Eli.

"Have you spoken to them about signing on to go to the Bluffs?"

"Not yet."

"You'd better get to doin' it, *mon ami*. Another day and Mac will be chopping down trees for their cabins."

Eli snorted. "Bodkin can't take his eyes off Aee, and Dixon looks like a dying calf when Bee is around. What chance do we have of getting them to sign on?"

"You won't know till you try, *mon ami*."

"I've been thinking that maybe MacMillan will help us hire some of the Osage, and we may be able to persuade Light to go along as interpreter —"

"— He won't."

"How do you know? Does he plan to spend the winter here?"

"He hasn't said."

"Mista Eli!" Linus came running toward the homestead. "Mista Eli!"

Eli stood. "What the hell's the matter now?"

Linus was gasping for breath when he reached them. All he was able to say was: "Yo . . . boat! Yo . . . boat!"

It was enough. Eli took off on a full run. In three minutes he was at the creek. He came bounding around the rhododendron bushes to the willows where the flatboat had been tied. It was not there, but the top of the shed and the mast were visible in the middle of the creek.

284

Eli swore. "Son of a bitch!"

"What? What — Ah . . . *mon Dieu!*" Paul exclaimed, breathing hard from the run.

"The cargo is ruined."

"All but what we stowed in MacMillan's caves."

"I'll kill him!" The name of the culprit was unspoken, but both knew who was responsible.

"Can it be fixed?"

"No way a knowin' that . . . yet."

"The bastard busted the hell out of it."

Caleb arrived with Zee riding astride his neck. MacMillan, moving fast for a man his size, was not far behind. They all stood on the creek bank surveying all that was visible of the flatboat.

"Lawsy, lawsy, mercy me." Caleb shook his head. "I's jist down here dis mornin'. It all right then."

"Paul and I were here before dinner. Washed and changed shirts," Eli said.

"Gawdamighty!" This came from Bodkin. "Did the crazy German do that?"

"It had to be *him*," Paul said. "He knew just where to put the holes to sink it."

"It's a damn shame is what it is." MacMillan walked to the edge of the bank. "We'll bring down the oxen and pull it out. It'll take some shovelin' to cut down this bank and make a ramp."

"I've no money to pay. I put it all in the cargo."

"I ain't heard nobody askin' for pay."

Eli swore again. "I should have shot the bastard when I had the chance."

285

"We can get the boat out and on blocks, but I don't know 'bout fixin' it," MacMillan said. "I ain't no carpenter. 'Course Linus can fix most things."

"I ain't worked on boats much 'cepts here, Mista Mac."

"Noah and I worked on a few down at Natchez," Bodkin said.

"Guess all that tobacco is ruined," MacMillan said wistfully. "For that alone, I could roast him over a slow fire."

"He's gone now. After what he's done, he'll get downriver as fast as he can. He knows if I lay eyes on him, I'll kill him."

CHAPTER NINETEEN

Light watched a formation of geese, their long necks stretched in flight, following their leader to the feeding grounds downriver. Flight after flight of the migrating birds had passed over the homestead the last few days on their way south. It reminded him that time was getting short and that soon, very soon, he would have to make a place for him and Maggie to spend the winter.

The effort of every man at the homestead was needed to get Eli's boat out of the creek, not only so that he could assess the damage, but also to allow MacMillan's boat passage down the creek to the river. The first day the men toiled from daylight to dark with shovels and makeshift tools, scraping down the bank and making a ramp of the slick mud.

Tired and dirty, they trudged up the path to the cabin. Aee came out with a pail of warm water for them to wash in. Eli noticed that she had taken to wearing a dress instead of the duck pants.

"I suppose this tickles you plumb to death," he said, when Aee snatched the wet towel from the nail above the outdoor wash bench and hung a dry one.

" 'Bout yore boat? Why'd I be glad a that? It's a sorrowful thin'. It's a doggone shame is what it is." Her dark brows came together and a woeful look came over her face. "I was hopin' ya'd be on the dad-blasted thin' and be gone from here by now."

"Mac invited me to spend the winter. I'm thinking on it." Eli grinned at her cockily, turned and splashed water on his face by scooping it in his two hands. He groped for the towel. When one was thrust into his hand, he brought it to his face. It was wet and gritty with dirt. He opened an eye to see Aee, with the clean towel over her shoulder, retreating into the cabin.

Confounded woman. Always had to have the last word!

Supper over, the men went to the yard. The women sat down to eat and then cleared the table. Light was glad to see Maggie pitching in to help. He had come to realize that since Maggie's parents had not required her to do anything about the house, it was good for her to be with the Mac-Millans where even the smallest child had a chore to do.

The next afternoon Caleb brought the oxen to the creek. Paul and Eli waded out to the boat and attached the ropes. When all was ready, every man, with the exception of MacMillan, who would drive the oxen, waded out to lend his weight against a pole. The flatboat moved sluggishly, creaked and shuddered. Every foot of upward progress was gained only by the constant, exhausting struggle of oxen and men.

When the flatboat was finally in position to slide up the mud-slick ramp, the men and oxen stopped to rest. Pine boughs were cut and laid to give the oxen footing when the struggling began again.

By sundown the boat was at last on solid ground and Eli could assess the damage. Boards had been pried loose both in front and back of the shed, which accounted for the quick sinking of the craft. The steering oar as well as the tools were missing and presumed to have been thrown overboard. The sacks of tobacco had been ripped open, the flour and whiskey barrels broken. It was unnecessary destruction because the flour, tobacco, salt and lard would all have been ruined anyway by the water. The whiskey would have been diluted with creek water, but not completely ruined. A keg of hand-forged nails, too heavy even for Kruger to heave over the side, had been tipped over.

Tools were precious items in the wilderness. They often meant the difference between life and death. The hatchets, hammers, saws, hewing tools, adzes of all sizes, augers, chisel tools, draw knives and planes all lay in the bottom of the creek. With these tools a man could build almost anything.

Bolts of printed cloth, bought from a store in St. Louis at a high price, were soggy and dirty. MacMillan said his womenfolk would wash the fabric so that it would not be a total loss.

"They are welcome to have it," Eli said.

As darkness approached, Eli wet and weary, carried the yard goods from the boat up the path to the cabin and dropped them on the ground outside the door. He looked so tired and so discouraged that Aee avoided him because there would be no pleasure in needling him.

The day had been long and miserable. The men washed in the buckets of warm water the women had carried to the sickroom. MacMillan provided dry clothing for those who didn't have it. When supper was over all sought their beds.

Maggie and Light, for the last few nights, after refusing to accept the offer by Caleb and Linus of their small cabin behind the potash works, had bedded down in the barn. They spread their blankets on the pile of grass cuttings and were grateful to be alone.

"Are ya warm enough, Light?" Maggie pulled the blanket up over his shoulders and fitted her body against his. He had been wet up to the waist when he came up from the creek.

"How can I not be, my treasure, with you in my arms?"

"I don't want ya to get sick."

"Don't worry. There is something I want to talk over with you."

"Something bad?" Maggie lifted her head from his shoulder. He moved his hand to press it down again.

"We need to make a place for ourselves for the winter. I had thought to ask Caleb to come with us and travel another hundred miles or so toward our mountain, but I don't wish to risk it in winter. I think we should move a few miles upriver and build a shelter. In the spring we will continue our journey."

"I go where you go, Light. I like it here, but this is not *our* home."

"Sweet wife." Light's arms tightened and he kissed the lips she offered.

"When do we go?"

"Soon. Tomorrow I'll help get the tools from the bottom of the creek. The next day I want to go to the Osage camp and tell the chief that I plan to winter here. They are my mother's people."

"Should I go with ya?"

"It would be better if you stayed here, pet."

"How long will ya be gone?"

"For a day and no more."

"I'll do what ya say, Light." Maggie's small caressing hand moved over his chest and down his flat belly. "Do ya want me, Light? I no longer have my woman's time."

Light drew a shuddering breath and turned to her.

"Want you, *chérie?* I shall want you till my dying day, or until I'm old and gray, whichever comes first."

"We'll be on our mountain, Light, when this turns gray." She tugged at the rope of hair tied behind his neck with a thong.

"You've not been sorry, *ma petite,* that you came with me? This is not an easy life." His fingers stroked her cheek.

"I'm not one bit sorry. I never want to go back."

Light rolled her onto her back and looked down into her face. It was pale and beautiful and smiling. Her breath was warm and sweet on his face. The soft utterance that came from her throat was an invitation he could not resist. Slowly, deliberately, he covered her mouth with his, pressing gently at first, then firmly with an urgency that sought deeper satisfaction.

The passion of this small woman excited him to immediate readiness.

"Ahhh . . . *mon amour —*"

The day dawned warm, windless and sunny. While Bee and the younger girls helped their mother shell corn to grind into meal, Aee and Maggie washed the yards of soggy cloth from Eli's boat.

At a bend in the creek above the homestead, MacMillan had built a log platform for the women to step onto when they dipped water from the clear pool to fill the iron wash pot. It was easier work than pulling the heavy buckets of water up from the deep well in the yard.

Now with the fire heating the water in the three-legged kettle and a wooden tub filled with rinse water, Aee and Maggie played with a lash, one sometimes used to drive the oxen.

Aee, aiming at a twig hanging from a branch, flipped the whip forward. The lash wrapped around the branch.

"Shoot!"

"When ya do that, the whip can be taken away from ya," Maggie said patiently as she unwound the leather from the branch. "Light says to give yore wrist a little jerk till ya learn how far the end will go. If it gets wrapped 'round somethin', there ain't no drawin' it back."

"I'll never be as good at it as ya are," Aee moaned.

"Ya will too. The leather on that whip is wider an' heavier'n mine. Try it again, Aee."

Aee threw the strip of leather back over her shoulder and stared at the twig she had missed before.

"I'm goin' t' think a that twig as the Swede's rear end."

Maggie laughed, then sobered and asked, "Why ain't ya likin' Eli? He give ya all that cloth."

"He's a palaverer an' a flummadiddler an' ain't fit to shoot!"

"Why'er ya sayin' that for? He is too fit to shoot!"

"Well, I ain't takin' no present from *him*. I'll wash his old cloth, dry it, and roll it up. Then I'm goin' t' poke it at him an' tell him t' give it t' the first married woman that catches his eye. I don't want it."

"Why don't ya want it? It'll make dresses for

yore sisters an' yore ma. He wants ya t' have it. 'Sides, Aee, there ain't no married women here but me an' yore ma."

Aee looked at the other girl and shook her head. At times Maggie was so *dumb*. She had no idea that Eli was smitten with her. But Light knew it; and if the stupid Swede didn't keep his eyes off her, there was going to be trouble.

"I'm not takin' anythin' from that struttin' rooster, an' that's that."

Maggie giggled and Aee joined her. One of the things Aee liked about Maggie was that her mood changed lightning fast. If she was angry it never lasted long.

"Go ahead. Think the twig's Eli's backside an' see if ya can hit it."

The whip came forward and again wrapped around the branch.

"Flitter-flatter!" Aee threw the whip down. "Missed the Swede's butt again!"

Maggie broke into peals of laughter.

"It's that heavy old whip, Aee. I'll get mine an' be back." Maggie darted away through the woods toward the homestead.

The past week had been one of the most exciting in Aee's life. She had not known white girls her age other than her sisters. Meeting Maggie had been a new experience. Aee didn't think, from what she had read, that married women were supposed to act the way Maggie did.

It was hard for her to consider Maggie a married lady. Married ladies wore dresses, cooked, gardened and had babies. They didn't go around using whips, throwing knives and talking to animals. The doll-like woman was going with her man into the wilderness where no other white woman had gone. Her husband adored her, Aee thought dreamily. It was plain that she loved him too. When he was near, her eyes were constantly going to him.

It's hard not to be envious, Aee thought now as she dipped lye soap from a crock into the iron pot. She wondered how it would be to be so close to a man that you shared his thoughts, his hopes, his dreams, and were willing to do whatever it took to make him happy.

It came without warning.

As she was putting the wooden lid on the soap crock, a rough hand covered her mouth and she was jerked off her feet.

Aee was so totally surprised that she didn't fight back for a minute or more. By that time she was in the sumac bushes that lined the clearing and was being dragged backward toward the creek. She was a strong woman; and when she began to struggle, it was difficult for her attacker to hold her. She dug in her heels and swung one fist upward, hitting only the arm that was dragging her. She jabbed with her elbow and hit a vulnerable place on the man's body. He grunted with pain and dropped her.

She was on her feet in an instant, whirled to face her assailant, and opened her mouth to yell. Only a squeak of a sound came out before a ham-like fist struck her in the face and knocked her off her feet.

A shower of stars flashed before Aee's eyes as she fell into a pit of darkness.

Still giggling over Aee's reference to the twig as Eli's rear end, Maggie ran to the homestead, darted into the shed where Light had left their packs, and picked up her whip. She coiled it, looped it over her shoulder and tucked the handle in the belt around her waist.

Maggie wished that Aee liked Eli as much as she did. He was unhappy and frowning most of the time, but that was because he was troubled about something besides Kruger sinking his boat. He had growled at her when she asked him why he watched Light and told her to tend her own business when she got after him for teasing Aee. Maybe he liked Aee. The only times he laughed were when he was teasing her.

With her pet chicken under her arm, Eee came toward Maggie as she left the shed.

" 'Lo, Miz Lightbody. What ya doin'?"

"I'm helpin' Aee wash."

"Want to hold Chicken?"

"Shore. What's her name?" Maggie dropped down on her knees and took the docile bird. It settled in Maggie's arms and closed its eyes.

"Chicken." Eee stroked the red comb on the top of the chicken's head.

"It's a good name. I had a dog once named Dog."

"Dog? I couldn't name her Dog 'cause she's a chicken."

Maggie returned her pet to Eee and stood. "I got t'help Aee."

"Can I come?"

"If yore ma says ya can."

"She won't let me. I got to hold the meal bag . . . and I don't want to."

"But ya got to mind yore ma. I'll be back when we get the washin' done, and we'll play a game of blind-man's bluff. Won't that be fun?"

"I guess so," Eee said begrudgingly.

Maggie ran through the woods toward the creek singin' one of her favorite ditties.

> Yan-kee Doo-dle is the tune
> Amer-i-cans de-light in;
> 'Twill do to whis-tle, sing or play,
> And just the thin' for fight-in'.

"Aee, Eee was wantin' t' come, but —"

Something was wrong. Aee wasn't there — and the crock of soap was tipped over. Instantly alert, Maggie stood as still as a doe. Then she heard a sound unrelated to the sounds of the woods — a muffled sound. Quickly, and as quietly as a darting wood mouse, she was through the sumac and into the clearing beside the creek.

There was Aee lying still as death on the ground! And Kruger was on his knees, pulling her skirt up around her waist. So intent was he on what he was doing that he hadn't heard Maggie enter the clearing.

"Get way from her!" The words burst from Maggie's mouth in a shrill scream.

Kruger jumped to his feet and turned to face her.

"I vas comin' for ya."

Maggie could see the craziness in his eyes. She took a deep breath, put her two fingers in her mouth and whistled two long loud blasts.

"*Verdammt!* Stop dat!"

Maggie jerked the whip from her shoulder and shagged it back when he took a step toward her. Her eyes never left his face.

The German watched her with an amused smile. The chance to get her had come sooner than he had thought. He had been watching since the two women had come to the creek and built a fire under the pot. When Maggie had left he had decided to take his pleasure with the other one until she got back, then he would take her away with him.

"Foolish voman," he muttered. "Ya tink to hold me off vit' dat silly vhip?"

The first blow answered his question. The tip of the lash caught him across the face, cutting a gash in his cheek, laying the flesh open to the bone. He stopped in his tracks and grabbed at his face.

"Ohhh . . . ow! Gott damn!"

Wild with fury, Maggie shagged the lash backward and with all her strength brought the thin strip of leather down on the arm he had thrown up to protect his face. He was bleeding where the forked tip had taken away skin. He let out another helpless bleat of rage, tried to catch the punishing strip of leather and discovered it was like trying to snare a striking rattlesnake.

Maggie went after him with a vengeance. Again and again, she cast, catching him on the ear, the shoulder, the neck. Flesh and blood flew. He backpedaled.

The only weapons Maggie had to use against this crazed man who outweighed her by more than a hundred pounds were the whip and her powerful voice. She used both. While she stalked him, she took another deep breath.

"Y-oo-al-al-al-ee. Y-oo-al-al-al-ee. Y-oo-al-al-al-ee!" The yodeling cry resounded throughout the woods.

"I kill dat breed, he come —"

Kruger managed to get the knife from the back of his belt. When he brought it forward, she opened the back of his hand and he dropped it before he could use it. He bellowed with rage and stooped to pick it up. Maggie's whip ripped open his shirt from shoulder to waist, drawing a long bloody line across his bared back.

She was tiring. She allowed the whip to wrap around his arm once, but jerked it away before he could grab it. Another mistake like that and the whipping would be over.

Otto Kruger was like a wild man. The blood that ran down his face mixed with the froth from his mouth. He roared with rage, but he did not retreat. Taking the lash full in the face, he threw out his arms and lunged at her.

"Drop, Maggie." Light's commanding voice came from behind her.

Kruger was only a few feet from her when she threw herself to the ground. Light's knife sailed over her, sure and swift. Kruger staggered back, stumbled over his feet and fell.

"She *meine* . . . voman —" They were his last words as blood gushed from his mouth.

Light stood over Kruger until he was sure he was dead. Then he knelt beside Maggie and took her in his arms.

"Mon trésor! Mon amour!" His voice was hoarse with worry.

"Ya killed him, didn't ya? I knew ya'd come."

"I killed him. I'll always come when you call, my sweet pet."

"Aee! He hurt Aee." Maggie turned her head to look around.

Eli, breathing hard, burst into the clearing. His eyes passed over Kruger lying on his back, Light's knife in his chest. Then he rushed to where Aee lay unconscious on the ground, her white limbs exposed.

"Godamighty!" He pulled her skirt down over her thighs. "What did that crazy bastard do to her?" he demanded of no one in particular.

She looked so . . . defenseless lying there. She was no longer the proud, lippy woman, but a young, pretty girl who had been overpowered by the German's superior strength. Eli turned

Aee's head. He could see that her cheek had been cut and bruised, and her lips were swollen and bleeding. He cursed again. *The bastard had hit her in the face with his fist.*

Then fear of something even worse than the blow came to his mind. Without hesitation he flipped up her skirt. Her underclothing had not been disturbed. *Thank God! He had not raped her.* Eli quickly covered her thighs again as her father and Paul arrived.

Aee was revived with a cloth dipped in the cold creek water. She sat up and stared dazedly about. What was the Swede doing there? He looked worried and was supporting her with an arm around her back.

"Don't try to get up just yet. He hit you pretty hard." Eli took the wet cloth from Paul and gently wiped the blood from her face.

"Where . . . is he?"

"In hell where he should have been sent days ago," Eli said passionately. "It's my fault, Aee. I saw him the day of the celebration and let him go. And I was sure he had gone downriver after he busted up my boat."

"Maggie?"

"She's all right."

In the safe haven of Light's arms, Maggie told him what had happened. The marks on Kruger's body spoke of the vicious fight the small woman had waged against the crazed man.

"If he'd caught the whip, I was goin' t' throw the knife."

"You did right, my treasure." Light gently brushed the hair back from her forehead and placed his lips there.

He was proud of her. She had dropped to the ground the instant he spoke so that he could throw his knife. But now, reaction had set in, and he trembled at the thought of the danger she had been in.

Maggie touched Light's cheek with her fingertips. "I knew ya'd come," she said again.

After making sure that Aee was all right, MacMillan squatted down beside Light and Maggie.

"Yore little woman shore knows how to use that whip," MacMillan said. "She held him off till ya could get here. Ma'am, I ain't never seen nobody move so fast as yore man did when he heard ya whistle. One minute he was there, next he was off like a shot. We knowed somethin' was wrong. It was like tryin' to follow a scalded cat. We couldn't keep up. Then we heared ya yodel. I ain't never heared nothin' like it."

"Is Aee all right?"

"She's got a busted lip. She don't seemed t' be hurt none, but she'll be mad as a hornet."

Maggie leaned up and put her lips close to MacMillan's ear.

"He . . . was goin' t' get in her . . . drawers. But he didn't —"

MacMillan was startled by the frank words. Then he nodded.

"I thank God for it. And ya too, ma'am, for savin' her."

CHAPTER TWENTY

"I ain't goin' to just walk off and leave the cloth in the washpot," Aee protested.

"To hell with the cloth!" Eli held her elbow securely in his hand and walked her back to the cabin. Then he stood by while her mother and sisters fussed over her.

With a wet cloth held to her face, more to hide it from the Swede and the rivermen than to ease the ache, Aee listened to her father telling her mother what had happened.

"Miz Lightbody whistled, then lashed 'im with the whip. Lightbody heared that whistle an' took off like a scalded cat. Little woman's got a powerful voice. Did ya hear that racket she made?"

"It was *odle, odle, odle,* Pa," Dee said. "Reckon I could learn it?"

"I bet ya could, sis." MacMillan pulled his second youngest daughter up onto his knee. "Why don't ya ask Miz Lightbody t' show ya how."

At Mrs. MacMillan's suggestion Dixon went with Bee and Cee to the creek to finish washing the cloth. The girls were leery of going there alone so soon after Aee had been attacked. Bodkin stayed at the homestead and turned the crank on the corn grinder for Mrs. MacMillan, who was still weak from giving birth. It brought to Eli's mind how readily the two rivermen had been accepted by the MacMillans.

Did Bodkin think he'd have a chance with Aee if he got in good with her mother? Eli scoffed at the thought of the two of them together. MacMillan's eldest daughter needed a firmer hand than the riverman would give her, and Eli decided to tell MacMillan so at the first opportunity. She would be miserable with a bumpkin like Bodkin.

As the thought came into Eli's head, he realized he had made a rhyme. Bumpkin Bodkin. A chuckle bubbled up and he glanced at Aee. She was looking at him. Their eyes met; she lifted her chin and stared at him defiantly. *Hell and high-water! He'd done it now. She thought he was laughing at her!*

The rest of the day was spent in almost awed silence.

Aee's and Maggie's narrow escape from the madman had shaken everyone at the homestead, even little Eee, who cried when she saw her sister's face. All felt relief knowing that the mad German was dead.

"God was with us this day," MacMillan declared as he and Paul left to dig a grave for Kruger.

They each took an arm and dragged the body to the knoll where the other rivermen had been buried. The soil was soft and the digging easy. They had almost finished when Many Spots and two of his warriors rode in to speak to MacMillan.

"How do, Mac."

"How do, Many Spots." The two men shook hands.

"Downriver we find big boom gun."

"How big?"

"This big." Many Spots curled his hands to form a large circle.

"A cannon?"

"Big," he said again, shrugged, and looked down at the dead man. "Who kill?"

"Sharp Knife."

"No Hair," the Indian said with disgust.

"Reckon he warn't worthy of hair."

"That is so. Where Sharp Knife go?"

"He went to look for the canoe this one came in."

"He will find it." Many Spots looked at Kruger's body with disgust. "Scalp with no hair! Nothing to hang on belt."

"It's a shame," Mac agreed dryly. "Seen any sign of Delaware?"

"Delaware go that way." Many Spots pointed across the river toward the south.

"That is good."

"This many canoe comin'." He held up two fingers. "Three, four days upriver."

"Trappers?"

"Bring furs and bear oil."

Having said all he had to say, Many Spots motioned to his warriors and they rode away.

Paul watched him leave, then turned to Mac-Millan.

"How does he know that? He's been *down* river."

MacMillan scratched his head. "Beats me. He may know the canoe carries bear oil because of the kind a canoe it is. When the dugout is made, two partitions are left in the middle. They pour bear oil in the center compartment. A skin is drawn tight over the top. Bear oil sells good in St. Louis."

Paul threw out a few more shovelfuls of dirt while he absorbed this information. When he thought the grave deep enough, he climbed out.

"Well, guess we know what the big noise was." MacMillan stuck his shovel in the pile of dirt beside the grave.

"Vega's boat blew up."

"Reckon Kruger did it?"

"It's sure we won't find out from him, *m'sieur*."

"Wonder where he stashed the canoe."

"Light will find it. He took Caleb and Maggie with him."

"Don't reckon he'll let her out of his sight fer a spell. She's got more guts than some men I knowed. She could'a run off, but she stayed an' fought the bugger. Kept him off my girl."

"She's a different kind a woman, *m'sieur*. I've never seen two people that were more suited to one another than she and Light. *Mon Dieu*, this bastard's heavy."

Not too gently, Paul and Mac lifted the body and placed Kruger in his final resting place. Mac-Millan looked down. Kruger's dead eyes stared up at him. He was a man far from home, being placed in a lonely grave with no one to grieve for him. But there was no pity in MacMillan's heart.

"Open wide ye gates a hell, yore son is comin' home."

"Very poetic." The homesteader's words were a surprise to Paul.

MacMillan grinned. "Read that some'rs."

The grave was filled quickly. When they were finished, Paul pulled his pipe and tobacco from his pocket, packed the bowl and offered the sack to MacMillan.

"Eli thinks Kruger may have filled his canoe from the boat before he sunk it."

"It's what I'd a done."

"What do ya think of my friend Eli, *m'sieur?*"

"Well . . . he's a moody feller. Can't say as I got anythin' against him. But I'm thinkin' he's got somethin' against Lightbody. Two of 'em don't talk much."

"It's nothing that won't be worked out . . . in time."

"Is it the woman?"

"He's worried about Light takin' her off into the wilderness all by himself."

"If anybody can take care a her, he can. I'd hate to be the one to try and keep her from goin' with him. 'Sides, a man ain't got no business

307

gettin' 'tween a man an' his woman."

"Eli knows that. I've known him since he was a lonely skinny lad working on the docks for a pence to give his ma. Grew up to be a good man. Honest and hard-working. I'd trust him with my life — and have many times."

MacMillan took his pipe from his mouth. "What'er ya singin' his praises for, Paul?"

"Am I doing that?" Paul chuckled, then answered his own question. "Guess I am. Eli's like a son . . . well, more like a brother. I'm not old enough to have sired him."

"It's plain ya want me t' think well of 'im."

"I do. 'Cause I'm thinking he's kind of sweet on your girl." Paul looked away and drew on his pipe.

"Aee? He's wastin' his time. She don't like 'im."

"Women act like that sometime," Paul said, as if he'd had vast experience with women.

"Like they don't like 'em when they do?"

"I got five sisters," Paul lied. "A woman is afraid a man won't return her affection so at times she acts as if she can't stand the sight of him."

"Hmm." MacMillan puffed on his pipe. "When any one of my girls takes a man, he'll be one she chooses."

"Be sure it's a good man, *m'sieur*. They're fine girls."

Paul and MacMillan went downriver to find out what they could about the big *boom* gun, as Many Spots described it. They had no trouble finding the site. The smell of rotting flesh would have led them to it even if they had not seen the circling scavengers and the iron barrel amid the charred rubble. Paul wondered why Many Spots had not mentioned the carnage.

They beached their canoe and walked along the sandbar strewn with charred debris. A small section of trees and brush along the riverbank had also burned. The pieces of bodies thrown out of reach of the fire were causing the stench and attracting the scavengers that had been picking and gnawing on the body parts.

"Mother a Christ!" MacMillan muttered when they passed part of a head with a few blond hairs attached to it.

Fish or crabs had nibbled on part of a torso that lay half in, half out of the water. A gold watch chain was hooked in the vest buttonhole. Paul turned away.

"We . . . should bury them, *m'sieur*."

"It would be the decent thin' t' do. Thin' is, I ain't sure I'm that decent."

"At least . . . the women —"

"— If we find somethin' to dig with."

In the middle of the afternoon, Light, Maggie and Caleb returned with Kruger's canoe. Caleb had suggested that the German might have gone upriver where the bank was high and several rock formations hung over the water. When they came to a place where the reeds were bent down, Light turned in. The canoe had been well hidden.

Caleb paddled the light birch-bark canoe back to the homestead. Heavily laden, it sat low in the water, and Light didn't think it would have lasted a day in rough weather. The German had taken a bale of tobacco, a keg of whiskey and tools to build a boat.

Eli was pleased to have the tools back. He was having a difficult time finding the ones Kruger had thrown overboard before he sank the boat.

When MacMillan and Paul returned, the homesteader gave a brief description of what had happened to the Vega boat to his wife and older daughters and a more detailed account to the men. The two crewmen from Vega's boat listened in chilled silence, knowing that they had escaped being on the boat by the skin of their teeth. They were more than grateful to the man who had taken them in. Already they had decided to stay here and help MacMillan build his village.

It was agreed that later the cannon might be salvaged and brought to the homestead. There was not much likelihood of anyone's running off with it.

Light took no part in the discussion. Come morning he planned to visit the Osage camp. After that he and Maggie would choose a place to spend the winter. With skins and fur bought from the Osage, he could put up a tight, temporary shelter in a few days.

Eli, on the other hand, was very interested in what Paul and MacMillan had to say about the explosion until he learned that nothing large enough to use to repair his boat had been left. He mulled over what he could do. The quickest way to get boards would be to use the ones from the top of his shed and replace them with a canvas covering. Then what? All that was left of his cargo was a few tools, the gunpowder stowed in MacMillan's caves, the rifles, a keg of whiskey and a bale of tobacco. It was not enough to pay for a winter's lodging at the Bluffs and to buy furs to bring back in the spring.

Aee came out of the house and went to the well. Eli stood. Knowing that the conversation had stopped and the men were watching him, he went to her and took the well rope from her hand.

"Let me help you."

"Why? I ain't no mamby-pamby town-woman." Aee kept her face turned from him.

"I know that."

"I ain't no *married* woman either."

Eli pulled the bucket to the top of the well and poured the water into the one at her feet. He didn't speak until he had lowered the well-bucket and tied the rope to the crossbar. He took her arm and turned her toward him. Even in the near darkness he could see the swelling on the side of her face.

"Why do you keep harping on that?"

" 'Cause ya can't take yore eyes off *her*. That's why."

"Don't you like Maggie? Godamighty! She

fought like a wildcat to keep that crazy fool off you."

" 'Course, I like Maggie. It ain't nothin' against her."

"I'm just worried about her going off with Lightbody."

"Well now, don't that beat all! Light's her husband —"

"— He's not. He's her . . . companion."

"What do ya mean by that?"

"They're not married. Leastways not by a preacher or a magistrate."

"Is that what's it about? That don't mean doodle-dee-squat. Ma and pa didn't stand up to a preacher. There wasn't one that'd marry a white man to an Indian. But Pa loved her and knew she was right for him. They married each other in their hearts. I'm thinkin', Swede, ya ain't got no notion a'tall about what goes on in a woman's heart."

Aee bent to pick up the bucket. Eli's hand covered hers, and she dropped the pail as if it were hot.

"I'll take it to the door."

Not trusting herself to speak, Aee walked ahead of him.

The meeting at the well had not gone unnoticed by Paul. He glanced at MacMillan and saw the man watching Aee and Eli. The seed he had planted was taking root.

The Osage camp of domed huts was in an up-

312

roar when Light reached it. He was extremely glad he had not brought Maggie with him. A warrior had caught his wife under a blanket with a young brave and had cut off the end of her nose, the classic Osage punishment for adultery. The brave was to be beaten by the indignant husband until his relatives or friends came forward with presents of sufficient value to persuade the outraged man to relent.

The husband took great care with his choice of weapon. The club of chokeberry was heavy enough to strike cruel blows, but not so heavy that the brave would die too soon.

After the brave was stripped, bound and thrown to the ground, the beating commenced. Knowing the young brave would be beaten to death if no one came forward with compensation, Light realized how far removed he had become from his own people. He tried to close his ears to the sound of the club hitting flesh and the groans of pain. Although he wanted to turn away from the boy's suffering, he watched. It would not do for Sharp Knife to appear squeamish.

The beating stopped when a gray-haired old man came forward leading a spotted pony. The husband looked at the pony with disdain.

"Grandfather, why you bring this skinny beast?"

"Because it is the boy's most prized possession. He rather die than part from him. I bring so he can see one last time."

"He die without the horse?" A crafty look came

over the husband's face.

"It is so." The old man struck his chest with his fist in a gesture of grief.

"Then he will die." The husband threw down the bloody club, jerked the rope from the old man's hands and walked away with the horse.

The wise old grandfather knelt, cut the bonds holding the young brave and helped him to his feet. He was dazed and blood ran from his mouth. A young girl came from the crowd to help lead the youth away. The crowd murmured at the strange end to the punishment.

Chief Dark Cloud stepped forward and raised his hand. There was instant silence.

"It is done, grandfather. Take him away and tell him to control what is under his loincloth."

He motioned to Light and walked into the circle of domed huts. A crowd followed them, then stopped when they approached a hut of tremendous size.

"Sharp Knife! Sharp Knife! Sharp Knife." The call came from the collective voices of the people.

Light lifted his hand in a gesture of friendship, then ducked into the hut. The chief sank down on a blanket, motioned for Light to sit, then began to fill his pipe. A powerful man in his early fifties, he wore his gray-streaked hair long and unbound. He was very large with the muscular, flat-bellied body of a much younger man. His eyes were fierce in their pride.

"It is good that you have come, Sharp Knife. Much has been said about how you saved Zee."

"It was my duty as an Osage." Light accepted the pipe, drew on it and handed it back.

"That is so."

"I came to tell you that I will be staying here until spring."

"You stay with Mac?"

"I stay near him, but in my own lodge."

"You are welcome here, Sharp Knife."

"I thank you, Chief Dark Cloud, but my woman would not understand the Osage way."

"She would approve of adultery?"

"No, but neither would she approve of cutting off the woman's nose, or beating the brave. It is her white blood that makes it so."

The chief shrugged. "It is of no importance that Singing Bird does not approve."

Light was wise enough not to argue. "I will continue my journey to the mountains in the spring. I came, Chief Dark Cloud, to buy hides to cover my lodge. I have the white man's coin to pay."

"We have no need for white man's coin."

"It is all I have."

"Because of you we have Zee. You will have the hides to build your lodge."

"It is good to be an Osage." Light drew on the pipe again. "When I hunt, I will bring meat to your lodge. Should your enemies come, I will be here to fight them with you."

The chief nodded.

CHAPTER TWENTY-ONE

Light chose a place among a stand of pine for his lodge. It would be shielded from the winter wind and near the creek that flowed into the river.

Many Spots and his warriors arrived two days after Light's visit to the Osage camp. They brought not only furs and hides but the willow poles needed for the frame. Upright poles were set in the ground and arched to overlap on top where they were tied together — the lower poles being at the ends, the higher near the center. The vertical poles were then interlaced with tiers of horizontal saplings and the dome-like structure took shape. A hole was left in the top to draw smoke, and the frame was covered with mats and skins. Stones were set in the middle for a fire and furs placed on the floor for warmth.

In less than two days the lodge was finished.

Eli watched with interest as Light's winter home took shape. He and Paul had been staying in the shed on the boat. It served as a shelter, but did very little to keep out the cold. Eli and Paul had talked over the idea of taking a canoe and going downriver with the trappers who had stopped a few days back. The two rivermen had decided that everything they had in the world was here, and here it would stay until their flatboat was repaired.

Work had stopped on the flatboat until planks for the deck could be hewn from downed oak trees MacMillan had cut the year before. It would not do to use green wood on the deck because when dried it would shrink. That backbreaking work on the oak was better suited for weather colder than the present warm autumn.

Bodkin and Dixon had decided to cast their lots with MacMillan and become the first residents of his village. Eli was certain that the homesteader's two older daughters had a lot to do with the decision.

Work began on a stockade-type cabin for the two men. Eli, Caleb and Paul cut trees, trimmed them, and used the oxen to drag them to the homestead. Under MacMillan's direction, the logs were cut to the proper length and set upright in a trench. The work continued from daylight until dark and the cabin took shape rapidly.

Autumn was also a busy time of year for the MacMillan women. Pumpkins and squash were gathered; some were dried, others stored in the dugout root cellar. Beans were shucked and corn shelled. The corn that was not made into hominy was ground into cornmeal or bagged for future grinding and hung in the rafters. Some meats were smoked and others salted. Fish was caught, skinned and placed in brine. Walnuts and pecans were gathered by the younger children.

Maggie was delighted not only with her first home, but that they would be near the MacMillans for the winter. Watching his young wife, Light was grateful for the patience of the MacMillan women. Maggie was as unskilled as the youngest MacMillan child when it came to preparing food for winter and other housekeeping duties. Knowing this, Mrs. MacMillan worked with her, or gave her jobs to do with one of the older girls.

Maggie was a willing helper but she occasionally ran off to look for Light. When she found him, she would throw herself into his arms and kiss him soundly as if all she needed to know was that he was there and that he was safe.

The middle of November brought a few flakes of snow. The first pole cabin was finished. The clay in the rock fireplace had slowly dried so that a fire could be built. Linus built a table, benches and shelves for the new owners and received ample praise for his work. Bunks were attached to walls and a scraped skin was stretched over the window to afford a measure of light. Although small, it was a snug and comfortable cabin.

MacMillan suggested building another cabin some distance from Bodkin's and Dixon's and the work began. Paul and Eli could use it this winter, and later, if they did not stay, it would become part of a homestead for a settler. Eli had not committed to settling here permanently. He talked of going back downriver in the spring to try to recoup his loss. Nevertheless, he appeared to Paul to be more content than he had been in a long while. He and Aee did not snipe at each other quite so much, but there was still a coldness between him and Light. They avoided each other when possible.

The crewmen, Paul and Eli were still eating at MacMillan's table. The work they would do during the winter, MacMillan assured them, would more than pay for the food they ate. The family enjoyed the evenings. The younger children had taken to Paul, and little Eee would often climb onto his lap. The men sat before the fireplace spinning yarns while the women cleaned up after the meal. They all missed Zee. Many Spots had taken him back to the Osage.

Aee continued to ignore Eli and had managed, so far, not to be alone with him. She was, however, aware every time he looked at her, but not once did she let him catch her looking at him. Her large brown eyes passed over him as if he were a fly on the wall.

Bodkin wanted to court her. Everyone in the family knew it and often teased her about it. Even though he was clean and pleasant, compared to Eli, he was plodding and dull. Sometimes when Eli was watching, she deliberately turned her attention to young Bodkin. This brought happy smiles to the crewman's face and disapproval to Eli's. None of this went unnoticed by Paul.

One evening, feeling she could sit still no longer under Eli's watchful eyes, Aee threw her shawl about her shoulders, picked up the bucket and went out to the well. The night was still and cold, the stars bright. She breathed in the cool pine-scented air.

At the well she lowered the tin bucket and waited to hear the plop as it hit the water. Suddenly a hand reached over her shoulder and took the well rope from her grasp. Aee jumped and let out a little squeak of fright.

"Scared you, did I?" It was the Swede's voice.

"Ya sneaked up on me!"

"You've been avoiding me as if I had the plague. This is the only place I can catch you alone. And . . . I was *not* sneaking."

"Then what would ya call it?" she demanded. "Ya certainly didn't come up behind me like a herd a buffalo."

"I could have been a Delaware. You shouldn't come out here alone."

"Why not?"

"You know why not. Did you think that poor love-sick Bodkin was going to follow you and you'd have a few minutes alone in the dark with him?"

"Linton Bodkin?"

"He's the only Bodkin here," Eli said dryly.

"Well . . . what if I did? It ain't no business of yores." Aee's heart was beating so fast that she was breathless.

"He's not for you," he said crossly. "Not by a jugful!"

"Well . . . I never —" she sputtered.

"Mind what I say, Aee. Stop leading him on. He's a decent enough fellow. It's not fair to let him think he's got a chance with you."

"Leadin' . . . him . . . on? How do ya know that he don't have a chance —"

"— You're stammering, Aee." Eli chuckled. "It isn't like you. You're usually ready with a smart answer."

"I . . . I could slap ya!"

"If you do, I'll slap you back. On second thought I'd rather kiss you." He poured the water into the bucket at her feet, swung the well-bucket back and tied the rope. "Come on. Your pa knows I came out here with you. I don't want him coming out with his gun." He picked up the bucket. "Come on," he said again when her feet seemed glued to the ground. "Or do you like being here in the dark with me?"

"I'd rather be here in the dark with a . . . with a polecat!"

He laughed.

"Don't ya laugh at me, ya . . . ya mule's arse!" She headed for the cabin, her face flaming.

He laughed again. "You ever been kissed, Aee?"

"No!" she gasped.

"I'm going to kiss you someday . . . soon," he said just as she reached the cabin.

Aee pushed open the door, hurried inside and retreated to the far corner of the room. She busied herself hanging her shawl on the hook.

Unable to keep the grin off his face, Eli followed. Every eye in the room turned toward them when they entered. Eli set the water bucket on the shelf.

"I think I'll turn in. Thanks for the supper, Mrs. MacMillan."

Eli was still smiling when he went out and entered the room in the side cabin where he and Paul were staying while working on their own cabin.

Light and Maggie cooked their meals in their own lodge. Light hung deer, turkey, goose and 'coon in MacMillan's smokehouse. There was no shortage of fish, nuts and root vegetables. The days were short this time of year. Light and Maggie spent long hours in the warm cocoon of their blankets, making love and making plans for their future.

It was an ideal time for Maggie.

"Will our home on our mountain be like this?" she asked one night. Snuggled close to Light, she could just barely see the outline of his features in the red glow of the fire in the middle of their lodge.

"Better, pet, because it'll be ours. We'll have a cabin with a floor. We'll have our own smokehouse and corral for our horses. You'll have a root cellar and a well and . . . a privy."

"A privy?"

"A privy, *mon amour*. My wife will not have to squat in the woods. In the winter, I'll set a trap line and we'll take the furs to a trading post."

"Is one there, Light?"

"There will be. People are moving west."

"Maybe Eli an' Aee'll come with us."

Light was quiet for a moment. "Why do you say that, *chérie?*"

"She likes him. Her face turns red when he looks at her."

"She talks to Bodkin —"

"That's to bother Eli. He don't act like it, but he likes her."

Light rolled her over and looked down at her. "I suppose you *just* know that too."

"Uh-huh. I wish you an' Eli liked each other, Light. He wonders about ya."

"Has he said that, sprite?"

"No. But he looks at ya . . . funny."

Light rolled onto his back and took her with him. The intuition of this small, wonderful creature never ceased to amaze him. The Swede seldom spoke to him but always listened intently when he was speaking to someone else. For a while it seemed that Maggie was the contention between them. Light was sure the Swede wanted her. He was still interested in her, but now it was a different interest, one Light couldn't put his finger on.

"I had a bath t'day in the washtub," Maggie whispered as if it were news of monumental importance.

"I could tell. You smell like soap."

"We put the tub in the girls' sleepin' room an' started with the littlest first." Maggie giggled.

"After Eee an' Dee, it was my turn cause Cee is bigger than me." Maggie giggled again. "Noah Dixon likes Bee. Did ya know that, Light?"

"I kind of suspected it, pet."

"Are ya goin' to love me again tonight, Light?" Maggie moved to lie on his chest so that she could kiss his face.

"Do you want me to?"

"Uh-huh."

He rolled with her again, locking his arms and legs about her.

"Ho! Ho! I've got a little vixen for a wife."

"Is . . . that . . . good?" she murmured between kisses.

"It is very, very, very good for your husband, *mon amour.*"

Because Light was more skilled at hunting than at carpentry, he was the designated hunter. It took a goodly amount of meat to feed fifteen people, and he had not forgotten his promise to take meat to the Osage camp. Each day while the others worked on the cabin, he took to the woods with his rifle, bow and quiver of arrows. For the first couple of weeks after his lodge was finished, he hunted through the area five miles east of the settlement, leaving the north and west for the Osage.

One morning, launching a canoe, Light paddled down the creek to the river. Here the Missouri made its great turn to the north, to continue northward over fifteen hundred miles to the distant towns of the Mandan that Meriwether Lewis had written about in his journal. Here, also, the character of the forest bordering the river began gradually to change. Patches of unwooded prairie appeared more frequently, especially on the south side of the river.

Crossing the river, he kept warily close to the south bank, paddling around the willows that leaned out from the bank. Suddenly he thrust his paddle into the mud to hold his craft motionless.

Above him on the bank not fifty feet away stood a huge buffalo bull. He was rubbing and scratching his back against the low branch of a pecan tree. Light loosened the paddle and let the canoe drift below the willows. He drew it to the shore, tied it and began to crawl up the bank that led to the grassy area above. Knowing that it would take two, possibly three trips to transport the meat across the river and also aware that scavengers could make off with what he left the moment he was out of sight, he decided to try and make the kill. Cautiously, Light reached the top of the bank and peered through a fringe of gooseberry bushes. He held his breath.

A half-hundred buffalo were peacefully grazing in the shallow valley. It was a small herd. Having not yet grown full coats of winter hair, their great bodies stood out boldly against the still green meadow grass. A few of them were lying down, contentedly chewing their cuds. Young calves, their reddish coats smooth and wavy, playfully butted each other. A number of the older animals stood placidly while tick birds strutted up and down their spines picking at parasites. Several of the beasts were within a hundred yards, easily in range of Light's long gun.

He was ready to lift the barrel and sight when the tick birds suddenly took flight. The buffalo herd, their noses to the wind, paid no attention to what had alarmed the birds. But Light was instantly alert. He carefully scanned the edge of the woods behind the beasts and discovered a circle of Delaware slowly creeping up on the herd.

Light counted twenty braves armed with hunting bows and spears and decided it was time to leave while they were intent on the hunt. He edged carefully backward until he reached the bank, then slid down to the canoe. Many Spots had reported that the Delaware had gone south. They had, but had stopped just across the river, within a mile of the settlement.

When he heard the first yips as the Indians charged and the thumps of hoofs as the startled herd stampeded, he pushed the canoe out from under the willows and paddled furiously for the opposite shore.

For several days Light watched the shoreline across the river through his glass. When he had returned after seeing the Delaware, he had instructed Maggie to stay at the MacMillans' whenever he was away and told the crew cutting poles for the new cabin that when they went to the woods, they should be well armed.

One morning when a heavy fog had lifted from the river, and after Maggie had gone to the MacMillans', Light trotted down the river path, stopping often to listen. Turning his ear to the north, he could hear the faint ring of the axe as the choppers worked felling trees. He continued east until he came to the sandbar where Ramon de la Vega's boat had blown up. The cannon was there, sunken in the sand. Most of the debris had washed away as the river had risen due to rains in the north.

Always cautious, Light squatted behind the now flaming-red sumac bushes that lined this section of the river and carefully scanned the area before he stepped out onto the sandbar. He looked up-river to see if a craft had come down near the bank. When he looked downriver, he noticed a canoe amid the reeds that grew close to the bank. The birch-bark craft, tied to the bank, bobbed on the gently moving water.

Skirting the bank, Light found a place where he could look down into the craft. It was Delaware and there were four paddles, which meant there might be up to four Indians roaming the area. The tracks led into the woods and turned west. They were easy to follow. Head up, his eyes checking from side to side, Light hurried along the path.

He knew where the Indians were headed.

The work on the cabin where Paul and Eli

would stay was progressing to the point where longer poles were needed for the roof. Caleb led them to a stand of tall straight pines a good mile above the homestead. This day they would cut and trim the trees; tomorrow they would bring the oxen to drag the poles to the homestead.

It was a cool, damp day and the work was going well. Eli was beginning to have a greater appreciation of the forest and the bounty it provided. He had always enjoyed physical labor, especially when he worked with Paul, who was as strong as a bull and also liked to compete. They often challenged each other to everything from arm-wrestling to seeing who could spit the farthest.

A dozen trees were felled before noon and Paul teased Caleb unmercifully because he couldn't keep up with trimming them. Aee had sent meat and bread for their noon meal. They sat down on a log to eat it. It was Paul's and Caleb's turn to tease Eli about the fine meal *they* were having because of him.

"It is good for us, is it not, Caleb, for a woman to be sweet on our friend?"

After they ate they took time out to sharpen their tools on a grindstone. Before starting back to work, Paul checked the loads in the rifles, and Eli checked the pistol he had stuck in his belt.

Caleb laughed. "Them Delaware ain't goin' to stand thar and let ya shoot 'em with that lit'le ole thin', Mista Eli. Ya ain't goin' to know they's here till ya start bleedin'."

"Light has been watching the shore with his spyglass and hasn't seen any more. He said the ones he saw could be a hunting party trailing that buffalo herd." Paul leaned his rifle against the log they had been sitting on and picked up his axe.

"One Delaware can kill you just as quick as a hundred." Eli patted the butt of the pistol in his belt. "That's why I'm carryin' this."

Eli and Paul selected a tall straight pine and the ringing blow of the axes was the only sound until Caleb began one of his low moaning songs.

> Donno where I goin',
> When I lay me down t' die —
> I be a poor soul a'rotten
> In dis deep hole where I lie.

"Good grief, Caleb. Can't you sing about something besides dying?" Eli straightened and looked over his shoulder at the man.

Swish. The arrow seemed to come from nowhere. It passed close to Eli's cheek and embedded in the trunk of the tree that he and Paul had been chopping. Eli jerked the pistol from his belt and whirled. A rifle barrel protruded from the bushes north of them. He lifted the pistol, aimed and fired. The shiny barrel jerked upward, then dropped.

Eli dropped the pistol and sprang for his rifle. Before he could reach it, Caleb's arrow pierced the chest of an Indian who had stepped from behind a tree to fire. A yell came from the choke-cherry bushes after the loud boom of Paul's gun.

Caleb was across the clearing before Eli could collect his thoughts. There was a dull thud. Paul and Eli crouched behind the log, waiting. *Were there more than three? Did Caleb need help?*

There was total silence.

Several agonizing minutes dragged by before Caleb returned. He dragged a Delaware by the hair on his bloody head and dropped his limp body beside the one with the arrow in his chest.

"Dat all dere is."

"There were three of the devils. I got one with the pistol. He's back there in the bushes."

"*Mon Dieu,* that was fast," Paul exclaimed.

"Dey quiet as a snake, dem Delaware." Caleb's foot nudged the one he had killed, then reached down and jerked the arrow free. "Dat damn good one. Ain't goin' to waste it."

"Be careful, Paul, he may not be dead," Eli called when Paul, holding his rifle in front of him, went toward the bush where Eli had shot the Indian. Keeping his eye on the bush, he stooped and picked up the rifle.

Eli had begun to reload his pistol when he heard Paul's agonized cry.

"*Mon Dieu! Mon Dieu!* Eli! You . . . killed . . . Light!"

CHAPTER TWENTY-TWO

You killed Light!

Eli could not believe what he'd heard. His throat swelled, his heart stopped, his feet stuck to the ground.

Caleb moved past him and somehow Eli followed. Paul was kneeling beside the still figure on the ground. Blood spread out over Light's buckskin shirt. His head lolled to the side. He looked young and small as if he were something that was no longer useful and had been discarded. The leather hat he always wore lay on a bed of leaves behind him.

The pounding of his heart and the lump in his throat made it impossible for Eli to speak. His numbed mind slowly played over what had happened. He had straightened and looked at Caleb a second before the arrow meant for him had struck the tree trunk. He saw the rifle come up out of the thornbush. He pulled his pistol and fired.

He had killed Baptiste Lightbody. In all his life he had never felt such crushing despair. *He can't be dead! He can't be dead! I'll never get to tell him —*

"He ain't dead."

It took seconds for Caleb's words to penetrate Eli's mind. He felt himself being pushed aside as the big Negro dropped to his knees and took the knife from Light's scabbard. Starting at the neck, he slit the scout's doeskin shirt to the waist.

"I can't find a heartbeat." Paul's fingers sought a pulse in Light's neck.

Caleb placed his ear against Light's chest. "He ain't dead," he insisted. "Dis hole not kill 'im dis soon." He pointed to the place in Light's chest where the bullet had entered. Caleb lifted Light's head. The back was soaked with blood. "Hit his hed on dis rock. Dat might kill 'im."

"He's not dead?" Eli whispered hoarsely.

"Almost. He lose blood. May die soon."

"Stop the blood!" Eli pulled his shirt off over his head and cut a hole in the sleeve with his knife. He ripped the sleeve from the shirt and handed it to Caleb, the rest of the shirt to Paul. "I swear I didn't know —" Eli clasped his hands and rocked back and forth. "Christ a'mighty! What've I done?"

"We've got to get him back to *madame*." After wrapping the sleeve about Light's head, Paul and Caleb wrapped the shirt as tightly as they could around his chest.

Paul looked up at his friend's ashen face. He had never seen him so shaken, not even when he had failed in an attempt to rescue three young children when a wharf collapsed at Evansville. He'd had nightmares for months after that.

332

"We can make a stretcher —"

"No time. I'll carry him," Caleb said firmly.

"Get the rifles, Eli. Eli," Paul said again when his friend continued to stare at Light's still face. He looked at Paul with dull eyes. "Get the rifles."

"What will Maggie say?"

"I'll get the tools. If Caleb can carry Light, we can carry everything else. Eli." Paul shook his friend's arm. "Move, Eli."

It was the longest mile Eli ever walked. Three times he offered to take a turn carrying Light and three times Caleb shook his head. After the third refusal Eli was convinced that Light had died and, knowing the guilt he was feeling, Caleb didn't want to add to it by having him carry the body of the man he had killed.

Before they reached the homestead, Paul went ahead to speak to MacMillan. The two men went to the house. When Caleb and Eli reached the yard, MacMillan and his wife were waiting beside the door to the sickroom. They stepped aside and Caleb carried Light inside.

"Where's Maggie?" Eli's face felt wooden.

"I saw her an' Bee go to the root cellar, but —"

Eli placed the rifles on the bench beside the door and walked away. Maggie and Bee came out of the cellar before he reached it. Smiling, Maggie ran across the yard to meet him.

"Eli! Where's yore shirt? It ain't summer."

She was wearing her buckskin britches and an

old wool jacket. He had never seen her so beautiful. Her eyes were shining, and her cheeks rosy, her red mouth laughing.

"Maggie, come —"

"Yo're goin' t' catch yore death a cold, is what ya'll do. Why'er ya sweatin', Eli?"

"Maggie, there's been an . . . accident."

"Did ya hurt yoreself?" When he didn't answer, Maggie took hold of Eli's arm. "Who's hurt, Eli?" Her eyes, large and suddenly fearful, searched his face. "Who?" Her mouth formed the word.

"Light."

"Bad?"

"I'm . . . afraid so. Miz Mac —"

"No." She shook her head vigorously. "Light's not . . . hurt."

"He . . . he was . . . shot."

"Light's not hurt! Yo're lyin', Eli. Yo're a liar! Yo're a liar!" she screamed. "Light's all right!" She darted around him and ran. She didn't stop until Paul grabbed her at the door of the sickroom. "Let go." Her clenched fist hit him on the side of the face.

"Don't fight, *chérie. Madame* will help him." Paul's hand gripped her shoulders.

Maggie twisted away from his grasp and bolted into the room. Aee and her mother were bending over the still form on the bunk. Maggie saw the blood on the chest of her beloved and the bloody rag wrapped around his head. From the depths of her soul came a soft keening cry of grief. It

334

was the most pitiful sound any of them had ever heard.

Outside the door, Eli clapped his hands over his ears.

"I swear to God, Paul, I didn't know it was him." Eli's eyes begged his friend to believe him. "All I saw was the barrel of the gun come up. Now I know that he was going to shoot the Indian — the one you shot. But at the time it seemed that . . . he was one of them."

Paul put his hand on Eli's shoulder. "It was an accident. No one will blame you."

"Maggie will."

"We must wait and see, *mon ami*. Light may not die. He is not big, but he is wiry and strong."

"You were right. I shouldn't have come looking for him. I wanted to see him . . . to hate him. I never thought I'd *like* him."

The soft sounds of Maggie's grief continued to come from the room. The sound cut into Eli's heart like a sharp knife. He walked away and stood in the cold damp air, facing the woods, feeling sick inside. After a while something warm slipped over his bare shoulders.

"Ya wantin' to come down with a sickness?" Aee moved around in front of him.

"How is he?"

"I don't know. Bullet went through him so Ma didn't have to dig for it. She dug out pieces of cloth. Caleb said it was a pistol shot when Ma asked. If it'd been a rifle shot it'd torn him to pieces."

"I didn't mean to shoot him."

"Ya did it?" Aee frowned. "Caleb didn't say. Guess I never thought —"

"Will he die?"

"Ma won't say. She says the crack on his head's bad. She's keepin' a wet rag on it."

"I didn't mean to shoot him," Eli said again.

"Ever'body'll know that."

"Paul don't."

"Why'er ya sayin' that? It was plain ya didn't cotton t' him. If it was 'cause he had Maggie an' ya wanted her, don't mean ya'd shoot him."

"Maggie loves him."

"That's plain enough," Aee said with less sympathy in her voice. "She's in there tearin' herself to pieces a grievin'."

"Do you think I shot him so I could have . . . her?"

She looked into his eyes for a few seconds before she spoke.

"I ain't got much use for ya most of the time, Swede. But I ain't think yo're that low-down."

Eli held her eyes with his. She tilted her chin and refused to look away or flinch when he ran a finger down her cheek.

"You're something, Aee."

"I know what I am. I'm a breed. Lived in the backwoods all my life. Don't know diddly 'bout livin' in a town." Her chin came up a little higher.

"You've got more gumption than all the town-women I've known put together."

Her brows lifted. "Even Maggie?"

"Maggie can't be put in the same pocket as other women. She's . . . different. Even you've got to see that." When Aee's lips began to curl in a sneer, he added, "She's one kind of woman, you're another. You're solid, Aee. Solid and dependable and resourceful. You'd do to winter with. Maggie's pretty to look at, like a . . . butterfly. Someone will always have to take care of Maggie."

"She's . . . pretty and I'm not."

"Who told you that?"

"I don't have t' be told. I got eyes. Ya got 'em too. Ya put 'em on Maggie often enough."

"Do you think a butterfly is pretty?"

" 'Course I do. Maggie's a butterfly. Ya said so. Then what am I? A horsefly?" Angry glints appeared in her eyes.

"I didn't say that."

"It's what ya meant." Aee reached up and snatched the blanket from around his shoulders. "I ain't carin' if ya catch a death a cold!" She marched off toward the cabin, digging her heels into the ground with each step.

"Christ-a-mighty!" Watching her rigid back and set shoulders, Eli was sure that this was the worst day of his life.

In the middle of the afternoon a norther swept down out of the northwest, bringing a flurry of snowflakes. Furs were brought in to keep Light warm. The fire Paul built in the small fireplace

337

hardly took off the chill until hides from MacMillan's storehouse were tacked to the walls along the north and west to hold out the wind.

Maggie sat beside the bunk holding Light's hand. Her face was tear-streaked, her eyes swollen. At times she laid her head on the pillow next to Light's and murmured in his ear. Paul put a kettle of water on the fire grate to heat, then settled down in the far corner. Maggie's voice, soft and pleading, was the only sound.

"Don't die an' leave me, Light. I can't go through them years all by myself. Ya promised to take me to our mountain. We'll have our babies there, an' grow old like ya said. When we die, it'll be t'gether on our mountain. Yo're my heart, Light. Wake up an' tell me I'm yore . . . treasure. I love ya. Ya always come t' save me when I call. I'm callin' ya now. Please come back t' me."

Her soft words droned on and on, pleading, telling Light she loved him. Paul discovered tears in his eyes.

"We'll have a cabin an' a root cellar an' a well. Ya said in the wintertime we'd stay in our blankets an' love each other all day if we wanted to. Wake up, my heart . . . wake up, my love. Yore Maggie's here."

When Maggie stopped talking for a while, Paul thought she might have fallen asleep. The only light in the room came from the fire. He lit one of the candles Aee had left on the table beside the bunk. She lifted her head and looked at him, her green eyes bleak.

"Miz Mac said Light was shot with a pistol. Indians use bows or rifles. They don't have pistols. Eli does. Did Eli shoot Light?"

"It was an accident, *chérie*. He —"

"Don't call me that. Light calls me *chérie*."

"I'm sorry, Maggie. When the Delaware attacked, Eli saw a rifle come out of the bush and he shot. He didn't know it was Light."

"Eli doesn't like Light. He said me and Light wasn't married to each other."

"He didn't shoot him on purpose."

Maggie shook her head. "How do ya know that?"

"I know the kind of man Eli is."

Paul had no more than said Eli's name when Eli came in carrying Light's packs. Maggie flew up out of the chair and attacked him with her fists.

Paul tried to hold her.

"Let her be, Paul." The packs fell to the floor. Eli stood there, taking every blow from her small fists, making no attempt to shield his face.

"Don't touch Light's packs!"

"I thought you might . . . need something in them."

"Get out! Get away from him! Ya shot him with that . . . old pistol!"

"I didn't mean to. Believe me. I had no idea he was anywhere near."

"Yo're a . . . liar! A pissant! A wart-hog! Aee said ya ain't worth . . . shootin'. An' ya ain't —"

"I'd give anything if it hadn't happened. I swear it."

"He saved ya when ya almost drowned and . . . thumped water out of ya! Ya'd a died if not for Light! Why did ya hurt him?"

She continued to call him every name she could think of and to flay at him with her fists. Finally exhausted, she threw herself into the chair beside the bunk, buried her face in her hands and burst into a storm of weeping.

"How is he?" Eli asked Paul.

"It's hard to tell." Paul lifted his shoulders and shook his head.

"I'll stay. You go eat."

"She don't want you, *mon ami*. Being here will upset her more."

"I've got to make her understand I didn't mean to shoot him."

"She's not in the mood to understand. Perhaps later."

"Did Miz Mac say anything? Does she think he'll . . . come out of this?"

"She said the shot went in under his collarbone and out under the shoulder blade. She doused it good with vinegar and put her Indian medicine on it. It's all she can do."

"His head? Is it bad?"

"She won't know until he wakes up."

After Paul left, Eli put more wood on the fire and sat down. Maggie didn't seem to realize he was there. She caressed Light's face with her fingers, and whispered in his ear.

"Yore treasure is here, Light. I'm stayin' right by ya. Nobody is goin' t' hurt ya. Ya want me t' sing to ya? Ya always smile when I sing."

Maggie placed her cheek on the pillow beside his head, and with her lips close to his ear, began to sing softly.

> Life's morn will soon be waning,
> And its evenin' bells be tolled.
> But my heart shall know no sadness,
> If you'll love me when I'm old.

"That's our song. Ya said ya'd love me when we're old. Ya want me to sing 'Brave Wolfe' for ya? I know all the verses." She continued to stroke his cheeks with her fingers.

In a soft musical voice, she sang verse after verse of the ballad of James Wolfe, hero of the French and Indian War. The lyrics told of his love for his English sweetheart whom he called "his dear jewel."

As soon as she finished one song, she started another. The quietness of her grief was the hardest of all for Eli to endure. How could he have thought she could be parted from Light? He was her heart, her soul.

Deep down inside Eli was a hollow place that longed to be filled. He had had grandparents when he was very young. His mother had provided lodging and food for the first ten years of his life, but not love. Then came Paul.

Baptiste Lightbody had everything that mattered.

Would anyone ever love him as much?

Aee came in with a plate of food. She stood just inside the door and listened to Maggie sing. Finally she moved and placed the plate on the table beside the bed. Flickering candlelight fell on Light's still face. Maggie appeared to be oblivious to anything but the man on the bed.

"Ma told me t' stay the night an' watch he don't go wild an' break open that hole," Aee whispered and sat down on the bench beside Eli.

"Maggie would rather have you here than anyone."

"It'll kill 'er if he don't . . . make it."

"He's lucky to have someone who loves him so much."

"Does she know ya did it?"

"Paul told her. Light saved my life, dived under the boat until he got my leg free of the sawyer, then thumped the water out of me. She wishes I'd died."

"What'd ya expect from her? A thanky?"

"Don't give me any sass, Aee. I've had a bellyful today."

"Ya really feel bad, don't ya?"

"I'd give my right arm to undo what I did."

"Have ya had any supper?"

"I'm not hungry. Will he wake up soon?"

"I don't know. Last year a riverman with a knock on the head lay here three days. When he woke up he couldn't see. Died two days after that. Buried him up on the knoll."

"Is this your way of cheering me up?"

"I ain't tryin' to cheer ya up. Ya ain't got

no cause to be so . . . cranky. Yo're sitting here with a hang-down face like it was ya that got shot."

Eli looked at her for a long while. "Leave it to you to put things in the right order."

Aee grinned at him. "Glad I can do somethin' right."

They sat quietly. The room was cozy and warm. The only sound was Maggie's singing. Eli was grateful for Aee's presence. He would have liked to hold her hand but feared she would jump up and leave if he made a move.

"Ya don't have to stay," Aee whispered. "Ain't nothin' ya can do."

"I can keep the fire going."

They sat in companionable silence, each glad the other was there. A low moaning wind swept around the corners and up under the eaves of the cabin. The candle burned down and Aee lit another.

When Maggie's singing stopped, they both thought she had fallen asleep until she lifted her head and put her face close to Light's.

"I'm here. Maggie's here."

Aee and Eli stood to look over Maggie's shoulder. Light's lips were moving.

"Mag . . . gie —"

"Here I am. Are ya wakin' up, Light?"

"You were sing . . . ing —"

"I'll sing all night long, if ya want me to."

His eyelids flickered, then partly opened and closed again.

"Don't go back to sleep," Maggie begged. "Stay awake a little while."

"Am I . . . hurt bad?"

"Miz Mac took good care of ya. She's good at doctorin'."

"I got to know —" His eyes opened wider and focused on Eli standing above Maggie. "Maggie. If I . . . if I don't make it. Take Maggie . . . home."

"Don't worry." Eli put his arm across Aee's shoulder and drew her close to him. "Aee and I will take care of Maggie."

Light closed his eyes wearily.

"I ain't goin' home, Light." Maggie's voice rose in alarm. "We're goin' to yore mountain like ya said."

"*Chérie,* my . . . treasure, I would like a drink of water."

CHAPTER TWENTY-THREE

Light was awake, alert, and worried about Maggie. He had slept through the night and most of the day. The first thing he saw when he awoke was Maggie's haggard little face hovering over him.

"*Chérie.* You have not slept."

"Ya feelin' better, Light? Miz Mac said yore t' eat if ya can. I'll feed ya. All ya got t' do is open yore mouth."

"When did *you* eat, *mon amour?*"

Tears filled Maggie eyes. "I don't know. Yo're better, ain't ya?"

"I am better, my pet." Light brought her hand to his lips.

"Tell me . . . I'm yore treasure, Light. I want so bad t' hear ya say it." Tears rolled down her cheeks.

"Don't cry, *ma petite.* In my dreams I heard my sweet treasure singing."

"I was singin'. I sung all the songs ya like."

"You've worn yourself out. You'll be sick."

"I won't be sick, Light. I promise. Will ya eat now?"

"My stomach is growling." Light rolled his head to the side and winced. "Did someone hit me on the head?"

"Paul said ya hit a stone when ya fell. I don't want t' leave ya, but I got t' tell Aee yore awake an' get ya somethin' t' eat." She started to the door and turned back. "Ya won't go back t' sleep?" She bent over him and her soft lips moved over his face.

"No, *amour*. Don't worry so."

"I hurt so bad, I almost died. I would've if I'd lost ya."

"I'll be all right."

"And in the spring we'll go to our mountain?"

"In the spring, *mon coeur*."

Eli was finding it difficult to get Aee alone so he could talk to her. Since two nights ago when he had put his arm around her and assured Light that *they* would take care of Maggie, she had avoided him. Every time she saw him coming she took off in another direction. She stayed so close to her mother she was almost her shadow. The feelings he had for her had been building. He wanted to know if she had feelings for him. At times he thought she did, and at other times he was sure that she disliked him intensely.

It had not snowed enough to hinder the work on the cabin Paul and Eli would occupy. In a few days they could move out of Bodkin's cabin and into one of their own. Bodkin was beginning to irritate Eli. He mooned over Aee and Dixon mooned over Bee. Bodkin was a good sort, but not the right man to hitch with Aee or take care of her properly. And the thought of him putting his hands on her raised Eli's temper to the boiling point.

It was mid-afternoon, and Eli and Paul were notching small three-foot logs for a "cat and clay" chimney for their cabin. A hole had been cut in the wall. The firebox, lined with river clay, had been moved up to it. The chimney was to be built up around the firebox and fastened to the side of the cabin.

Eli saw Aee leave the house with Eee's chicken under her arm and head for the shed where the laying hens were kept. He dropped his adze and leisurely walked down the path past the cow pen to the open shed door.

Paul leaned on his axe and grinned openly as he watched his friend glance around to see if anyone were watching before he stepped inside.

It was gloomy inside the shed and smelled of hay and animals. In a far corner Aee was struggling to open the top of a stick coop with one hand while holding the chicken with the other.

"Damn ya! Don't ya do-do till I get ya in the pen. Ya already did it in the house and Ma's fit t' be tied. Eee's bawling woke up Frank. It's all yore fault, ya dang-blasted little pissant."

"Now, now, now, Aee. You shouldn't swear."

So startled she almost dropped the chicken, Aee spun around. Blood rushed to her face and her legs began to tremble. How did that damn Swede know she was here?

"What'er ya doin' in here?"

"I followed you." Eli grinned unabashedly and unhooked the wire holding the top of the coop. "You better put Chicken in there before she do-dos on you."

Aee dropped the chicken inside and took off for the door. Eli closed the lid, hurried after her and caught her before she reached it.

"Wait a minute." He held onto her arm. "What's the matter with you? Why do you run every time I come near?"

"Run? Why'd I run from you, Mister Town-man Nielson? Ya don't scare me."

"I think I do. Are you mad because I told Light that you and I would take care of Maggie? Or is it because I put my arm around you?"

"*That* didn't mean nothin'. But ya lied to Light when ya said 'me and Aee.' *You'd* be the one to take her. Ya'd sure not want *me* taggin' along."

"You and me," Eli insisted. "I said it to put his mind at ease, but I also said it, you stubborn little bunghead, because I *meant* it."

"Did ya foller me out here jist to tell me that twaddle?"

"Yes. Paul saw me come in here, and I don't doubt that Mac's eagle-eye was on me too. I wasn't trying to hide it."

Aee's heart was thumping as if it were trying to get out of her chest. She didn't want to look at Eli, but she couldn't help herself. Her eyes kept going back to his lips, his beard, his nose, his eyes. Her silly stomach was quivering like a dish of jelly.

"Now that you've said it, I got t' go." She tried to dart around him, but he caught her and pulled her into his arms.

"Not till I kiss you."

"Ya can't —"

"Why not?"

" 'Cause . . . 'cause —" Her face was so close to his that all she could see was his mouth.

Lordy! A man was about to kiss her. Not any man, the wonderful, beautiful man she dreamed about every night.

The kiss was far from what Aee expected a kiss to be. His lips were soft and gently seeking. His beard against her face was a silken caress. He pulled her closer, lifting her as he kissed her. She breathed in the fresh, masculine scent of his body. The taste of his mouth was in hers. A tingling heat built within her. Aee felt the throbbing beat of her pulse, high in her throat, fluttering to her very ears, as she slowly drew her mouth from his so that she could look at him.

Eli made a kind of a groaning sound, unable for the moment to do or say anything. He could only look at her. His heated gaze took in her smooth golden skin, sweetly curved mouth and her eyes, large soft brown eyes that looked back at him in puzzlement.

"That was sweet. You're sweet," he said huskily. When she said nothing, he whispered, "I want to kiss you again." She still said nothing, and he lowered his lips to hers again.

Slowly, deliberately, his mouth covered hers, pressing gently at first while he guided her arms up and around his neck, then wrapped her in his. His kiss deepened when he realized she was leaning into it. Everything was softly given and softly received. Caught in the throes of desire, she pressed herself against him.

"Do you like kissin' me?" he asked, moving his lips a fraction away from her.

"I didn't think it'd be like this."

"What did you think it would be like?"

"Not . . . nice, like this."

"Two people have to like each other for kisses to be nice . . . like this."

"Then, ya like me?"

"Damn right, I like you."

"Ya don't act like it . . . sometimes."

He chuckled, hugged her tight and kissed her again.

"Don't pick a fight with me now, sweet thing. I want to make the most of being here alone with you."

"Ya can kiss me again . . . if ya want to."

"If I want to? Christ-a-mighty! I've been dying to kiss you for days and days and days —"

The soft utterance that came from her throat was a purr of pure pleasure as their lips met again. She leaned into him, oblivious to everything but the feel of his arms encircling her, the hard strength of his hands that lay flat on the taut swell of her hips, pressing her to him with urgent force. Her heart hammered crazily against his chest.

It was the most wonderful, exciting moment of her life.

"Aee! What the hell ya doin'?" MacMillan's harsh voice blasted the silence.

Aee jumped when she heard her father's voice. She would have run from the shed, but Eli's hand tightened on hers and held her beside him. What she felt was total embarrassment. Blood rushed to her face. She couldn't look at her father or Eli. She tried again to tug her hand from Eli's, but he wouldn't let go of it.

"Pa . . . I —"

"Go to the house!"

"Mac, wait. I grabbed her and kissed her. Aee didn't do anything."

"I ain't blind. I could see it. She warn't fightin' ya off, that's certain."

"I've been going to talk to you — was as soon as I knew how Aee felt about me. With your permission, I'd like to . . . walk out with her. Court her."

"Ya want to court her? Why didn't ya come right out an' ask like a man? Hidin' out in the shed a-huggin an' a-kissin' ain't no decent way a courtin' to my way a thinkin'."

"We wasn't hidin' out, Pa." Aee had found her tongue at last.

"That's what I'd call it." MacMillan's eyes stayed for a while on his daughter's red face,

351

then went back to Eli. "Ya got a notion t' take my girl to wife?"

"Pa!" Aee screeched. "Ain't nothin' been said . . . 'bout that."

"Then it's time it was. It's goin' to be a long winter. I got more t' do than be a watchin' ya don't go slitherin' off in the dark with 'im an' gettin' . . . ah . . . with a babe."

"I resent that!" Eli was shocked and angry. "I would never dishonor Aee."

"Didn't say ya would. But there's times the juices run high in a young buck, especially in cold weather. I ort t' know. Got six younguns now." He chuckled. "Ever'one of 'em got planted in the wintertime."

Aee was so humiliated she could not look at her father. She wanted to melt and run down into the ground and never have to look at him or Eli again. The thought of running to the river, wading out into the current and drowning herself crossed her mind. Then her father did the unexpected thing. He turned to leave.

"I said my piece, Eli. Ya've said yores. Ya can court her, if ya've got a mind to an' she's willin'. Ya ort to know one thin' right up front. She ain't goin' to be easy to deal with. I spoilt her. Let her have her own way too much of the time. She can be stubborn as a mule an' meaner'n a cornered she-wolf with two pups hangin' on her tits. But I'll say one thin' in her favor — she's a crack shot."

Relief flooded Eli when he saw the glimmer

352

of amusement in MacMillan's eyes.

"That's good to know, Mac. But I was counting on a woman who could cut and tote a load a firewood, kill and skin out a bear, and chew deerhide to make me soft moccasins. Can she do that?"

"I ain't knowin' 'bout the bear —"

"Hush-up! Both of ya. Ya make me so mad. I got some say in this —"

"I got t' go. Say it to Eli." At the door, MacMillan turned for a parting remark. "I'll be watchin' for when ya come out."

On the way to the house MacMillan passed Paul, jerked his head toward the shed and winked.

Alone in the sickroom Light sat up on the side of the bunk. He had to be careful not to move his head too fast, or breathe too deeply. Maggie seldom left his side. She was bitter toward Eli for shooting him and stood guard in case he came near. Paul had explained that the shooting was an accident. Light had no doubt that it was exactly that. He had arrived at the cutting site just as the Delaware were springing their unexpected attack. There had been no time to make his presence known.

What worried Light now was how he was going to pay MacMillan for his and Maggie's keep until he was able to hunt again. Never in all his life had he been beholden to anyone. It was humiliating, almost as much as having to use the chamber pot.

The first few times the need arose he had let Maggie help. His wonderful Maggie, a cherished part of himself. He knew every curve, dip and secret place in her body and she knew his as well. He had turned on his side on the edge of the bunk and she held the tin pot. But when he needed to sit on it, it was a different matter. He asked her to leave. She pleaded to stay. Finally she left in tears, but minutes later Paul opened the door and came in.

If not for the dizziness in his head Light would have been able to manage, but as it was, he was grateful for Paul's strong arm that helped him back upon the bunk.

Later in the day Eli walked in.

"Paul says you're feeling better."

"I am."

Nothing else was said. Eli picked up the chamber pot and went out. When he returned, he moved it under the bunk and stood awkwardly looking down at Light.

"You didn't need to do that," Light said.

"I think I did."

The door flew open. Maggie bolted into the room and got between Eli and Light's bunk.

"Ya come to hurt him again? Get out. Go on. Shoo! Shoo!" She fluttered her hands in a shooing motion.

"*Chérie*," Light reached for Maggie's hand. "Don't fret yourself."

"He hurt ya, Light. I don't want him here."

"I've told you that I didn't mean to shoot him,"

Eli said in an exasperated tone. "Why don't you believe me?"

" 'Cause I ain't wantin' to. Stay 'way from him."

"Godamighty! You think I came in here to attack a man lying flat on his back?"

"Ya do and ya'll get my knife in ya. I can throw it. Not as good as Light, but I could hit ya, big as ya are."

Eli looked over Maggie's head and spoke to Light.

"I came to tell you that Paul and I were lucky enough to get two big bucks this morning. MacMillan's smokehouse will be full. There'll be no shortage of meat."

"I thank you for that too."

"Too," Maggie echoed. "Ya ain't thankin' him for shootin' ya, are ya?"

"No, sweet pet."

Eli spun around and went out the door. Damn! He had missed his chance again. The burden of what he had to say to Baptiste Lightbody was bearing down hard on him. He wanted it over and out of the way so he would be free to plan his life with Aee.

They had walked out last night with Mac's approval. Eli had taken her to Light's lodge and built a fire. They had talked for several hours — the longest uninterrupted time he had spent with her and the first time they had talked without sniping at each other. He had been surprised and pleased with her intelligence and her common-sense approach to life.

It had been difficult, there in the cozy lodge with his sweet woman in his arms, but he had managed to keep their kisses from getting out of hand.

Eli had not realized until now what it meant to love a woman and have her love him in return. The feeling was so warm and wonderful that when they left the lodge, he felt that he was walking several feet above the ground. In all his thirty years, he had not known such a love between a man and a woman existed. Since falling in love with Aee, he had a better understanding of how it was between Maggie and Light.

"*Chérie,* you are being unreasonable."

"I don't like him anymore." She had a sulky look on her face. "He hurt ya, Light."

"It wasn't as if he shot me deliberately. He had no way of knowing I was not a Delaware —"

"I don't care," she said stubbornly. "I don't know why Aee likes him. She's lettin' him court her."

"You told me last night. Does it make you sad that he's courting her?"

"No. Aee's happy. She smiles all the time. Bee teases her, her pa teases her. Mr. Bodkin isn't happy. He wanted to court her too. I'm glad she chose Eli."

Maggie began to smile, then giggle. Her magnificent green eyes shone like polished stones.

"I ain't still mad at him, but I ain't tellin' him

356

yet. I want him to feel bad 'bout hurtin' ya. But I told Aee. She said it wasn't nice of me t' carry on like that. But she won't tell him."

"Ah, *ma chéri*. What will I do with you?"

She leaned over him. "Ya can kiss me. I've missed our lovin'." They exchanged tender, sweet kisses. "When can we go to our lodge?"

"Soon, pet. As soon as I can protect you should the need arise."

Maggie lay down beside him. He pillowed her head on his uninjured shoulder. His doubts that perhaps someday she would prefer a man like Eli, one who was completely white, had vanished. He pressed his lips to her forehead.

"Tell me how it'll be when we get to our mountain," she whispered.

CHAPTER TWENTY-FOUR

When two days of exceptionally warm weather went by, Light began to chafe at being cooped up in the room. He now dressed with Maggie's help and tended the fire. Mrs. MacMillan had removed the bandage from around his head and, according to her, the other wound was healing too. She thought it a miracle he hadn't come down with a fever.

The accident had made Light realize how easily his life could be taken. His worries about Maggie and what torments she would endure if she were left alone in the wilderness confirmed his resolve to speak to Caleb. The Negro had expressed an interest in the new land. Other than Jefferson Merrick or Will Murdock, Light knew of no one more capable to entrust with Maggie's safety than Caleb.

The men at the homestead were taking advantage of the good weather to work on the potash. Eli had become interested in the byproduct gleaned from burning patches of forest to use for farmland. MacMillan had convinced him that potash sold well in the east.

Eli and Aee had put their heads together and were trying to figure out a way to make soap that had a nice smell to it. Eli thought it would sell in St. Charles and St. Louis. They had even named it "Wilderness Flower."

Maggie related the news to Light. She described in detail, to his amusement, the dresses Mrs. Mac had cut from the fabric Eli had given them.

Bodkin, she told him, had been moping around since Aee had begun walking out with Eli. Lately Bodkin had turned his attentions to Bee. This had not sat well with Dixon. Maggie thought it great fun to watch the two men vie for the attention of MacMillan's shy daughter. Bee had taken to putting her hair up in a new way and making sure the clean side of her apron was turned out at mealtime.

Light was bored and tired of inactivity. He had asked Caleb to bring a hide from his lodge so he could make Maggie an extra pair of moccasins. Mrs. Mac suggested that he not work his arm and shoulder for a few more days.

This afternoon he had taken a small whetstone from his pack and sharpened his knives. He had just finished and was putting them back in his pack when Eli came in. Light half-expected to see Maggie dash in behind him. A smile flickered across his dark face.

Eli read his thoughts.

"Aee is going to keep Maggie busy so I can talk to you. All women like new dresses . . .

or so I'm told. They're making one for Maggie today."

"I hold no ill feelings about the shooting," Light said abruptly, thinking that the only reason for Eli's visit was to apologize.

"I was hasty —"

"There was no time to let you know I was there."

"I know that, but Maggie will never forgive me. It tore her to pieces."

Light said nothing. He wasn't a man to speak unless a reply was required.

"I know it's bothering you that you're not holding up your end here at MacMillan's right now. I'd feel the same. Paul and I will furnish meat for the homestead until you're on your feet." Eli's grin was somewhat boyish. "Neither of us is the hunter you are, but we'll make out."

"I'm obliged."

Eli stood on first one foot and then the other. Now that he was here, he didn't know how to start. What he had to say to Light couldn't be blurted right out.

Light sensed Eli's unease, and he felt a bit of apprehension. What did this man have to say that was so hard for him to spit out?

"Lightbody is a name I've not heard before," Eli began. "Did your folks come from Canada?"

Light looked at him squarely, his black eyes snaring blue ones and holding them. There must be something more important than curiosity about his name lying behind the question.

"My father did."

"Was he French?"

"He was. My mother was Osage, as you know."

"How did you get the name Lightbody? It's not French."

"My mother named me Lightbody because I was small at birth. Indian children do not necessarily carry their father's name."

"I didn't know that." Eli looked down at his feet, then at the wall, avoiding the questioning gaze of the man who sat on the bunk. "What was your father's name?" Eli waited in a vacuum of uncertainty for the answer.

"Pierre Baptiste."

Eli's rigid shoulders slumped. He had not been aware that he was holding his breath until the air came from his mouth in a rush.

"Yes," he said. Then again, "Yes."

Light sensed that this was a very important moment for Eli and waited patiently, as was his way, to discover the connection with him. Eli seemed unable to speak.

Finally Light broke the silence. "Why are you interested in my father's name?"

"Because . . . because my father's name was also Pierre Baptiste."

The words were totally unexpected. The implication did not register at once with Light.

"How can that be? You said you were Swedish. Baptiste is a French name, a common name. There are probably many other Frenchmen by that name."

"That may be true, but none of them with a son named Baptiste Lightbody. You're my brother, Light. Like it or not."

Light was stunned. He looked at the tall man standing in front of him and suddenly it hit him why Eli had looked so familiar to him. Eli's eyes and eyebrows were like Light's father's and he held his head slightly to the side as Pierre Baptiste had done. Light looked for other similarities, but found none. He remembered his father as being a big man, even bigger than Eli.

"I understand that this is hard for you to take in all at once. I've had five years to think about it." Eli pulled up his shirt and unwrapped a doeskin belt from around his waist. He unfolded it on the bunk and took out a letter. "Ten years ago my father sent this letter up the Ohio to Sloan Carroll at Carrolltown. He had known him many years ago. In it he inquires about me. He felt that he had been wrong to go and leave me behind. But, as the letter relates, his life with my mother was far from pleasant.

"Five years back Sloan discovered my whereabouts and sent a message for me to come see him. Until that time I had thought I had no blood kin anywhere in the world." Eli handed the letter to Light.

Light took the paper but did not unfold it. He looked hard at Eli.

"If what you say is true, your father is what

is known as a squaw man. Whites look down on a white man who marries an Indian woman and begets half-breed children. How do you feel about that?"

"At first I was angry that my father left me with a mother who despised me because I was his son; I was resentful that he had taken up with an Indian woman. But, now . . . well, time has a way of sorting things out. Read the letter."

Light folded back the single sheet of paper. The ink had faded until it was nearly impossible to make out all the words. He did see his mother's name, Willow Wind, and a reference to "my son, Baptiste Lightbody." The paper had torn apart at the fold, but his father's bold signature, Pierre Baptiste, was unmistakable. Light folded the paper carefully and handed it back to Eli.

"It's in bad shape. Could you make out the words? I've been trying to save it until you could read it."

"I saw my mother's name and mine. I've no doubt my father wrote it."

Eli returned the letter to the doeskin belt and wrapped it about his waist. He sank into the chair, relieved that the words were out at last but uncertain about how Light felt about what he had just been told.

"The letter was in better condition when I got it, but I've folded and unfolded and read every word a hundred times. Obviously, Pierre Baptiste loved your mother and pitied mine. He wanted to know if I still lived and, if I did, where I was." Eli paused. "My impression was that he was a good man who probably *had* to marry. He just was unable to live the kind of life my mother demanded."

Light nodded, then said: "He was a good father. He loved my mother and was not ashamed of his half-breed children."

"My mother was Swedish. When she was a young girl, she came with her parents to Louisville, a town up on the Ohio. She was their only child and they doted on her. My grandparents baked bread and cakes to sell. We all lived together in the back of their store. I don't know what my father's work was during this time, but I don't believe it was in the bakery. He left when I was so young that I don't remember him at all."

Eli was silent for a short while before he continued.

"Mother had fits of yelling and hitting and crying. She would fly into a rage that lasted for days. I was five or six when my grandparents died. I remember them and how they did everything they could for my mother and me. The only loving attention I received when I was a child was from my grandma.

"The bake shop shut down after Granny and Grandpa died. We lived for a while on the money they left us. Mother constantly harped on the fact that my father had deserted me and what a rapscallion he was. She said I was a bastard, which I know now was not true. I was not to use his name or speak it. I was never to forget that I was a Nielson.

"She insisted that I go to the docks every day and seek work. She was determined that I not be lazy like *him*. As I grew older I came to realize Pierre Baptiste may have had a good reason to leave us. Sloan Carroll told me that he left with the blessing of my grandparents and that they had assured him they would take care of Mother and me. They did until they died five years later."

Light sat quietly, but his mind was far from quiet. It was a struggle to accept this man as his father's son. He knew of men who had sired offspring by several different women and then had gone away and left them. This was not something the father he knew would have done.

"My mother died when I was eleven," Eli told him. "I went to the shack we lived in and found her. She had hanged herself or one of her . . . friends had hanged her. I've wondered all these years if something happened before she met my father to make her not . . . quite right in the head or if she had been that way since birth. I don't think ill of her. I want you to know that. She was my mother and gave me life. She couldn't help being the way she was."

"What did you do after she died?"

"I met Paul. He was footloose like me. He was about sixteen, I'd say, and had run away from a bad life in Canada. He didn't speak a word of English. I didn't speak a word of French, but we got along. He was like a father to me, although we are nearly the same age."

"Didn't you think of looking for your father?"

"Not once. I was scared to death he would find me. It had been drummed into my head ever since I could remember that he was the devil come to life."

"What changed your mind?"

"My mind wasn't changed about finding him. Sloan's message had reached Louisville and had lain around there for several years while I was freighting farther up the Ohio. I happened onto it by accident when I returned there to buy freight goods. On a trip downriver, Paul and I stopped at Carrolltown. Sloan gave me the letter. I was shocked to learn that my father had even thought of me. Since our first visit to Carrolltown, Paul and I have become friends with Sloan. We have visited in his home many times."

"You've known about this for five years?"

"Sloan also told me on that first visit that he had received word from Jefferson Merrick that my father had been killed. That is how I knew to inquire of Merrick when I came looking for you."

Light was silent. He thought of that time. A party of Sauk Indians had ambushed his father while he was checking his trap lines and had killed him. His mother had been devastated. At times he could almost hear in his mind the keening sounds of her grief when she heard the news.

"At first I wasn't very interested in finding you. I kept thinking about it. The more Paul told me to forget it, that you would not care to hear from me, the more curious I became. And to tell you the truth, I almost hated you because you'd had *my* father during the years you were growing up and I'd had no one but a mother who didn't care if I lived or died.

"I wanted to see you. I wanted to assure myself that I was a better man than you are. I also wanted to know what kind of a man my father was, and you were the only one who could tell me. Knowing that there was another man in the world who had the same blood in his veins that ran in mine has gnawed at me for five years. I wanted to know what he was like."

"You expected to see a savage with war paint on his face." It was a flat statement.

Eli grinned sheepishly.

"I didn't expect you to be quite so civilized or that you would have a woman like Maggie."

"You think I *am* civilized?"

"At times yes, at other times no." Eli had answered as truthfully as he could. "I wondered *if* you were after you killed the three rivermen, and I was sure you *were* when you toted the small man home on your back."

The statement required no answer and Light gave none.

Paul came in. He looked first at one and then the other.

"I see you are both alive. *Mon Dieu!*" Paul sighed with relief. "I'm glad it's over."

Light, as usual, said nothing.

Eli was uneasy about what Light was thinking. Was he disappointed to learn that his father had sired a son and gone away and left him? It was common for a white man to leave his half-breed sons, but not the other way around.

Light's impassive face revealed nothing. Eli stood and held out his hand.

"I'm glad I got to know you, Light. If I can ever be of any help to you, you need only let me know."

Light hesitated, then put his hand in that of his newfound brother.

When he was alone again, Light lay down on the bunk and stared at the ceiling. The news Eli had given him had surprised him but had not shocked him as much as Eli thought. Since his father's death, Light had searched his memory for bits and pieces of information about his father's life before he came to the land west of the big river. He could recall no mention by his father of family, friends, or even places he had visited east of the river. Pierre Baptiste's former life must have been very painful for him to have blotted it out so completely.

He had a brother. Light did not think it would make much difference in his life. He and Maggie would go on to their mountain. Eli's life would continue here, or on the river. Yet it was good to know that his father's blood would be passed down throughout the ages in the white man's world from which he came and the blood of his mother's people would be carried on by his and

368

Maggie's descendants.

The door flew open and Maggie came in.

"Looky, Light. Look at my new dress. Me an' Aee made it —" She paused, tilted her head and looked at him. "Why was ya smilin', Light? Ya was smilin' in here all by yoreself."

CHAPTER TWENTY-FIVE

The stream beside the homestead trickled to life.

Spring came like the sun breaking through a rain cloud. One day the thin layer of snow disappeared, and new sprigs of grass showed green on the hillsides. Huge flocks of geese, passing overhead in a V formation, their long necks stretched, followed their leader on their long northward journey. Unending swarms of ducks and cranes came from the south to settle on the river. Noisy swirls of gulls stopped to rest on the sandbars.

The winter had been short and pleasant. The weather had not been so harsh that it prevented work being done in the potash shed and on Eli's flatboat.

On a cold winter day following Christmas, Aee and Eli had stood before the entire population of MacMillansville and said their vows. They had promised to love and to cherish each other until parted by death. In his happiness Eli failed to recall how he had scorned such a ceremony, outside the realm of church or law, that had united Maggie and Light. Aee, beautiful in a pure white dress, radiated happiness. The couple went to live in the new cabin and Paul moved back in with Bodkin and Dixon.

During the winter Eli and Light came to know each other as brothers. Light was still reserved and quiet, but Eli understood that that was his nature. Aware that Eli was curious about their father, Light shared his memories of an educated man who had taught him to read and to write. Pierre had talked with his son of the world around and above him. He could read the stars, a fact that made Light think now that he might have been a seaman at one time. He was a man, Light said, who was comfortable with himself and had taught his son to hunt and to fish and, above all, to respect nature.

Eli listened intently to every word. His resentment toward the father who had deserted him had faded long ago.

When Light had told Maggie that he and Eli had had the same father, she had been delighted with the news.

"He's yore brother! Now I know why I wanted ya t' like each other. I just knew there was somethin'."

As soon as winter began to wane, Light and Caleb began work on the canoe that would take them up the Missouri and into the Osage River. They planned to travel that river to its beginning and there to swap the canoe and other trade goods for horses to take them the rest of the way to the mountains.

371

The day before their departure, Eli came to the dock where Light and Caleb were waterproofing, with a mixture of buffalo tallow and ashes, the middle section of their canoe, where they would keep such things as gunpowder and food. Eli had brought them a dozen knives that had been well oiled and wrapped in a hide, along with two rifles, a keg of gunpowder, several small sheets of shiny tin to be used as mirrors and ten yards of dress goods. He had already given Caleb, without Light's knowledge, a leather bag of gunpowder and two extra rifles.

"I know what you're going to say," Eli said when Light shook his head. "These goods are for Maggie." On his face was the grin that had irritated Light in the past, but that he now understood was a sign of uneasiness. "I want to make sure she doesn't walk all the way to your mountain. Use these things as trade goods. Aee and I insist. This is the last thing we can do for our brother."

"You have already given me tools."

"The tools were a gift to . . . Maggie" — Eli laughed at the absurdity of the excuse — "to help build her new home."

"I have nothing to give in return."

"You saved my life and you've given me friendship. That is worth far more." Eli's big hand came down on Light's shoulder.

"I will send my first winter's catch of mink furs to make a coat for my brother's wife."

Eli felt a lump in his throat. It was the first

time Light had referred to him as brother. In an attempt to cover his feelings, he joked.

"If mink is that plentiful, I may go with you."

"You are welcome."

"I would be tempted if my first son had not decided to arrive in the fall."

Light's smile lit his solemn face.

"Mac went to the well six times before he got a son. What makes you think you'll get one the first time? Huh?"

Eli fingered his beard. "I hadn't thought of that. But now that I do, I think that it will not be so bad to have a daughter. It's a most enjoyable trip to the well."

Their eyes met in companionable understanding. Eli regretted that they had known each other for such a brief time as brothers and friends.

"I will leave sign along the way if you and Aee should decide to come out. Paul would be welcome, as you know."

"Send word back with anyone coming this way. MacMillan is known along the river, and I expect in a few years he will have a village here."

"And you, Eli?"

"I've spent my life on or along the river."

Maggie came running down the path toward them.

"Does she ever walk?" Eli asked with a broad smile.

"Not if she can run," Light replied.

"Light! Aee and Eli gave me this goods. It's to make clothes for our first babe." Maggie held a bundle of cloth in her arms.

"Then, *ma petite,* I guess we'd better make a trip to the well and get one."

Maggie looked puzzled, then she laughed. "Get a baby out of the well? Light! Ya made a funny."

Light looked over her head and winked at his brother.

The parting was both happy and sad.

Maggie put her arms around each of the younger MacMillan children.

"Take care of Chicken, Eee. And Dee, keep working with that whip Caleb made ya. Yore goin' t' be a better yodeler than me, Cee, if ya keep goin' like ya are." She hugged Bee and whispered, "Decide soon 'tween Bodkin an' Dixon or they'll kill each other." Bee giggled, then burst into tears.

"Miz Mac, good-bye, good-bye," Maggie said. "I'll remember ya and little Frank always." She cried a little when she said good-bye to Aee. "Ya learned me a lot 'bout lots a thin's, Aee. I wish ya was comin', but I know ya can't. Ya be good to Eli, but don't take no sass off him."

Maggie hugged Eli for a long moment, then backed away and looked up at him.

"If I hadn't found Light, I mighta taken ya for my man, Eli. But I'm glad Aee got ya."

With tears running down her cheeks, she shook hands with the others, then ran for the canoe, leaving Light and Caleb to say their good-byes.

Light and Caleb, with Maggie between them,

picked up the paddles and the journey began. Maggie looked back at the small group standing on the riverbank. Aee was crying. Eli had his arm around her. They were all waving.

Maggie waved, then turned her face toward the west and began to yodel as she had never done before.

"Y-oo-dal-oodle-al-dee-hee. Y-oo-dal-oodle-al-dee-hee. Y-oo-dal-oodle-al-dee-hee —"

The musical sound was wild, haunting, unearthly. It rolled over the water. It echoed up and down the river and spilled into the hills beyond. It was music such as no living creature had ever heard before. It went on and on and on until it was lost in the distance.

On a bright sunny afternoon forty-eight days later the trio rode into the foothills of the Rocky Mountains.

The trip from the Missouri River had not been uneventful.

They had met a party of Osage, near the time they were to end their journey by canoe, and had traded the rifles, a small sack of gunpowder and three knives for four half-wild ponies that Maggie tamed within a day.

Light was able to converse with the Osage, although they spoke a different dialect. Though they lived far away, they had heard of Sharp Knife and his rescue of Zee, medicine man of an Osage tribe to the east, and had treated Light with much respect. He had sent a message back to Dark Cloud to relay on to the MacMillans, to say that they had reached the end of their water journey and were well.

A band of Kiowa overtook the travelers shortly after they had left the Osage River and would have killed them were it not for Caleb. The Kiowa had never seen a black man before, nor any man with the strength to lift a huge log over his head. To Caleb's amusement, they thought him a god and camped nearby for two days while Caleb performed feats of strength. The Indians offered him many ponies and his choice of a maiden for a wife if he would come with them. When he refused they became sullen. They rode off, somewhat appeased, when Light gave them two shiny pieces of tin, a knife and a length of Maggie's yard goods. For several days, however, Light and Caleb were careful to watch their back trail.

On the grassy plains they had waited two days for a mile-wide herd of buffalo to pass, and later they had crouched in a cave while a whirling, destructive wind passed overhead.

After reaching the foothills of the mountains, they rode on for another week, awed by the majestic, snow-capped mountains, the dense forest, the clear mountain streams and the abundance of wild game. Light remarked that it was like what he imagined the Garden of Eden to be.

One morning they broke camp, not knowing that this was the day that they would forge a life-long friendship with the Cheyenne Indians. The sun was breaking through the mists that hung over the valley when they came upon a small group of Indians on a ledge overlooking a deep gorge. Two of them lay on their bellies, looking down.

A squaw with a papoose in a cradleboard sat apart from the others. She rocked back and forth, keening with grief. Light spoke to them in Osage but they shook their heads, not comprehending. Two braves with drawn bows flanked the strange trio, eyeing Caleb fearfully.

The cry of a child caught Maggie's attention. She slid from the pony's back and, ignoring the Indians, went to the rim and looked down into the gorge. Light followed quickly, holding the back of her belt lest she slip over the edge.

Fifteen feet down, clinging to a spindly tree growing out the side of the rock wall, was a small child. He whimpered in terror, his arms and legs wrapped around the trunk of the sapling. A hundred feet below him a stream rippled in the sunlight.

"Ahh! He's so scared, Light. What can we do?"

"Get the rope, Caleb, and lower me down."

"No!" Maggie said quickly. "The tree will break under yore weight. I'm lighter. Let me go."

"I cannot risk it, *chérie*."

"If the tree breaks, he'll die, Light."

"Missy be right," Caleb said. "The tree'll hold her, not you."

The Indians looked from one to the other, not understanding what they said but knowing the strange people were trying to help the boy. When Caleb brought out the rope, a young man with beautifully etched features and a face dark with worry motioned for them to put it around him. Light talked to him, using his hands to explain the tree would break under his weight.

Maggie threw her hat on the ground. Light secured the rope around her. He tested the knot several times, then pulled her into his arms.

"*Mon amour,* when you reach the boy, have him put his arms and legs around you, and back off carefully. We will not let you fall."

"I know that, my love. I'm not afraid."

Caleb and two of the Indians held the rope even though Caleb could have easily done it alone. Light, trying not to look at the bottom of the rocky gorge, lay belly-down on the edge of the rim and felt the rope slipping through his hands as his beloved was lowered to the tree below. He called out to Caleb when Maggie's feet touched the trunk to test it to see if it would hold her weight.

With his heart in his throat, Light watched her crawl carefully out onto the trunk that grew almost straight out from the cliff. With her eyes on the boy she talked to him in the quiet voice she used to calm an excited animal. The child couldn't understand the words, but the tone soothed him and he stopped crying.

"Don't be scared, little boy. I'm comin' for ya. Hold on till I get t' ya. Ya'll be with yore ma in a little while. My name's Maggie. I'm goin' t' live here in the mountains. I'm almost t' ya. Now put yore arms around my neck. That's it. Put yore legs around me too. I'll hold ya tight and ya won't fall. Light an' Caleb'll pull us up. First we got to back off this tree trunk. It's startin' to wiggle. Light said be careful an' I do what Light says."

While she was backing, Light took up the slack. When she reached the side of the cliff the men began to pull her and the child slowly upward. As soon as she was within reach, Light and the Indian grabbed her beneath the arms and lifted her and the boy up and away from the edge.

With a cry of gladness the father reached for his child.

In a clearing back from the trail, the Indians, Light and Caleb sat beside a fire and smoked while Maggie played with the baby and the boy. Light was able to understand that the father of the boy was the son of a chief named White Horse and they were on their way to their summer camp. They had seen only a few white people and never a black man.

When they were ready to leave, Maggie hugged the little boy she had saved and told him how brave he was. He looked at her with big solemn eyes and hugged her back. The boy's father took the necklace of blue feathers from around his neck and placed it around Maggie's. She smiled because she thought it pretty; she was unaware of the significance of the gift — that from this day on she and her husband would be protected by the Cheyenne.

Maggie wanted to give something to her new friends before they parted. She went to the edge of the cliff, lifted her head and began to sing.

Flesh of my flesh, heart of my heart,
forever, hand in hand with wond'ring steps
through the wide forest we go . . .

Her voice was high and sweet and wild. It had the carrying quality of a bell. The echoes filled every crevice of the mountain and resounded into the valley. When she finished she yodeled.

"Y-oo-dola-dee-y-oo-la-dee — Y-oo-dola-dee-la-lee —"

The Cheyenne stood in awed silence.

Far away on a mountainside, a hunting party paused, lifted their heads and listened.

A doe, bending her head to drink from a stream, paused, stood still and quivered. And the cougar who was ready to spring on the doe opened its wide mouth and let out a roar, alerting the doe, who darted away.

Maggie had made her presence known in the mountains.

Two days later, they skirted a series of hills, crossed a narrow valley and followed an animal trail up into the pines. Light stopped and Maggie moved up beside him. In the clearing the grass was green and knee-high. A rock-bottomed stream of clear mountain water zigzagged to the meadow below. Birds flitted from bush to bush and wildflowers grew in abundance.

This was the place Light had seen in his vision. He and Maggie looked at each other. He began to smile and Maggie to laugh.

"We're here, Light. This here's yore mountain."

"Yes, *mon amour*. We are home."

Maggie slid from her pony and ran to the highest point. She threw out her arms and began to dance.

"We're home," she yelled. "Y-oo-dal-la-dee-hoo — ! We're ho . . . me, ho . . . me, ho . . . me. Y-oo-dal-lay-dee-hee!"

Across the valley, the Cheyenne, with his small son riding in front of him, stopped and held up his hand in a distant welcome to his new friends.

EPILOGUE

Light and Maggie spent the rest of their lives in the cabin they built that year on what was to be known as Light's Mountain. The Cheyenne became their friends and protectors. They called Light Sharp Knife and Maggie, Singing Bird — the names given to them by the Osage.

Caleb's blackness and his strength were assets to him. He was adopted into the tribe and took an Indian maiden for a wife. They had many children, who came often to visit with Light and Maggie after Caleb and his wife were gone.

Two of Maggie's babies were stillborn, but two lived. They were named Eli and Paul. Paul left the mountains to explore the world beyond. Eli inherited his father's love of the mountains and the forests. He roamed the Rockies, but he always returned to the homestead.

When in his old age Light's health began to fail and he could no longer go on long hunts, he knew the time was drawing near when he would leave his beloved woods sprite. His life had been good. Forty years before he had found his mountain. He and Maggie had shared a rare and wonderful love. Light worried about leaving her alone, even though he was sure that young Eli would take care of her. He shielded her from knowledge of his pain, hoping to spare her grief for as long as he could.

One summer day they walked hand in hand down the same winding path that years ago had led them to the site of their mountain home. They reminisced about Jefferson Merrick and Annie Lash, Will Murdock and Callie. They spoke of the day they left St. Charles and the vows they had made on the bluff overlooking the river. They recalled the meeting with Eli, Paul and the mad German. Light remembered his shock at learning that Eli was his brother. They wondered if MacMillan's village had grown into a town, if Aee's and Eli's first child had been a boy, and if Bee had married Bodkin or Dixon.

They talked about Roman Nose. When he was a little boy, Maggie had gone down the side of the cliff to rescue him. Now a powerful chief among the Cheyenne, he came to see them each year when he returned with his tribe from their winter camp to the south. He often brought his father, White Horse, to visit with Light; and when they were ready to leave, Roman Nose would ask Maggie to yodel.

Maggie was still slim and spirited, although her dark curls were streaked with gray and she walked now rather than ran. Today she went ahead of Light down the path to peer into a robin's nest she had been watching.

"They've not hatched yet, Light," she called, then to the old wolf-dog that trotted at her heels, "Ya keep away from here, Moses. That mama robin's scared yo're goin' t' eat her babies. 'Course I know ya'd not do it." She patted the rough head. "Go find yore lady friend. Ya been itchin' t' mate lately."

The dog, its gaping mouth and sharp white fangs capable of snapping off her hand, licked it and whined as if he understood what she was saying. Then he bounded away.

Light watched her and the dog. In all their years together he had not known of an animal she could not tame. She was still the beautiful, wild, shy forest creature he had brought to his mountain so long ago. A gentle smile lit his usually grave countenance.

Mon Dieu! How he hated to leave her.

Overhead, thunderclouds began to gather and in the distance low rumbles of thunder could be heard.

"We should go back, *chérie*. A storm is coming."

Maggie came to him as she always did when he called.

"It's here a'ready."

It was raining steadily when they reached a towering pine and took shelter beneath its spreading branches. Standing close, Maggie wrapped her arms about his waist and lifted her lips to his. Light kissed her lovingly and then raised his head to look at her. She was his love, his life, the other part of himself. He smiled into her emerald eyes and his arms tightened around her. She placed her head on his shoulder.

"I like t' see ya smile, Light. Ya know that I love ya more'n anythin'."

"I know, my sweet treasure. And I love you —"

The words had scarcely left his mouth when a bright flash forked down out of the darkened sky. It was followed closely by a sharp crack of thunder.

When twilight came and they hadn't returned to the cabin, young Eli became concerned about his parents. The howling of Maggie's wolf dog led him to them. He found the two of them lying beneath the tree. Light was holding Maggie in his arms. They looked as if they had just lain down to sleep for a while. He buried them together on the grassy knoll where their two babes lay sleeping and where Maggie had danced and sung the day they had come to Light's Mountain so long ago.

The love story of Light, the scout, and Maggie, the beautiful woods sprite, became a legend. Their story was told and retold along the Missouri River, across the great grassy plains, and through the Rocky Mountains. The tale was passed down from generation to generation among both the Indians and the pioneers who followed Baptiste and Maggie Lightbody to settle the country beyond the great river.

It is said that if you are in the mountains and if you listen carefully, you may hear Maggie singing to her lover.

> When my hair has turned to silver,
> and my eyes shall dimmer grow.
> I will lean upon my loved one,
> through my twilight years I go.
> I will ask of you a promise,
> worth to me a world of gold;
> It is only this, my darling:
> that you love me when I'm old.

The legend lives on . . .